Where Your Heart Belongs

DENSIE WEBB

Where Your Heart Belongs
Red Adept Publishing, LLC
104 Bugenfield Court
Garner, NC 27529
https://RedAdeptPublishing.com/
Copyright © 2026 by Densie Webb. All rights reserved.

---

*To my writing village, which helped me every step of the way.
You know who you are.*

"Absence diminishes mediocre passions and increases great ones, as the wind extinguishes candles and fans fires."
Francois de La Rochefoucauld

Prologue

As the screen on my laptop brightens, I lean over to skim the headlines—protests in Paris, a bomb in a market in Iraq, the deficit at a record $2 trillion with no end in sight—the usual global horrors.

But tucked between world events are these words: "Cillian Byrne, 43-year-old lead singer of the Irish rock group The Swifters, found dead..."

My bagel pops up from the toaster, an exclamation point to the devastating headline.

I collapse in my chair as the last bit of breath escapes my lungs. My fingers pause in midair then click the link on the screen. The spinning wheel turns, the page refusing to load. I stare out the kitchen window, my chaotic thoughts desperately trying to rewrite the words on the page as my crippled heart struggles to accept the finality of it. The harsh morning sun shines an unwelcome light on my dark regrets.

So many regrets.

I fight the urge to throw my aging laptop across the room. I imagine the screen cracking, the keyboard destroyed, and relief. But then the article comes into focus.

And there he is under the bold headline, in pixelated black and white, looking just as beautiful as the night we met.

So young.

We both were.

My youthful decisions have long since proven to be their own punishment. Now, I'll forever be left with questions that can never be asked, never be answered. I can't delude myself that Cillian is a ragged remnant of my past. No, I can't erase him, no matter how hard I try, not when he is so very much a part of my present.

I wipe my sweaty palms on my robe and return to the words dancing on the screen with no rhythm.

"Byrne, lead singer for The Swifters, was found dead at his home in Killgantry Village, Ireland, yesterday morning following a brief illness."

It doesn't feel remotely real, yet my first thought is that I should have sensed something was wrong. It's a crazy, stupid thought that at the same time feels absolute. We'd once been connected in every way—physically, emotionally, intellectually—until we weren't.

"Byrne had amassed a loyal fan base over the years, with two gold records and one platinum record to his name. Former band member Damian O'Leary said he and Byrne were working on a new album from his home studio at the time."

Has Sloane seen the news? No, she would have called. She was my lighthouse, protecting me from the crashing waves of heartache, helping me find my way. I have to let her know. We'll likely reminisce, maybe laugh at the memories, then she'll let me cry it out for what I hope will be one last time.

A musty hope chest of memories, one I keep locked away and rarely acknowledge, has cracked open. The contents are exposed, and the smell of naphthalene is making it hard to breathe. I jerk to standing, sending my chair teetering back on two legs before it crashes to the kitchen floor, and I slap my still-trembling hands over my mouth to stop a guttural scream from filling the room.

I pace the perimeter of the now-claustrophobic kitchen before I set the chair upright and slump back down in it. My face feels flushed, my head suddenly too heavy to hold upright, and I rest my cheek on the cold metal of the computer.

As I conjure up his image, I can almost feel the warmth of his skin next to mine and hear the music from that first night.

Part 1: BEFORE

Chapter 1

Twenty-two years earlier

The focus that night was on loud music, strong drinks, and dancing with abandon. As restless seniors at the University of Texas, we were primed for the slog of college to be done and for getting on with our lives as if only good things lay ahead. Armed with my newly legit ID, I marched into a dive bar, flush with entitlement. The familiar tang of spilled beer and stale cigarettes hung in the air as the three of us quickly staked claim to a wobbly table next to the small stage and an even smaller dance floor. Sloane, Leah, and I ordered three Mexican martinis, and we began our favorite pastime: rating the guys hanging at the bar on a scale of one to ten, estimating their odds for a successful hookup, and creating stories about couples who, at least on the surface, were wildly mismatched.

By the time the band stepped on stage, we were on our second martinis, digging into a bowl of thick guac with warm chips and enjoying a nice buzz. I hadn't given much thought to the band or the music we'd paid to hear, but when the lead singer stepped up to the mic, the stage became my sole focus. He gave his lean body a good stretch, and his ripped T-shirt rose just enough to expose the dark line of hair that disappeared below his waistband. He pushed his long sandy hair back from his face, leaned in, almost kissing the mic, and surveyed the crowd before assuming a rock-star stance.

"Cheers. We're The Swifters, all the way from Ireland, and we're chuffed to be here in Austin."

He possessed a delicious accent. The only Irish voices I'd ever heard came out of the mouths of actors. In real life, I found the melodic sound richer, far more seductive.

Or maybe it was just him.

He waxed poetic about their music and about Ireland before the band kicked off their first set. I listened, enthralled, as he closed his eyes, investing his whole body in the song. If he'd been kissing the mic before, now he was making love to it.

At one point, I could have sworn he looked right at me. I told myself his attention was at best my imagination or at worst a part of his act: pick a girl out of the audience, make goo-goo eyes, and he would have a fan for life. Anyway, he was probably an asshole, a player, a narcissist. Otherwise, he wouldn't be up there on stage, charming girls like me.

Sloane grabbed my hand, yanking me from my fugue-like state, and dragged me to the dance floor. She gyrated seductively, and we both flung our arms in the air and stomped our feet in time to the music. Leah jumped from her chair to join us, and I abandoned all self-consciousness, reveling in the joy of living in the moment, something that didn't come easy to a small-town girl from Johnson City—only an hour and a half from Austin but a universe away.

I figured by the time I sat back down, he would have zeroed in on another "fan for life." *So be it.* I'd already added him to my very selective sex-fantasy roster that had gotten me through long dry spells, and that would be enough. It would have to be.

When the music stopped, he announced the band was taking a break. The three of us, winded and laughing insanely at what bad dancers we were, collapsed in our chairs, debating whether another drink was a good idea. We dug out and pooled our cash and figured we had enough money for another round and a cab home, so "why the hell not" was the consensus. That was when I sensed a presence next to me, and I turned around. He was taller than he seemed on stage. He was backlit, and I could just make out his facial features.

He asked, "Was it any use?"

I cocked my head like a terrier reacting to a high-pitched sound. "I'm sorry?"

"Did you like it—the music?"

I'd like to say him talking to me was what I'd hoped for, but a mile-sized canyon lies between fantasy and hope. I placed my hand above my eyes as if looking out over the horizon. Yep, it was really him, asking me if I'd liked his singing. I nodded. He squatted next to me, so I had to look down at him, and he hung his arm over the back of my chair.

"Can I get you a drink?"

When I didn't respond right away, he said, "I'm Cillian, by the way."

"I'm sorry?" That was the second time in the span of a few seconds.

His laugh was as expressive as his singing. His smile revealed a single dimple in his left cheek, giving him a childlike appearance—quite the opposite of the persona he projected on stage. He leaned in close so I could better hear him. His warm breath in my ear took my own away as he said, "Think 'Kill' then 'Ian.'"

I pulled back to face him and pouted. "Poor Ian."

It took him a second, but he laughed and said, "Ah, you're one for the craic. But just so you know, it's a fine Irish name."

"Good to know," I said before taking the last sip of my drink. Cillian was now my favorite name of all time, especially when he said it.

"And this is where you tell me *your* name, luv."

"Zezelia, an unusual name here. My friends call me Zee."

He looked at my empty glass. "So, what are you having? Zee, is it?" He stood up and looked around the table. "Ladies?"

Sloane and Leah had been zapped with a stun gun but managed to answer in unison, "Mexican martinis."

He looked confused.

"You're in Texas," I said.

"Ah, okay. I better get my round in. So, three?"

I watched him take four long strides to the bar. Sloane and Leah leaned toward me in a single, coordinated move.

"We will fucking kill you if you blow him off," Sloane said.

Their warning was based on my well-established habit of declining invitations to enter some horny douchebag's orbit.

I shrugged and smiled, but my insides were churning, my head scrambled with questions. *Is he for real? How many girls does he hit on every night? I'm no groupie, but maybe just this once? If I do what I'm thinking of doing, what I really want to do, would my mother somehow find out and disown me?* Okay, that last one was ridiculous, but the thought flitted through my brain just the same.

Before I had time to ponder answers, he was back with a tray of drinks, smiling that smile and serving us as if he were the bartender and we were his favorite customers. He'd gotten a draft for himself.

"Band with benefits," he said. Still standing, he took a sip and gestured to the empty chair at the next table. "Can I join ya?"

"Sure," I said.

There was no way I could have known that my simple one-word response would be so catastrophically consequential, knocking me off my clearly marked life path and pushing me down a rocky detour.

He sat down next to me, and I couldn't help but stare at the thick sandy hair he so casually swept behind his ear, revealing a small piercing; at his solid forearm as he lifted his mug to take a long drink of his beer; at his dimple, which deepened when he turned to smile at me. The intensity of his gaze had me anticipating the feel of his full lips on mine, but the moment was broken when he suddenly turned his attention to the stage. The rest of the band was milling around, laughing together in a way that suggested they weren't just fellow members of a band but longtime "mates" as well.

Cillian stood and cupped his hands over his mouth to amplify the sound. "Lads!" He motioned them over, and one by one, they jumped down from the stage, grabbed empty chairs, unaware or unconcerned that the previous occupants had simply left for the bathroom or to get another beer, and joined us at the tiny table. I couldn't ignore the what-the-fuck looks from the other girls in the club. I was sitting at the cool table, and the star quarterback was leaning in. But that description didn't do justice to what was actually happening. When Cillian sat back down, he scooted closer until our bare elbows touched. The contact ignited an unmistakable current, a connection—a disturbance.

"Damian, Sean, Ronan, this is Sloane and..." He paused. "Leah, right?" he said, pointing at her. "And this, lads, is Zee." The simple act of him singling me out for an introduction had me smiling like an idiot. I no longer cared if I was the designated groupie for the night.

"Are you all from Ireland?" It seemed like a decent enough conversation starter—I hadn't yet heard the others speak.

"All from the same tiny village, yeah."

"How long have y'all been together?" I was shouting to be heard over the canned music blasting through the speakers. "The band, I mean."

"Feels like it's been donkey's years."

"Donkey's what?"

"A long time—three years." He bit his lower lip and nodded to himself as though mentally reviewing the long months of struggle, then he looked at me. "Trying to see if we can make a wee bit of money here in the States before we go back. Don't want to go home empty-handed, yeah?"

"When do you go back?" The idea of him flying across an ocean and being thousands of miles away triggered a ridiculously premature pang of disappointment—an unexpected, uncharacteristic, and unwelcome reaction.

"Haven't decided, right, lads?" He glanced across the table. Sloane was already making out with Damian, her arms draped around his bare neck, and Leah was in dude heaven, sandwiched between Sean and Ronan and giggling like a schoolgirl. It was anybody's guess which one of them might get lucky later that night, though my money was on Damian. His long lashes shifted the odds in his favor. And Sloane had a thing for floppy-haired guys in muscle shirts.

Cillian leaned in, and once again, I felt his warm breath on my neck. "Going for a smoke. Join me? I think we can leave 'em to it."

He took a swig of his beer before he touched my hand—an invitation more than an expectation—and led me through the crowded bar. The graffiti-covered metal door creaked closed behind us, and my ears buzzed from the sudden silence. A lone car drove past, music blasting from the rolled-down windows. The silence rose again as the car flew down the street, heading east. Cillian leaned against the brick wall layered with peeling blue paint, pulled a pack of cigarettes from his shirt pocket, and offered me one.

"No thanks. Don't smoke."

"Good girl." He leaned in and whispered, "It's a filthy habit, but lookit."

That was the third time he'd leaned in so close. I was bursting with a combination of alcohol and anticipation. I took a breath of the warm air, grateful for the soft summery breeze floating down Seventh Street. The night felt electric with promise.

He wrapped his lips around the filter, lit the cigarette, took a draw, and blew smoke up and away from me. I'd broken up with my last boyfriend because he refused to quit—one of the reasons, anyway. But Cillian made smoking sexy. It was confusing.

"So," I said, again trying to get a conversational rhythm going, "Swifters? Where'd that name come from?"

"Jonathan Swift—you know, the Irish author?"

"*Gulliver's Travels* Jonathan Swift?"

He tossed his barely smoked cigarette into the street and combed his hair back from his face with his slender fingers. "That's the one."

"Huh..."

"I read a lot when I was kid," he said as though he felt he needed to provide more of an explanation. "I was a wee book nerd. *Gulliver's Travels* was one of my favorites. Years later, I understood it was about a lot more than some crazy adventure. When we formed the band, it seemed right. Damian and them were okay with it."

Not only is he a hot singer, but he's a reader too? I imagined him propping himself up in bed, a lamp on the nightstand, shedding light over his shoulder, a book in hand, him frowning in concentration—a sexy image if ever there was one.

"So you've read it, yeah?" he asked as his eyebrows shot up.

"In high school. And we watched an old movie based on the novel."

"The book was deadly," he said.

"Agreed."

"So, Zee," he said as he stepped closer, "you from around here?"

He had a wicked grin that exposed a slightly protruding incisor that somehow only added to his innocent sex appeal.

"Around, yeah. About an hour and a half away, but I go to school here."

"Ah, Zezelia's a uni girl."

I couldn't tell if he was impressed or making fun. "Yeah, almost done. Only one more semester to go."

"And then what?"

"Not sure. Maybe travel, see the world—if I can scrape together enough money."

"Yeah, travel, definitely," he said. He hesitated before smiling. "Maybe Ireland?" He was closing the space between us. "I'd be happy to be your personal tour guide." His look was an unmistakable prelude to the kiss I'd been thinking of since I first spotted him on stage. He gently pushed a strand of my hair behind my ear as a lock of his fell onto his forehead. He leaned into me in agonizingly slow motion, and my heart battered my rib cage. I closed my eyes in anticipation.

His lips were centimeters away from mine when I heard Damian's voice. "Watch yourself, girlie. He can be a right bollocks, that one."

I turned toward his voice—only his head poked out from the exit door—and Cillian stepped back. "Eh, shut yer gob, Damian."

Damian shrugged it off. "In you go, nice and quick. Break's over."

Cillian stood in front of me, his hands shoved into his pockets. "You'll be around later? We'll be done at midnight. Have to pack up and all, but maybe we could get in a round? And I'll tell ya what's good to see when you make it over to Ireland."

When we went back inside, he climbed onto the stage and whispered something in Damian's ear, and when he stepped up to the mic, there was no mistaking who he was zeroing in on that time. For the rest of the set, I couldn't take my eyes off his mouth, those lips that had been so incredibly close to mine.

"Thank you! That's it for us tonight. We're The Swifters!"

I'd lost all sense of time, and the band was wrapping up. The bar had seriously thinned out, and I felt bad for them. Even Leah and Sloane had left.

Before she walked out the door, Sloane had leaned over and yelled in my ear, what I think was intended as a whisper, "He's not a good kisser." She was dishing on Damian, of course. But Sloane was notorious for being hypercritical of her hookups, of which there were many. She made her exit at about twelve-thirty, after checking with me to make sure I felt safe, and dragged a reluctant Leah with her. They both hit me with the thumbs-up and lewd hip thrusts in a laughing fit as they stumbled their way to the exit. I prayed Cillian hadn't caught their departing act.

I watched the band unplug, box things up in a well-orchestrated rhythm, and lug equipment out to the white van I'd seen parked outside. Theirs was a "one-band show"—no roadies, no hordes of fans, just four Irish guys wanting to make music and hopefully, eventually, some money.

When they were done, Cillian came and sat down next to me. Our previous almost-kiss had felt natural, and I was so ready for it. But now that he was close to me again, looking at me so intently, I felt like we were starting from scratch. *Is he waiting for me to say something? Does he want to pick up where we left off and jump right in with a kiss?*

"Y'all sounded awesome!"

"Ya think so?"

"Absolutely!"

He glanced around the almost empty room. "You may be in the minority."

"They were drunk and ready to go home. It doesn't mean they didn't like it. The Swifters' sound is destined to be a hit."

A few more seconds passed before he leaned in closer and said, "You're crazy beautiful, but you already know that, eh? Especially when you're complimenting me." He smiled.

It could have sounded like a cheap pickup line, but something in the steady tenor of his voice made me feel as if he were running his fingers through my hair and confessing long-held feelings. And I believed him. I thought, *If he doesn't kiss me soon, I'm going to die.* Then his hands were gently caressing the back of my neck, and he kissed me. His lips were soft but insistent. He tasted of beer and pheromones.

When he pulled away, he wiped my bottom lip with his thumb. "I swear to ya I've been wanting to do that all night."

Sometimes, a kiss is just a kiss, but that one was much more.

He stood, and I thought, *Was that it? He wanted to kiss me, he did, and now he's going to walk away?*

Then he asked, "What would ya like to drink? It's on the house."

If the night was going to end up like I hoped it would—now more than ever—I figured I'd better not have another one. I was already anticipating his mouth on mine again, his slim body naked next to mine in a hotel bed somewhere nearby. I definitely wanted to be fully present for that.

"You know, I think soda and lime would be the smart choice right now."

He winked at me again, a gesture that, on any other guy at any other time, would have come across as smarmy. Coming from him, it felt like a second kiss.

"Be right back."

I watched him walk away, and his absence triggered a shocking sensation that the room contained less oxygen. I inhaled deeply, relieved I could still breathe.

He returned with the drinks, took a sip of his foamy draft, and wiped his lips with the back of his hand. "So, Lady Zee, tell me something about yourself."

"Like what?"

"Well, I could ask, 'Do you come here often?' but I'll start with 'What are you studying at uni?'"

"It's not sexy—social work. I wanted to get a double major with business, but my grades weren't good enough to get into business school."

"Sounds serious enough. Never made it to uni myself. Music and the band sort of pulled me away."

"Some record label will snatch you up."

"Knock on wood." He banged his knuckles against the table.

"So you do that in Ireland too?"

"Silly superstition having to do with tree spirits or some shite, but my mam always did it, and it stuck. Now, it feels like I'm inviting disaster if I don't. Anyway, we figure we'll give the band another year or two, and if we can't break through, then it's back to Ireland and slog for a living for the next forty years."

He huffed a breath and shook his head as if his denial of that future would make it go away.

An extended silence followed his last comment. All I could think was that I wanted him to kiss me again. And he did. As he leaned in, he slid his hand around the back of my neck, moving his fingers as if playing the keys on a piano. The delicate movement of his fingers against my skin showed he was feeling the moment as much as I was.

When he pulled away, my heart was beating double-time. "How long will you be in Austin?"

He gave me a knowing look. "Not long enough."

Time was clearly of the essence. I leaned in to kiss him again, and he pulled me onto his lap. I fit perfectly. His body heat blended with mine, and I felt him hard beneath me as he slid his fingers across my bare skin under my shirt. I forgot about school, about my mom, about my last disaster of a one-night stand. *This will be different.* It was already different. I didn't know how long our lips and tongues were in sync before bright lights overhead intruded, and the bartender shouted, "Last call!"

I looked up and blinked twice. The place was empty, save for a couple of frat boys passed out at the bar. Cillian's bandmates were nowhere to be seen. I thought of how bedraggled I must look in the bright lights of the bar. He, however, looked adorable in a scruffy man-boy kind of way. I was ready to take the next step. I had come prepared. The blue foil packets, neatly stored away in my purse for a while, were burning a hole in the inside pocket.

He planted one last kiss on my lips before he slid me off his lap and stood. "You coming tomorrow night? I feel like we've some unfinished business here."

Disappointment must have been evident on my face. He smiled at me. *Is it arrogance or understanding?*

"So, tomorrow night?" he asked with a hint of uncertainty.

Standing on my tiptoes, I cradled his two-a.m.-stubbled face, kissed him, and with a soft moan let him know that I was all in.

Chapter 2

I woke the next morning to Sloane perched cross-legged in a chair pushed up against my mattress. She had a supersized Longhorn coffee mug in her hand.

My head was on fire, and my mouth tasted like dirty socks.

"What the hell, Sloane?" I croaked.

I managed to sit up, and she handed me the mug. I took a sip and shuddered.

"It's cold."

"Well, you should have woken up sooner. I've been here awhile."

"Do you make a habit of watching me sleep?"

She answered with a click of her tongue and a dramatic eye roll.

"We want to know what happened last night with your Irish rock star."

"Zap the coffee in the microwave, and when you come back, I'll share," I said as I threw back the covers and plodded to the bathroom.

"Leah, she's up!" she yelled loud enough for our upstairs neighbors to hear.

I was going to have a disappointed audience of two. They were surely hoping for something more titillating than my recounting of a two-hour adolescent make-out session in the bar.

I brushed my teeth, washed my face, and tied my bird's-nest hair back into a ponytail, all the while replaying my time with Cillian the night before. While it hadn't ended the way I'd anticipated, it was pretty amazing. Or maybe the three martinis I'd downed earlier in the evening had draped a dreamy haze over the actual events.

I was deep in concentration, staring at my raccoon eyes in the mirror and trying to recall if I'd made any missteps or said anything to humiliate myself, when Sloane pounded on the door.

I took a breath and opened the bathroom door. Seated side by side on the end of my bed, they were waiting for me to hold court.

"Y'all are too much. I'm telling you right now you're going to be disappointed. Nothing happened," I said, my words thickened by my own disappointment.

"Nothing? Like nothing at all?" Leah was taken by surprise.

"Well, not *nothing* nothing. A lot of kissing, touching, you know, but no sex. We never left the bar. They kicked us out around two in the morning."

"So you stayed in the bar and just made out until they closed?" Sloane was incredulous.

"Yep."

Sloane frowned. "He didn't ask you to go back to his hotel room?"

"Nope. But he did invite me to come back to the club tonight."

"You're going, I assume? A second chance to see him naked?"

"Jesus, Sloane, maybe you should go have sex with him and get it out of your system."

She stood and raised her hands in surrender. "I won't say another word." She made a zipping motion across her lips. "At least not until tomorrow morning."

Leah handed me my newly reheated coffee.

I took a sip. "Ahhh, thank you. It's just right."

"You up for breakfast tacos?" she asked.

"Sure. Let me get dressed, pop a couple of ibuprofen, and I'll be ready for some hangover food."

As I dressed, I couldn't stop thinking about Cillian and wondering if he was thinking about me. Not my usual MO. I found most guys not worth the mental energy or the hassle. A couple of one-night stands had taught me a thing or two, mainly that they weren't for me. I hated how they made me feel—about both the guys and the experience itself. I preferred long-term relationships, but I hadn't been in one since my freshman year. So I didn't know why I was obsessing over this Irish guy, whom I'd met less than twenty-four hours before and who would be leaving in a few days, never to be seen again. *Maybe I shouldn't go to the club tonight. Maybe I—*

My thoughts were cut short by the ringing of the phone in the kitchen.

"Zee, it's your mom!" Leah called.

Listening to my mother's admonitions and lectures about focusing on school and tightening my money belt was the last thing I needed or wanted right then. I reluctantly shuffled my way to the kitchen, and Leah handed me the receiver.

"Morning, Mom," I answered in a deep monotone, my voice still not fully recovered from the night before.

"Zezelia, are you coming down with something? You sound sick."

"I just woke up."

She sighed, and I swore I could smell her nicotine-laced breath over the phone.

"It's almost noon! Don't you have finals you should be studying for?"

I guessed the question was rhetorical because she didn't take a breath before she informed me that she wanted to drive into Austin and meet me for coffee. To say that my mother and I had a contentious relationship would be an enormous understatement. Our visits often ended with raised voices and hurt feelings. Leaving home and moving to Austin for school was one of the happiest days of my life.

"Oh man, I can't, Mom. I'm meeting a study group in the library in a couple of hours, and it will probably run late into the night."

"What about tomorrow?"

"Um, I'll let you know, okay?"

Lies—both hers and mine—were the cement that held us to-gether.

Later, as the remnants of my hangover faded, along with the last of the daylight, I watched the digital numbers on the clock flip in excruciating slow motion. Sloane and Leah pounded on my door and marched in before I could respond. Sloane shoved a handful of bright-gold condom packets in my direction.

"Just in case Cillian is running low. I think the ones you carry around in your purse have passed their expiration date."

At 8:30, I decided to walk to the club despite the heat, hoping the exercise and distance would help calm my internal quivering. As I made my way down Sixth Street, I saw that some of my fellow students had started early. There was always something unsettling about watching drunk people act out when I was stone-cold sober. I couldn't decide if it was a feeling of missing out on the fun or hop-ing to God that I didn't look and act like that after I'd had a few. That night, I was planning to keep my drinking to a minimum—just enough to calm my nerves but not so much that important nerve endings were numbed.

It was 9:00 when I pulled on the metal door handle, walked in, and waited for my eyes to adjust to the dark. It was 9:05 when I placed my elbows on the bar, stood on my tiptoes, leaned over, and waved to get the bartender's attention. It was 9:15 when she handed me a gin and tonic with lime, and I took a sip. Piped-in rock music filled the air. I straightened and turned around to see if the band was setting up. Nothing was happening on the stage yet, so I turned back to the bar and took another sip.

It was 9:20 when Cillian came up behind me, slid his hands around my waist, leaned in, and whispered in my ear, "You came."

I turned around and was greeted with my first kiss of the night. He took my hand and led me to the same table we'd all gathered around the night before. A sloppily handwritten sign that said Reserved sat in the middle. Before I sat down, he pressed his body against mine and kissed me passionately, confirmation of how that night would end.

"We have a break at eleven," he said. "Don't disappear on me."

His eyes lingered. The noise, the chatter, and the smell of the place faded into the background.

"I'm not going anywhere. I promise."

I switched from gin and tonic to club soda and lime, and as he sang and moved to the music, I found myself trying to interpret his every word, his every movement, desperately wanting to know everything about him—his family and what he was like in school. *Was he popular, or was he bullied? What about previous girlfriends? Has he ever been in love?* I needed to know who Cillian—I realized I didn't know his last name, and he didn't know mine. I was trying to envision a past I knew nothing about and a future that was a blank page, anxiously waiting to be written. I was overcome with an inexplicable but unshakeable certainty that whatever happened in my life, Cillian and maybe even Ireland would play a part in it.

At one in the morning, the band finally wrapped up.

"Thank you! Great audience! We're The Swifters!" Cillian announced to the people still there.

The band had given it their all once more, but few people were there to appreciate their efforts. He jumped down from the stage, leaving the guys to do the heavy lifting, and beelined to where I sat at the bar, passing the time with Genevieve, the bartender. In the hours I'd spent nursing my drink, I learned she was in graduate school and working nights to pay at least part of her tuition. The plan was to get out of the bartending business after graduation and into the CPA business.

"I love numbers," she said with a conviction that would have rivaled Cillian saying, "I love music." I could see her hungry eyes tracking him as he headed my way, but she was being cool, respecting the fact that for that night, at least, he was with me.

He took my hand and planted a soft kiss on my lips. "I thought that set was never gonna end. So, Lady Zee, you ready to go?"

"Go? Go where?"

"I know a place."

So there would be no make-out session in the bar until the lights flickered on. We were evidently skipping the prologue and getting straight to the juicy part. I thanked Genevieve and left her a tip on the mucked-up bar.

As we walked away, she raised her fist and shouted, "Numbers rule!"

"That was odd," Cillian said, eyebrows kinked.

"She's actually very cool. And smart. Studying to be a CPA."

"CPA?"

"An accountant."

"Really? Head for the numbers? Maybe I'll look her up so she can handle my money when the band makes it big." He chuckled.

He clearly had no idea she wanted to fulfill a lot more than his accounting needs.

The street was deserted, save for drunk stragglers leaving bars. Cabbies knew it was closing time, and they would soon be showing up en masse. In the meantime, Cillian slid his warm hand under my shirt and around my waist, pulling me close, and we made out under the glow of the streetlight. I felt the rapid beat of his heart against my chest. *Can he feel mine?* I was more present than I'd ever been, but at the same time, I felt as if I were standing outside myself watching, not convinced my outsized feelings were real.

He pulled away suddenly, took a step to the curb, and held out his arm, and a cab appeared like magic. He held the door open and gestured for me to climb in. The cloth seats of the cab smelled of weed and tacos. He slid close to me and put his arm around my shoulders, and I laid my head on his chest like that was what "we" always did. His scent imprinted on my "olfactory sensory neurons." Of course, I didn't know that was what was happening at the time. Only later did I learn that term in a conversation with Leah when I tried to explain the effect he'd had on me. She was studying nursing and always shared tidbits of medical information—some of which I would have preferred she keep to herself. But in that moment, I only knew that it felt as right as anything I'd ever experienced.

"Where y'all headed?" the cabbie asked.

"The Driskell Hotel," Cillian answered.

I jerked my head up. "The Driskell? I'm impressed."

He leaned in and whispered in my ear, "That's the idea."

When he'd said, "I know a place," I assumed that might've meant a dark spot to park the van, climb in the back, and fog up the windows—or maybe a back room in the club. A night at the Driskell was definitely not what I expected.

"Where y'all from?" the cabbie asked with a thick Texas drawl, the question clearly directed at Cillian.

"Ireland. You been?"

"Me? Nah. Never left Texas."

Cillian grinned at me and shrugged. I'd never been out of the state either, but I kept that bit of biographical information to myself.

"You're looking deadly tonight," he whispered.

He pulled my legs over his and leaned in, his lips a breath away from mine, never touching. The sensation was more erotic than if our lips had been frantically pressed together. His hand was on my knee then my thigh, and as his fingers inched slowly upward, my breath caught.

"Wait, wait." I exhaled the words, pushing his hand away. I glanced up to see the driver watching us intently in the rearview mirror.

"Woman," he breathed the word through closed teeth as his head dropped back. His eyes were open, staring at the roof of the cab, and his hand fell away from my leg. I instantly missed it.

"You're killing me," he whispered, his head tilting to look at me.

"It's a bit much, that's all."

I reached for his hand, and our fingers laced together. He raised his head and faced me.

"So you don't want me to take you home?" His voice was low, soft, private.

I wanted to tell him that I'd never wanted any guy as much as I wanted him right then, but if his fingers had slid just a couple of inches upward, I would have noisily embarrassed myself in the back seat of the cab, providing a titillating show for the cabbie.

"No, the Driskell. Definitely the Driskell," I said in my most sultry voice.

Chapter 3

We pulled up to the entrance at the Driskell Hotel, and while Cillian paid the driver, I gawked at the hotel's façade. I had seen the Driskell plenty of times as I drove by, but I'd never stopped to take it in up close. Built in the 1800s, it looked like it had been airlifted from another time and place. It was where celebrities and dignitaries stayed when they came to Austin, not penniless college students and struggling musicians. The uniformed doorman opened the door to the lobby, and I stopped short. Gleaming marble floors, towering columns, and stained-glass ceilings—I'd never been in the presence of such opulence.

He slid his arm around my waist.

"I'm not dressed for this place," I said.

He cocked an eyebrow and smiled. "Neither am I. What harm?"

Translation: soon, we wouldn't be dressed at all. It was a little after one in the morning, and we were the only guests around.

"Is the band here as well?"

"Just you and me," he said, and he took my hand.

As we made our way down the long lobby entrance to the check-in desk, the squeak of my Vans echoed off the marble floors, further reminding me of where I was, making me ask myself what I was doing there.

"Good evening. Welcome to the Driskell," the girl behind the desk said.

Cillian handed her a credit card. She glanced at the name. "Thank you, Mr. Byrne. I'll have your keys in just a second."

Cillian Byrne. I wouldn't have to embarrass myself by asking the guy I was about to have sex with to tell me his last name.

"Ah, I see your reservation."

A reservation? He wanted this as much as I did. He signed a receipt, and she handed him the key and his credit card. "The elevators are around the corner. Breakfast is served from six thirty a.m. to eleven a.m., and the fitness center is twenty-four hours."

"We won't be needing the fitness center." He squeezed my hand.

She looked down at the floor around us. "Do you need help with your luggage?"

"No luggage, but thanks," Cillian said. It came out as "tanks," which I found absolutely adorable.

I followed her gaze to the empty spot where luggage should have been, and I felt my face redden. When I told him, "Definitely the Driskell," I was feeling confident, sexy. Right then, I felt like a little girl trying to fool my way into a very grown-up club.

"Enjoy your stay, Mr. and Mrs. Byrne."

I almost threw my neck out as I jerked my head up. So I was the missus, at least for the night.

As we headed to the elevators, I whispered, "You signed us up as a married couple?"

"You never know. I read about how Texans can go on like they're holier than thou. Didn't want to chance it."

He pressed the elevator button, and as soon as we stepped in and the doors shut, he bent over, slid my hair away from my shoulder, and kissed my neck. His hot breath on my skin triggered an involuntary gasp. He whispered in my hair, "I think you're going to be the best thing that's ever happened to me, Zezelia—" He stopped, pulled back, and looked embarrassed. "I don't know your last name."

"It's Owens. Zezelia Owens."

The elevator doors slid open. "Well, Mrs. Zezelia Owens Byrne, care to join me in our hotel room? With a balcony, I might add."

"Why, yes, I would, Mr. Byrne." I was trying my best to play it cool and go along with his little joke, but if my stomach twisted any further, I was going to require a trip to the ER instead of a night at the Driskell.

He put the key in the door and pushed it open. Holding it for me, he said, "Zee, look, the room is grand."

Some unknowable force pushed me into the room, and the door slid shut behind me. He sat on the king-size bed and held out his hand to me. My lips trembled with excitement, but he quelled it with a kiss. There was no going back.

"Do you want something to drink? We can raid the minibar," he said as he rubbed his hands together like a kid about to open his first Christmas present.

"Uh, sure." I thought sex was next on the agenda, not a mini bottle of booze.

He stood and opened the fridge door. "Wine, champagne, beer?"

"How about club soda?"

He cocked an eyebrow. "One club soda coming up."

He twisted off the top and handed it to me. I took a sip.

"You know, the original club soda was made in Dublin in 1877."

I snorted a laugh, and a bit of club soda shot from my nose. "You just made that up."

"No, I swear, it's real. Look it up." He turned back to the fridge and grabbed a beer.

After a few more sips of our drinks, he took the bottle from my hand and set it and his beer on the floor. He gently pulled me close and peppered my neck, my cheeks, my lips with butterfly kisses. I wasn't used to such tenderness, and a lump formed in my throat.

He pulled away to look me in the eye and said, "I'm glad you're here."

"Me too."

The next few minutes were an awkward blur of shoes, T-shirts, and jeans being shed and tossed into the corner of the room. The only sound was the echo of our heavy breathing as we tumbled back onto the bed. He took me by surprise when he pulled back and sat upright, looking down the full length of me.

"Zezelia Owens, you are the most beautiful thing I've ever seen."

In that moment, my need for him was smothering in its intensity. It felt brutal. No other moment in my life could ever match it, I was sure.

He whispered in urgent tones, "God, I want you."

He pulled a condom seemingly out of thin air and laid the foil package on my stomach. He slowly ran his tongue down my neck and circled my nipples before tracing my stomach, my hips. I arched my back with each touch of his lips. *I want... I want more.* He slid his way back up, our bodies never separating, and he kissed me. But I couldn't concentrate on his lips, with his fingers between my legs. The anticipation was almost too much.

"Is that good?" he whispered in my ear.

The guys I'd been with never asked me if I was enjoying myself before they took the plunge.

"Yeah," I said while trying to catch my breath. "Really good."

He took his own sweet time and skillfully took away what was left of my breath. He once again kissed his way down my body, and when his warm tongue hit just the right spot, I gasped and grabbed fistfuls of his hair. My mind emptied of all thought, all worry. All I could think of was the silky feel of his tongue moving in just the right rhythm.

"Cillian," I moaned. "Oh God." I'd never been particularly religious, but what was happening bordered on the spiritual, and I melted into the bed sheets.

When I was on the verge of exploding, he suddenly stopped, raised himself onto his knees, and slipped the condom on. The heavy-lidded look of desire that had overtaken him almost pushed me over the edge. Then he was inside me. He uttered a guttural moan as he sang my name.

I'd read once that an orgasm is like a sneeze—you feel it building and building, then it releases all at once, out of your control. But that description fell woefully short. When it happened, it was what I imagined mainlining heroin would be.

The hours that followed passed in a blur of skin and sweat and a depth of physical and emotional connection I'd never come close to with anyone else. Each stroke of his hand, each whisper, each kiss ignited my desire. Each time our bodies came together was more intense than the time before. I wanted it to never end.

But in a few hours, we would be leaving our fantasy escape, and I would realize that it had been a temporary high, a biological cocktail of endorphins, oxytocin, and dopamine—shaken, not stirred—a completely immersive experience never to be repeated. I wasn't sure what I had been doing until then that passed for sex, for intimacy. But I feared I would spend the rest of my life chasing that same high and come away sorely disappointed.

My head rested on his chest, and I listened to his rapid heartbeat, a rhythm I wanted to memorize. My hand wandered up and down his beautiful body as we talked, sharing our pasts, our present, and our hopes for the future.

"What's your dream for the band?"

He stared at the ceiling. "To make it big. To hear my songs on the radio. To have a gold record hanging in my own recording studio."

He propped himself up on his elbow and stroked my hair with his other hand. "I know how mad that sounds. God, I sound like a right prick. But that's my dream. What about you?"

"I just want to be happy, whatever that turns out to be."

He frowned as if deep in thought before he said, "When I was in sixth year, we had to write a report about what we were going to do, what we wanted to do after graduation."

"In the sixth grade?"

"Sorry, no. In the States, I guess that would be your senior year."

"Ah, okay."

"Anyway, the teacher said we needed to know the difference between our motivations to do something and our goals. I wrote pretty much what I just told you."

"That's awesome that you knew what you wanted to do even then."

"Well, my point is that you said you want to be happy. But that's not really a goal. That's your motivation. So what would you say is your goal? What do you want to do that would *make* you happy?"

"Oh, well, I guess my immediate goal is to graduate."

"Would that make you happy?"

I thought for a second. "It would make my mother happy."

He frowned again before pulling me closer. "But what would make Zezelia Owens happy?"

I was too embarrassed to admit my lofty goal of creating a nonprofit to help single mothers like my mom get a degree and start a career.

"Hey, I'm only twenty-one," I said. "I've got time to figure that out. I wasn't like you, having a clear vision of what my life goals were when I was kid."

"Fair enough."

Eventually, he got up and headed to the bathroom. I sighed and rolled over to his side of the bed to watch him walk away and soak up his warmth that had seeped into the pillowcase. As he closed the bathroom door, I spotted a few scraps of paper on the floor below his side of the bed, next to his rumpled jeans. I leaned over and picked up the tiny squares and quietly unfolded one. Poems were scribbled on lined notebook paper and napkin scraps—no, not poems, they were song lyrics, beautiful emotions jotted down on paper that had been folded into tiny two-inch squares. I was opening another square when he emerged from the bathroom. He stopped short.

"You took those from my pockets?" he asked with a tinge of anger.

I felt such shame for my unintentional snooping. "No, no. They were on the floor." I swallowed hard. "They're beautiful."

He held out his hands, and I placed them in his open palms.

Looking down at the papers I'd handed over, he quietly said, "They're not finished. I haven't shown anyone yet. Not even the lads."

"I'm sorry, I shouldn't have opened them, I—" I was devastated that my curiosity might have ruined our short time together.

Standing naked beside the bed, the papers clutched in his hands, he looked like a little boy in a man's body, desperately seeking approval, and he asked, "So you liked them, yeah?"

That was the moment I completely understood the lyrics to every love song I'd ever heard. I had fallen deeply, hopelessly, irrevocably in love with Cillian Byrne.

I woke the next morning, disoriented and pleasantly sore.

"Mornin', Zee."

Cillian was propped up in bed, hotel pen in hand, scribbling on the papers I'd unfolded and read the night before.

"What time is it? You been awake long?" I asked, rubbing my eyes with one hand and pulling the sheet over my bare breasts with the other.

"About an hour, and it's eight thirty."

He leaned over and kissed me. His reddish scruff had grown to a respectable pre-beard level.

"You've already had coffee?" I asked.

"That obvious? I'll make you a cup so we'll taste the same."

That was my first ever "morning after," and I wasn't quite sure how to act. Eric, my boyfriend from my freshman year, lived at home, and we'd had to get creative about where and when to have sex, but we never had a sleepover. And my previous one-night stands were always in the guy's apartment with multiple smirking roommates, and my encounters were more the variety of "do it and get the hell out of there" to avoid the walk of shame in the morning.

Cillian slid out of bed and poured me a cup. He was wearing one of the white terrycloth robes from the bathroom—it made for a mouthwatering confection.

He tugged at the collar. "I'm thinking we should nick a coupla these."

"Oh yeah? I'm thinking not."

"What's the fun in that?" He shrugged and returned to the business of making coffee. "Milk, sugar?"

"A little of both, please."

I sat up, pulling the sheet with me, and he handed me the cup. "You Yanks' idea of coffee is, well, shite. Go to Europe if you want the real thing."

"So I've been told."

He cocked one eyebrow.

"Several European classmates at UT. They've made no secret of their disdain for American 'coffee,' complete with air quotes."

"There must be some place around here with better coffee than this, yeah?"

I shrugged before I said, "I saw you writing on those papers. More song lyrics?"

"Trying."

"Can I see?"

"I don't want you to look again until I feel they're done. You've inspired me."

"Really?" His words made me feel like Helen of Troy launching a thousand ships.

"So," he said, as he scooted closer, "what should we do today?"

"You don't have to rehearse or something?"

"Nah, thought we'd spend the day together, maybe walk by the lake. I hear it's lovely. We can get a bite—unless you have plans."

I thought about how I should be studying, how my mother would kill me if I flunked out, how Sloane and Leah would be dancing on one foot then the other, waiting for me to dish on my night with Cillian. But my heart was drunk, my desire at a painful peak, and my willpower was ebbing by the second.

"No plans."

He took the coffee cup from my hand, set it on the nightstand, and kissed me. "Well," he said, his voice lowered, "checkout isn't until eleven."

I pulled his robe tie open and sprinkled his smooth chest with kisses. I no longer cared about my coffee breath or his. I just knew that I wanted him. If I couldn't have him at least one more time before checkout, I would die in room 367 at the Driskell Hotel. He quickly shrugged off the robe and pulled the sheets down, exposing me from head to toe.

"Let's make the most of it." He exhaled those words into my neck, and I didn't care if I flunked out or if my mother never spoke to me again. Sloane and Leah could wait. All I cared about was the now—with Cillian.

When we finally pulled apart, I glanced at the digital clock on the nightstand: 10:30 a.m. "It's time," I said, breathless.

We jumped from opposite sides of the bed and headed to the bathroom. Cillian opened the shower and motioned for me to enter. "After you, Mrs. Byrne."

"Why thank you, Mr. Byrne. I believe I will."

He looked even hotter drenching wet, his long hair slicked back. It was a test of wills for us not to start up again under the warm water spray, but the clock was ticking. *Just one more lingering kiss,* we told ourselves. But of course, shower sex was something I put on my list of things I wanted to experience again.

By the time we got out and dried off, we had five minutes to get downstairs to the lobby and check out.

"Where are my trousers? My pants?" he asked as he frantically scanned the room.

"Here," I said, tossing them to him from behind the chair in the corner.

We dressed as if we were in the midst of a fire drill, flames lapping at our feet. Cillian opened the door and ran down the hall to the elevator. I couldn't keep up, but he held the elevator doors and motioned frantically for me to get in. We jumped in together, looked at each other in agreement and, laughing hysterically, pushed all the buttons, like children whose parents had told us absolutely, under no circumstances, to touch the elevator buttons. Out of breath, we reached the lobby at 11:05 and turned in our key. The desk clerk let our tardiness slide, and we made our way to the exit and into the bright sunlight. It was like emerging from a warm, dark cocoon as I tried to reorient myself to the more familiar surroundings of Austin streets. The spell of hot sex and soft murmurings was broken.

The night before and that morning had been spectacular, a span of time I would remember always. In the literal light of day, I was sure Cillian would kiss me goodbye and go on about his day, go on about his life, despite his suggestion that we spend the day together. After a few more nights at the club, he would be on the road then return to Ireland. My heart was already sick with longing.

He pulled me close, and squinting against the sunlight that revealed specks of gold in his green eyes, he asked, "What would you like to do today, Lady Zee? The day is ours."

My heart was filled to the brim with a frothy kind of happiness.

Chapter 4

Despite our having just showered, our clothes carried the heavy aroma of the club from the night before.

"I think we really need to change clothes before we go any-where," I said.

His brow furrowed, and he hesitated. He sniffed his armpit, scrunched his nose, and gave me a thumbs-up.

It was almost noon when our cab pulled up in front of my apart-ment.

"I guess this is me," I whispered as I leaned in for a deep kiss.

I pulled back, and when he sighed, drawing me back in for an-other kiss, the cabbie cleared his throat.

"I'll be back in an hour."

I nodded and scooted out of the car. As the cab pulled away from the curb, I turned to watch, and Cillian was craning his neck to look at me out the back window. My heart was so full, I feared it might rupture.

When I opened the door to the apartment, the air was hot and muggy. The air conditioning couldn't keep up with the unseasonable heat, and the place was stuffy, the walls permanently infused with the smell of fried eggs and coffee. Sloane and Leah, dressed in the faded and ripped T-shirts they typically slept in, were sitting at the kitchen table, knees up to their chests, sipping coffee in chipped mugs from our eclectic collection. When they saw me, they stood and broke in-to loud applause and a series of ear-piercing finger whistles, a skill I had never mastered.

"Seriously?" I said, laughing at their over-the-top greeting.

Sloane pulled out a chair for me as if she were the maître d' showing me to my table. "Come, come. Have a seat."

Leah poured me a cup, and I took a sip. I slowly took another sip then another, creating a dramatic pause for maximum effect.

"Okay, so?" they asked in synchronized rhythm.

I set the mug on the table, placed my palms down, and leaned forward, shifting my eyes between Sloane and Leah before I proclaimed, "Amaaazing!"

They squealed in delight.

I sat back, satisfied with their reaction. "And... we spent the night at the Driskell, if you can believe it."

Leah sighed and placed her hand over her heart. She was an incurable romantic, a character flaw I was certain would someday be her undoing.

I provided the CliffsNotes version of my night with Cillian. I wasn't about to reveal the deep well of feelings I had fallen into. Sloane, whose lexicon lacked the word "romance" or anything romance adjacent, would have rolled her eyes, clicked her tongue loudly, and thrown me a double-knotted jute rope to pull me out of the well.

"So you going to hook up again?" she asked.

I cringed at the implication that Cillian was nothing more than a hookup. It had been a wildly intense one-night stand, to be sure, but it had felt like so much more. "He's coming here to pick me up in about an hour. So yeah, probably."

"The band is playing again tonight, right?" she asked. "Maybe we can all go to the club—a chance to get to know Ronan or Sean a little better," Sloane said and let loose a seductive shimmy.

"What about Damian?"

"Leah can have him if she's interested."

"Gee, thanks, Sloane. So, what, I get your sloppy seconds?"

Sloane shrugged. "Whatever. He's not my type after all. And you said you thought he was cute."

I stood and grabbed my coffee, leaving them to sort out their boy preferences, and headed to my room. A note was stuck to my door: *Was he as good as he looks?*

When I laughed, Sloane yelled from the kitchen, "That was in case we were asleep when you came home!"

An insistent knocking on the front door stopped me from stepping into my room.

Sloane answered without checking to see who it was, despite her exposed butt cheeks bouncing beneath the edge of her T-shirt.

"Sloane, honey, do you always answer the door half naked?" my mom asked.

I choked on my own saliva, coughed, and hoarsely eked out, "Mom, what are you doing here?"

"I thought you'd be happy to see me," she said in her well-honed guilt-trippy tenor. "I wanted to surprise you."

I was struck mute. She came over to me and pulled me into a tight hug. I stiffened, horrified that any movement would stir the scent of sex that clung to me like heavy perfume.

"You're going to be studying so hard I thought you deserved a treat."

"Mom, I told you I would let you know. I have plans."

"Plans? You mean studying? I think you can manage an hour away from study time to refresh and restart your brain. And spend time with your mother."

In full panic mode, I stuttered and stammered my way through the next sentence. "I... I, um, can we meet for dinner? Like I said, I have plans."

She frowned and placed her hands on her substantial hips.

"And what exactly am I supposed to do in the meantime?"

I couldn't tell if she was gearing up to scream at me or to turn on the waterworks. I could never tell.

"Maybe we can get a quick coffee?"

"I guess it's better than nothing," she said with a sigh.

"I just need to jump in the shower first."

My fire-alarm dressing drill that morning at the hotel had been good practice for my rapid shower and change.

My hair still dripping wet, I walked into the kitchen, where she was chatting with Sloane and Leah. "Okay, I'm ready. Let's go," I said, as I shifted from foot to foot.

"Calm down, Zezelia. I was having a nice conversation with Sloane and Leah."

Sloane and I had been friends since middle school, when we used to argue over really important stuff like whose boobs were bigger, hers or mine, and who we would rather marry—Leonardo DiCaprio or Ethan Hawke. She and my mother had a carefully crafted best-friend-and-mother-of-the-best-friend relationship.

"How about that coffee shop I took you to last time?" I asked. "You know, the one down the street?"

"That place smells like *marijuana*," she said, lowering her voice when she uttered the "m" word. "I don't feel comfortable there. Can't we go someplace nicer?"

"Uh, sure."

My mother bid Sloane and Leah goodbye and headed to the door. I motioned for Sloane to come close and whispered, "If Cillian shows up before I get back, apologize for me and tell him I'll be here as soon as I can. Just let him know I haven't stood him up."

"Got it."

The "nicer" place was farther but still within walking distance. Despite insisting she wanted to spend time with me, she didn't say much on the way there. We ordered our coffees and grabbed a table next to the window that looked out onto the campus.

"So," we said in unison and managed to laugh at ourselves.

"You first," she said.

"I've been here for most of the last three years, and you've never just shown up like this before. Is everything okay?"

She waved her hand in a dismissive gesture and said, "First of all, I told you yesterday that I wanted to drive in. Anyway, everything's fine."

"Okaaay?"

"But I was thinking…"

Oh, here it comes.

"Graduation is just a few months away, and I was thinking maybe you could move back home for a while before you, you know, get a job and go off on your own."

She might as well have said she was moving to Kyrgyzstan and wanted me to pack up my life and tag along.

"Where is this coming from? I thought you liked having the house to yourself."

"I never said I didn't enjoy you living at home."

She didn't have to.

"I haven't made solid post-graduation plans yet. Let me see if I can get an internship or a job first. Can I think about it?"

She gave me a look, the one that let me know how disappointed she was, before downing the rest of her coffee. She leaned over to dig something out of her purse, and for the first time, I noticed her gray roots showing. My focus shifted to the envelope she was handing me.

"What's this?"

"Open it," she said, smiling.

It contained photographs of me as a toddler. In one, I was holding tightly onto my mom's hand, as if I had never wanted anything more in my little life than for her to love and protect me. I'd never seen them before. She looked shockingly young.

"Where did you find these?"

"I came across an old roll of film and got it developed. You were such a beautiful little girl." She sighed.

My mother had never been one to be sentimental or nostalgic. *Is this a new tactic for laying on the guilt?*

I survived coffee and a few bites of the blueberry muffin she ordered for me despite my insistence that I wasn't hungry.

"I really should get back, Mom."

"So soon?" she said, her bottom lip displaying her displeasure.

"Yeah, sorry. But thanks for the coffee and the muffin."

"You barely ate it. Let me get a takeout container so you can have it for later."

Before I could protest, she was on her way to the counter, delaying our departure that much more. She returned and carefully placed the mostly uneaten muffin into the Styrofoam clam.

"Maybe you'd like another coffee to go? I could—"

"No!" I snapped.

She jerked her head back, and I immediately regretted my curt response. I thanked her again for saving the leftover muffin for me, and we headed out. She lit a cigarette as soon as we stepped outside. The sight of her lighting up was a stinging reminder of home and how claustrophobic I felt there. I couldn't do it. Moving back home would be a huge step backward. When we finally reached my apartment, I hugged her goodbye and thanked her yet again.

"Wait, I need to use the bathroom before I head back."

She walked up the front steps and opened the front door like she lived there.

I scurried after her, hoping she would be quick about it and finally be on her way.

When I trailed in behind her, Sloane looked as panicked as I felt. She knew my mother. If she collided with Cillian, it would set off a nuclear bomb. I could almost hear the clicking of a Geiger counter from the fallout. Thank God, Cillian was late. Under any other circumstances, his lateness would have convinced me that he was a no-show, and I would have felt preemptively foolish for letting my feelings careen out of control. I would've spent an interminable amount of time waiting, obsessively replaying and analyzing every conversation we had, every touch, every sigh, certain that I had read more into them than was actually there. But right then, all I could think of was my mother walking out the door and driving off as soon as possible.

She was still in the bathroom when there was a knock on the door. I glanced out the window. Cillian's van was parked out front. I had no choice but to answer. I opened the door to his dimpled cheek and a look of bright happiness. He had showered, shaved, and changed into clean clothes. *Did I really spend the previous night naked with this gorgeous guy, touching, kissing...?*

"Sorry I'm late." He leaned over to give me a kiss but stopped short when he spotted Leah and Sloane, spectators at a much-anticipated event.

"Mind if I steal Zee away again?"

"*Again?*" My mother's timing was impeccable. Her hands were back on her hips.

She pointed an accusatory finger at Cillian. "So *he* is your *plans*?"

I cleared my throat. "Cillian, this is my mom. Mom, this is my friend, Cillian."

"Nice to meet you, Zee's mam." He offered a handshake.

She made no move to reciprocate and stepped back.

I felt my face redden with anger and embarrassment, and I created space between myself and Cillian. "Mom, I can explain."

She was judging Cillian from top to bottom. "Oh, no explanation needed, Zezelia. I'm pretty sure I understand—*everything*."

She looked from Cillian to me and back again. Her eyes trained on him, she said, "Zezelia, I don't even know what to say. I'm so disappointed in you."

Sloane and Leah let loose syncopated gasps. My accidental audience of two couldn't help but react.

Never one to mince sharp words, she often opted for passive aggression, but right then, she was opting for straight-up aggression.

"Mom, it's not what you think." That was a bald-faced lie. The situation was exactly what she thought.

"I can only imagine what you were doing last night—instead of studying!" she said, as she jerked her head in Cillian's direction without looking at him. My night with Cillian had been far more than she could've or should've imagined.

Poor Cillian. Poor me. I didn't want my time with Cillian to end on such a sour note, but I wouldn't have blamed him one bit if he had mumbled an excuse, hurried out the door, and sped away in his van, never to return.

"Ms. Owens, is it? I take full blame." He raised his hands in surrender. "Zee and me were just going to get some breakfast. I promise ya, I'll have her back to study for her exams in no time."

He clearly thought he could help by stepping up and coming to my defense. He didn't know my mother.

She slowly turned to shoot her patented death-ray stare at him. "Did I ask you?"

He glanced at me, and I subtly shook my head, trying to convey a message—*Please don't say anything else. You'll only make the situation worse.*

I gently nudged her aside and whispered, "Mom, I'm sorry, but it's not Cillian's fault. I promise it's just breakfast, and I'll come back and study."

Just above a whisper, she said, "You've already wasted valuable time. You have only one more semester. Don't put your future at risk for a boy. Any boy. Not a single one of them is worth it." She glanced at Cillian and turned her laser focus back toward me and lowered her head and her voice. "What kind of accent is that anyway, and what kind of name is Cillian?"

Cillian stepped back, and she gave him one last bloodcurdling stare before I escorted her out the door and to her car. She stopped short, and I could tell she was gearing up for another round.

Before she could rev up, I said, "Mom, I'm fine. My grades are fine. Please don't make a bigger deal out of this than it is. He's a nice guy, and he offered to take me to breakfast before I buckle down. That's all."

She unlocked the car door and tugged on it furiously, trying to pry it open. The door had never been the same after a fender bender several years before, and she couldn't afford to get it repaired. She turned toward me and leaned back on it. Agitated, she rattled the keys.

"Don't lie to me, Zezelia. You have to focus on your education. Do I have to remind you how lucky you were to have gotten that scholarship? Don't put your future in jeopardy because of some boy you think is cute. You know perfectly well that I know what I'm talking about."

Yeah, I knew—in spades. She'd been lecturing me about the lecherous tendencies of the opposite sex since before I hit puberty. She was utterly convinced that her past experience with men, or at least one specific man, was indicative of the entire male species.

I didn't have a clue who my father was, but I knew my mom had been left pregnant and alone with no family and, to hear her tell it, no friends. We had food stamps, Medicaid, and public housing when I was little. A few years later, she won a housing lottery with the city, and we moved into the house I grew up in, where she still lived. She scraped by, working odd jobs, and the minute I turned sixteen, I started a part-time job as a hostess at a nearby restaurant after school and on weekends to help make ends meet. We were never homeless, and we always had food on the table—but resentment and regret had oozed out of every pore of her body my whole life. I tried to empathize. But sometimes, like now, my empathy reserves dried up.

She kissed my cheek, got in the driver's seat, and rolled down the window to leave me with her parting words, her eyes glistening with unshed tears. "Zezelia, honey, don't let your life circle the drain and disappear like mine did."

I watched my mother drive away, her words reverberating in my head. *She feels like her life disappeared?* I knew she had a boatload of life regrets. *Who doesn't?* I guess I didn't fully realize the depth of her disappointment. I vowed then and there to make her tell me about her past, about my father, and to ask her about the choices she had made that, looking back, she would have chosen differently.

When I turned back toward the house, Cillian was standing in the doorway, looking confused and a little concerned. I didn't know how to explain to him what had just happened when I didn't fully understand it myself. I went back into the house and mumbled my way through a superficial explanation—that I was an only child and my mother was overprotective, that she only wanted the best for me, which meant graduating with honors. No distractions were allowed.

"I'm the youngest of eight, so I can't relate to being an only child, but I understand parents not being happy with your life choices. Is your da in the picture?"

"No. I don't even know who he is or what he looks like. They were never married."

"Sounds like that was a good thing. Marriage is a problem—at least in my family."

"I thought you said your parents had a solid marriage until your father died."

"Yeah, they did, but my sister's marriage is shite. Her husband is a right wanker."

"She doesn't want to get a divorce?"

"You have to understand divorce was illegal in Ireland until just a couple of years ago."

"Are you serious?"

"Yeah, but there's still social pressure to stick it out no matter what, and my parents never believed in divorce. You know, the Catholic thing."

"And what do you think?"

"What do I think about divorce?"

"About marriage."

He hesitated. "I think it's a piece of paper. If two people love each other, they don't need a contract that binds them together—for better or worse. If things go to shite, you should be able to just walk away without getting the government, the church, or your family involved."

He wrapped his arms around me, and his mistrust of marriage and my mother's harsh words had to be relegated to the past, where all bad things belonged.

Chapter 5

Cillian had to perform that night, and Sloane and Leah tagged along, never letting me forget their envy or their pride in my status of being "with the band." Each night, Cillian seduced his audience—and me—a little more. During band breaks, he would pull me to a back corner, press me against the wall, and kiss me to the point of breathlessness.

"Only two more hours till we're alone," he whispered in my ear.

Those two hours felt like an eternity.

While I had to share him with the crowd at night, the days were for just the two of us. I introduced him to breakfast tacos, migas, and horchata. He'd gotten a recommendation for a café near Lake Austin that served Turkish coffee and strong espresso that satisfied his need for "real" coffee. We were that nauseating couple that you wanted to knock senseless, always touching, kissing, and whispering in over-the-top PDA.

My heart and my belly were full.

We opened up more about our families—mine tiny, his unusually large—where we saw ourselves in five years, in ten years, in twenty years—a thought that made us both laugh at the impossible-to-imagine image of us as fortysomethings with graying hair, me in mom jeans and him with a middle-aged paunch in place of his almost concave abdomen.

We talked more about our lofty visions for our futures, his far loftier than mine.

"I want the band to be a household name."

"Nothing like shooting for the moon," I said.

"What is it you Yanks say? 'Go big or go home'?"

"Wow. Well, I've been thinking about what I want to do since you asked me the other night at the Driskill. I guess I want to get an MBA—if I can get my grades up and get another scholarship—score a good-paying job with great benefits and maybe even stock options, and then I can help my mother get out of debt."

"After the confrontation I witnessed at yours, I thought things were not so great between the two of ya."

"It's complicated. She got laid off from her job, so she's collecting unemployment right now. She's way too young for Social Security, which wouldn't be much anyway. You're right that we have issues, but it's always just been the two of us, and she managed to keep a roof over my head, which wasn't easy. And, I mean, she's still my mom."

"Is that what you want or what your mam wants?"

My insides squirmed. "Sometimes it's hard to know the difference.

"What about *your* family?" I asked to shift the focus away from me. "What do they want you to be, for you to do? They're okay with the traveling band gig?"

"You're going to laugh, but my mam wanted me to be a priest... like my older brother."

I couldn't help but chuckle. "No way. You have a brother who's a priest?"

"Yeah, he's a good lad. Just wanted to please our parents and do some good in this shite world. I even thought about it for a second or two." He hesitated then smiled. "It was the celibacy thing that was doing my head in."

"Obviously."

Between our nights at the club, the after-hours rendezvous, and our days spent together, few hours were left for sleep. We were both running on fumes, fueled by the high of our incredible mutual attraction.

I hadn't been privy to the discussions, but Cillian had somehow convinced his bandmates to let him have the van after they were done each night. It wasn't the Driskell, but a blanket in the back of his rented van in an empty "car park," as he called it, at Zilker Park after dark, surrounded by the band's equipment, suited us just fine. I would have loved to bring him to my place and the comfort of my bed, but my mattress squeaked when I rolled over at night, and the walls were thin. Sloane and Leah would no doubt have had their ears pressed against the sheetrock. But I didn't care where we were. I just wanted to feel his lips on mine, his hands on my body, feel him hard inside me. At least the van offered the illusion of privacy. I'd lost count of the number of times we'd had sex, which had begun to feel much more like making love.

At two in the morning, we parked in our usual spot and immediately began ripping off shirts, pants, and anything got in the way of us touching each other. A sheen of sweat covered us both. I was basking in a serious afterglow. I couldn't believe something so good was actually happening to me.

"Zee, ya know we're leaving tomorrow, heading to the West Coast. Have a couple of nice gigs lined up."

My bubble of contentment burst with a deafening pop.

I abruptly sat up and wrapped my arms around my knees. "I know that," I said, my irritation clear. I had been deluding myself. He was setting up his it's-been-fun speech to let me know our time together was coming to an abrupt end.

"Don't be thick about it."

"I don't even know what that means."

"Don't be mad. You knew I'd be leaving."

Yeah, but I didn't know I would feel like this. I had shoved aside my responsibilities to my mother, to myself, and to my academic future just to be with him. I was spectacularly unprepared. *What have I been thinking?* He was leaving Austin, leaving me, and I would be left to deal with an emotional hangover of my own making.

He gently touched my back. "This isn't the end, luv. I'll be back."

"Uh huh," I said, my voice infused with sarcasm. "It's okay." I shrugged his hand off. "It's been fun, right?" I said, wanting to beat him to the punch.

He sat up, took my chin in his hand, and turned my head to face him. "Fun? It's been that, alright. But I think we both know it's been a wee bit more than that, yeah?"

"Has it?"

"You know that it has. That it is."

I wanted to believe him, I needed to believe him, and I let him wrap his arms around me as I buried my nose in his chest to breathe him in. Even if I never saw him again, even if my body screamed with the ache of missing him, I wanted to remember the smell of his skin.

Chapter 6

When Cillian left, I didn't ask him for details of his itinerary, and he didn't offer any. I just knew the band was headed west and he promised he would stay in touch. He said over and over again how much he would miss me. But our time together had been so sexually charged that I had to consider the very real possibility that we were just two people who were incredibly, electrically sexually compatible—two random stars that with million-to-one odds had collided in time and space—nothing more.

How could I expect this gorgeous guy with the delicious accent, who just happened to be a lead singer in a band—catnip for girls like me—to be a part of my life beyond the one amazing week of sex and promises whispered in moments of passion? The rational part of me, the thinking part not clouded by lust, told me not to hold my breath waiting for him, or I might die of asphyxiation, another term I had picked up from Leah.

But one small part of me, the part whispering in my ear that maybe, just maybe, my feelings were based on more than the lingering reverberations of a series of toe-curling orgasms, was certain that it had been something more, something deeper, and that he really would miss me as much as I was already missing him.

Then one week stretched into two with no word from him. I threw myself a surprise pity party, complete with a crying jag or two, before making a supreme effort to pull myself together and be attentive to my real life, not to a memory that was already blurring around the edges. I somehow managed to cram for exams and, with some extra credit, keep my grades up—and keep my mother happy.

Those fourteen days of waiting were interspersed with pep talks from Sloane and Leah forcing me to listen to hard truths, telling me to chalk it up to experience, saying I would have other Cillians in my life, and they urged me to snap out of it.

"Experiencing incredible, if short-lived, sex is better than having no sex at all," Sloane said to me. Her bastardization of Tennyson didn't make me feel any better.

At the end of week two, I thought I detected a dim light at the end of my Cillian-crazy tunnel. If I followed that flicker of light, maybe I could come out the other end stronger than before, lesson learned. At least I now knew that feelings like I'd had with Cillian were possible. Maybe Sloane was right. I would find another Cillian, one that wasn't in a traveling band and didn't live thousands of miles away.

I was lying on my bed, headphones over my ears, listening to music and studying, when the kitchen phone rang. I removed the headphone from one ear. I heard Leah answer, but I couldn't make out what she was saying.

Then she came barging in my room and whisper-shouted, "It's Cillian!"

I ran past her into the kitchen and picked up the receiver lying on the counter, took a couple of deep, calming breaths, and answered as if his call was nothing special.

"Hello?"

"Zee, it's Cillian."

The sound of his voice was simultaneously titillating and torturous. "Yeah, Leah told me," I said flatly. I heard the irritation in my voice. The call was already not going the way I'd imagined over the previous two weeks.

"You okay? You sound—I don't know—strange."

"I'm good. You?"

"Um, did I call at a bad time?"

I would've burst into flames if I didn't voice my hurt and frustration over his lack of communication. I didn't care if I sounded needy. I *was* needy.

"It's been over two weeks since you left. Why haven't you called?" My regret was immediate. I didn't want to be *that* girl.

"Here, now, don't be like that. This leg of the tour has been insane. I woke up this morning and realized it's been two weeks since I left. Couldn't believe it. I'm knackered, and I've no privacy. I wanted to call you without the lads breathing down my neck. Anyway, I called to tell you that we'll be back in Austin in a fortnight. 'Back by popular demand,' as they say, and—"

He sounded so sincere, but I had to make a split-second decision whether to believe him.

"I'm not going to be your Austin fuck buddy, Cillian."

Silence.

He cleared his throat. "What? Seriously? Is that what you think?"

"What else am I supposed to think? All that talk about how much you were going to miss me—oh, never mind. Obviously, you had more important things on your mind."

"Are we rowing, then? Maybe me calling was a mistake."

"Maybe it was."

"It's like that, is it? Right, yeah," he said and hung up,

I slammed the phone onto the cradle before I slumped onto the floor. *What just happened?*

Leah rushed in. "You okay?"

"I think I just fucked up."

I thought I was done crying, but I was wrong.

She sat next to me on the floor and put her arms around me. "Please don't cry. You're going to make me cry."

"I'm so stupid. I've been moping around, waiting for him to call. For what? He said he's just been busy, but that's bullshit."

"Let me get you some tissues."

She jumped up and headed for the bathroom. The phone rang again, startling me. I swallowed hard, stood, and looked at the caller ID: same number. It was Cillian again. I stared at the phone for two more rings, three more rings, my heart beating faster with each one. On the fourth ring, I picked up the receiver.

"Hey."

"Zee, don't hang up."

"I won't."

"I'm not sure what just happened, but maybe let's start over?"

"Okay." I sniffled.

"Are you crying?"

"What do you expect? I thought... Never mind what I thought. I—"

"If you thought that I can't wait to be with you again and that I wish I was there with you right now, then you're thinking right. But if you're thinking that you're nothing more than a 'fuck buddy,' as you put it, then your thinking is shite."

"So, how long is a fortnight?" I asked softly, an apology woven into my voice.

He sighed. "That's better. Two weeks. Playing at the same club. I'll call to let you know when we're on our way."

"Okay."

Before he could say goodbye, I said. "Wait. Cillian?"

"Yeah?"

"I'm sorry."

"I know, luv. Me too."

Chapter 7

While I waited for a "fortnight" to pass, I accepted my mother's invitation, which she issued more as a mandate, to come home for a visit. Leah let me borrow her car, and in a little more than an hour, I was pulling into the driveway of our two-bedroom clapboard house, which was in desperate need of a fresh coat of paint. The neighbors evidently still believed broken washing machines and spare car parts were smart landscaping choices.

Mom peered out the window from the edge of the curtains before meeting me at the door.

"So, I made it," I said.

She hugged me and asked as she turned and walked back into the house, "How was traffic?"

"Not too bad."

"Come on in. I'm making us chocolate chip cookies."

When I was a kid, I'd considered Nestle Toll House cookies from refrigerated dough the ultimate in haute cuisine.

"Smells yum," I said, but the distinctive base note of tobacco overwhelmed the soothing scent of chocolate and butter melting in the oven.

She headed toward the kitchen, and I cocked my head as I watched her walk away. Her pants swished, loose around her hips. "Mom, you've lost weight. Are you dieting again?"

She was always trying to lose weight and, in the end, failing. Growing up, I remember her trying liquid diets, the Atkins diet, Weight Watchers, the Scarsdale diet, the cabbage-soup diet, and a host of other diet plans I couldn't remember the names of. Maybe she had finally succeeded.

She didn't answer.

"Mom, did you hear me?"

"Oh, yeah, sorry. My mind was a million miles away. Actually, I have been trying to take off a few pounds."

"Well, it looks good."

She smiled and pulled a cigarette from the pack on the counter and lit up. *In the kitchen. While baking cookies.* It drove me nuts.

I sat at the kitchen table, where I had consumed countless Pop-Tart breakfasts and dinners of SpaghettiOs, mac and cheese, sloppy joes, whatever was on sale and could be bought with food stamps. She did her best with what she had. It was hard on us both.

She pulled the cookie sheet out of the oven, set it on a rack to cool, and sat opposite me at the table.

"I can't believe this will be your last year of school."

"Yeah, only one more semester to go." I raised my hands and my crossed fingers in the air.

"You and Sloane have any celebrations planned after the graduation ceremony?"

"Not yet, Mom. Maybe when it gets closer, we'll think of something. Anyway, you know Sloane. She's not a planner. It'll probably be something last minute."

She rarely asked me about my social life. Maybe the scene with Cillian had placed it front and center in her mind.

"But, you know, I'm not sure I even want to walk the stage. Seems stupid."

"What? Zezelia Ann Owens, you are walking that stage and getting your diploma."

"You know that it's not really my diploma, right? It's just a binder with the school emblem on it. The real thing comes in the mail later."

"I don't care. I've worked too hard to secure a better future for you. I want to hear your name called, have the dean shake your hand, and watch you walk away with that binder with the UT seal on it. Do you hear me?"

She set a plate full of chocolate chip cookies on the table as if it were a bribe. I grabbed one, stood, leaned against the kitchen counter, and took a bite of the warm, chewy goodness.

"Yeah, well...I'll think about it."

Her exaggerated sigh spoke louder than any words could.

She took a cookie and nibbled on it. "So, how are Sloane and Leah?"

"Good, you know, about the same as when you saw them last."

I immediately regretted bringing up that day, the day she accidentally met Cillian.

"So," she said, taking a fortifying breath before she spoke. "Are you going to see that Irish boy again, or has he moved on?"

Of note, she didn't ask me if I had moved on.

"That Irish boy's name is Cillian, and he's not in town right now, but he'll be back in a few days."

"Just be careful."

If she means be careful with my heart, it's too late for that.

"Zezelia, you've got to know there's no future there. Okay, so he's cute, but he's in a traveling band, probably has young girls falling all over him at every stop, and he lives on the other side of the world."

My growing anger was rooted in what I feared to be at least a partial truth in what she'd said.

I grabbed another cookie. "I want to take a shower and crash early. If that's okay with you."

"Whatever you want."

So now *it's whatever I want?*

Sleeping in the room I'd grown up in somehow felt both intimately familiar and strangely foreign. The sheets had long before been washed thin, and they smelled bleachy, like they always did, but they no longer smelled like home to me. I nestled in and began replaying my greatest hits—my relationship with my mother, my life after graduation, and my relationship with Cillian—though not necessarily in that order—before I finally drifted off to sleep and into dreams where Cillian was the headliner.

In the morning, I sat on the edge of the bed and looked around with fresh eyes. My poster of Nirvana was gone, leaving an outline of where it had hung for years. The U2 poster was still intact. I walked over to my dresser. Things were missing—my jewelry box full of rhinestones and glittery things from my middle-school years, along with my makeup bag overflowing with cracked blush, dried lip balm, and clumpy mascara. I had thought it all made me look sophisticated and grown-up. I could still hear my mother's stinging comment. "You're wearing too much makeup. Makes you look cheap."

"Zezelia? You awake?" she called from the kitchen. She had no doubt heard me walk across the room. The floors always creaked, an impediment to me sneaking in or out when I was younger.

"Yeah, Mom! I'm up!"

"Coffee's ready!"

Still wearing the T-shirt I slept in, I threw on my sweatpants and went to the kitchen.

"Morning," I said.

"How'd you sleep?"

"Really good, actually. I haven't been sleeping so great lately." I sniffed the air. "Is that cinnamon rolls I smell?"

"Yep. Almost ready."

Those cinnamon rolls had always been our Sunday-morning splurge. My favorite part was when Mom let me whack the tube against the kitchen counter. I would close my eyes, waiting for the loud pop before the container twisted open, the dough oozed out, and the yeasty smell wafted up to my eager nose.

"Mom, have you started to clean out my room? I noticed some things are gone."

"Not just your room—my room, the garage. Some of that stuff hasn't been used in years, decades even."

"Before you toss any more stuff, can you check with me first?"

She was slathering icing on the cinnamon rolls. "Come home more often, and we can do it together."

She served us two each.

"Breaking your diet?" I asked, smiling. "No judgment."

She shrugged. "I guess so," she said before taking a bite.

"So, how's the job search going?" I asked.

For a forty-year-old woman with no degree and no specialized skills, jobs for her were "as rare as hen's teeth," as she liked to say.

"Still looking, but no one wants to hire me. Too old."

"Mom, you're not old."

She rolled her eyes at me. "Anyhow, I've got unemployment for now. It won't be much, but I think I can make do until you start working."

It took a second for me to process her words. She was counting on me to make enough money to support us both. I wasn't sure how to respond.

"Mom, I doubt I'll make a lot right out of the gate."

She swiped a glob of icing from the cinnamon bun and licked her finger.

"Have you thought any more about moving back home for a while?" she asked with studied nonchalance before looking me in the eye. "It would make things more affordable for both of us."

So, this is her ulterior motive for asking me to come home and bribing me with chocolate chip cookies and cinnamon rolls?

"I haven't even started applying for jobs yet. Sloane did mention something about us being roommates after graduation. So, we'll see. Okay?"

Was it panic or frustration I detected in her eyes?

Aside from her asking me again to put my life on hold and come back home for an open-ended stay, the weekend passed uneventfully. My backpack was packed, and we were sitting in the kitchen, drinking coffee before I left for Austin.

"Zezelia, I want to apologize."

"Apologize? For what?" I thought she might apologize for pressuring me to move back home, for expecting so much of me, or for being a taskmaster instead of just being my mom.

"For anything I've ever said or done that was insensitive or hurt your feelings. If I could go back…"

"Mom, where is this coming from? Are you talking about Cillian? It's okay."

"It's not just that, though I'm sorry about that too. I lay awake at night thinking of so many things I wish I hadn't done, hadn't said. I don't know…"

I couldn't believe what I was hearing. Her apology was long overdue, but I was grateful for it just the same. I came around to where she was sitting, bent over, and wrapped my arms around her. "Mom, I know we've had our issues, but it's okay, really."

"Despite everything, I've always only wanted to protect you, to stop you from making bad decisions and having to live with the consequences, like I did. I just want what's best for you. I want you to know that." She took a breath and patted my hand resting on her shoulder. "Okay, enough of that. More coffee before you take off?"

I guess that was that. She'd said what she wanted to say and was ready to change the subject. I followed her cue and stood, looking down at the top of her head. Her roots were showing more than they had when we went for coffee. "So, you've decided to go *au naturel*?"

"What?"

"Your roots. You're going gray?"

"Oh yeah, I'm going to save money on hair dye."

"Mom, I'm sure we can find something inexpensive. I'll help you touch up the roots."

Money. Our life had always been about money or the lack of it. And now, she was looking forward to sharing the financial burden of worry with me.

Chapter 8

Cillian returned to Austin, and I went to the club that first night solo. I planned to play it cool, not aloof—that hadn't gone over so well on our phone call—but I didn't want to convey the level of feverish excitement I felt. I had to be in control of the situation, of myself.

I shook my head to reset my thoughts, stood straighter, smoothed my tank top, and flipped my hair back over my shoulder before pulling open the door to the club. I was returning to the scene of the crime—or the scene of a miracle—which one remained to be seen. Cillian was on the stage with his back turned as he and the guys were setting up. I waved at Genevieve, and as I was making my way to the bar to say hi and grab a drink, Cillian jumped down from the stage and pulled me into the same dark corner where we had kissed before. Our bodies collided.

Definitely a miracle.

He pulled his lips away with a sucking sound. "God, I missed ya. Don't think I realized just how much until this very minute." He wiped his thumb across my bottom lip before gently kissing my forehead. "Did ya miss *me?*"

"You have no idea."

He gave me one last kiss and said, "That'll have to do for now." He took me by the hand. "Come say hi to the lads." He led me to the edge of the stage and pulled me close to his side.

"Boyos!"

They all stopped what they were doing and turned in my direction.

"You remember Zee," Cillian said.

Sean and Ronan raised their hands and nodded in vague acknowledgement. Damian stepped forward and leaned over, his hands resting on his thighs. "Hard to forget with you saying her name every five minutes."

"Jaysus, Damian. Thanks for that."

"Good to see you again, Zee," Damian said before he returned to setting up equipment, satisfied he had sufficiently embarrassed Cillian.

Cillian ushered me to the table closest to the stage. I always hated sitting alone in a movie, a restaurant, or a bar. But with my eyes trained on Cillian, I didn't feel alone.

He repeated his speech about Ireland, about music, which still felt fresh to me, then he said into the mic, "I've written a new song that we're going to play for the first time tonight. I hope you like it." He was addressing the audience, but he was looking at me. Then he closed his eyes, stepped back, and lowered his head, gathering his energy, creating a force. When he stepped up to the mic again, he had transformed into the lead singer of The Swifters. It was one of those heart-skips-a-beat moments I read about in novels—a visceral reaction. It wasn't normal, the effect he had on me. Even when we weren't touching, I could feel his touch through his words. Control was a concept I could no longer grasp.

"This song is dedicated to someone who recently came into my life—proof that miracles do happen."

Then he began to sing.

Every morning, I wake up
With thoughts of you on my mind.
As the days go by, my feelings
Get stronger but harder to define.

You've come along just in time
To save me from myself,
To unlock my heart.
If this is love, you've got to let me know,
Just don't take too long,
'Cause I'm not that strong.

I immediately recognized the words from the scraps of paper I'd unfolded and read in the Driskell. But new words were also there, words he said I had inspired. As the beautiful lyrics left his lips and filled my heart, my body absorbed the music and became a part of me. I wanted to freeze that moment in time so I could thaw it out when I needed a reminder of just how great life could be.

The next few days were a blur of music and bodies intertwined. We talked more about our lives outside of our protective cocoon. We drew palpable energy from one another, which regenerated each time we came together, and we would emerge recharged and ready to take flight.

"How's uni?" he asked as he traced the lines of my body with his fingers.

"Fine. Somehow both boring *and* stressful. But it'll be over soon."

"How soon is soon?"

"Another semester. As soon as I'm done, I'll have to focus on finding a job—like, a real job."

"In Austin?"

"Moving away is not an option. It wouldn't go over too well with my mom." That was a PhD-level understatement.

"What happened to you wanting to travel, see the world?"

I turned to face him. "I can't believe you remember that."

"Yeah, especially the part where I offered to be your tour guide in Ireland."

He smiled. I was certain he must practice in the mirror, perfecting the smile that showed his dimple in the best light. He was flirting—unnecessary, seeing as how we'd just had sex. But I welcomed the warmth it generated.

"Well, the closer I get to graduation, the farther away the idea of world travel seems to be."

"Zee, you can do whatever you want. My family were dead set against my choice to sing in a band thousands of miles away from home. But I did it. I'm doing it."

"But your mom has all your brothers and sisters still in Ireland, right? They have each other. For better or for worse, I'm all my mom's got, and she's all I've got."

"Fair enough. Maybe give it some thought. You'll never be this young again."

"That's deep. Did you just come up with that?"

"Nah, it's from a song."

"Of course it is." I chuckled.

Without a word, he sat up, grabbed a pack of cigarettes on the blanket and lit up. He blew smoke into the air, and I watched it float above his head. He wrapped his long arms around his knees and began to rock back and forth.

"What is it?" I asked, wondering if my flippant comment had come across as insulting.

He took another puff and snuffed out the cigarette. "Come with me," he said, not turning to look at me.

"Come with you where?"

He lay back down and rolled over on top of me, his skin melding to mine.

"I want to be with you. All the time. I want you to come with me on tour."

My brain was scrambling to make sense of his words. "Cillian, you know I can't do that. I'm almost done with school, and I need to start working, making money. I can't just run away with you."

"But I need you." His soft hair trailed my cheek, and he exhaled the words into the nape of my neck. He was teasing me, promising an endless supply of whatever this was. If I went with him, I would be changing the trajectory of my life, of my mother's life—flaunting fate.

"I want to be with you too. But I can't. I... I just can't." I started crying, miserable and mad that he expected me to make that choice. He was asking the impossible of me. I wasn't sure if he wanted me to prove my love, to satisfy his selfish needs, or to create an unbreakable bond between us. I wanted him in my universe. But that was asking too much of me.

"Don't cry, Zee. I'm sorry. Really, I'm sorry. I shouldn't have asked. It's just that I think about you all the time."

"Me too, but my situation is complicated. You know that."

"Life's only going to get more complicated as we get older, yeah? Now is the time for us to experience life, and I want to experience everything life has to offer—with you."

He was whittling away at my will, my determination to do the right thing—for me, for my mom. My next words surprised even me. "Can I at least think about it?"

"Well, promise me you'll think hard before you say no."

When he left that time and each time after that, I stopped wondering whether he would return to me. He wanted and needed me as much as I wanted and needed him. Still, each absence became a test of my patience and endurance, a test I was failing miserably. Despite the time between his Austin appearances stretching longer, the slack in the thread that connected us had been pulled taut. It was easy to forget that we'd met only three months before, but those months had reshaped my present and were slowly refiguring my imagined future.

The Swifters were getting more gigs and performing at larger venues as they zigzagged across the country. I had taped a US map to my wall and stuck a push pin in every stop. Cillian would call from the road, and I would always ask, "Where are you now?" He was responsible for booking all the gigs. Between that and late nights, he was burning the proverbial candle at both ends.

I was pushing a pin into Santa Barbara when the phone rang. I ran to answer, and he started talking before I even got a chance to say hello.

"Zee, this gig has been deadly!" he said, breathless. "I think we have a shot at getting an agent!"

I could barely make out his words through the background clamor, but the word "agent" came through like fireworks.

"Oh my God! That's awesome!" I so wanted to be there with him to celebrate. I raised myself up on my tiptoes, and gripping the phone with both hands, I said, "Tell me everything!"

"So, this scout watched our last set and came backstage, handed me her card, and said to ring her, that she wanted to talk. She actually said she'd heard 'buzz' about us. She's based in Los Angeles."

"What did the guys say?" I asked.

"Sean was banging on about all the shite he was going to buy when we get a contract. I was like, 'Are you feckin' serious? We haven't met with her yet, and you're already spending?' Sometimes, it feels like Damian and me are the only ones who are bleedin' serious about the music, you know?"

"Oh, Cilly, I'm so happy for you."

"Well, it's just a meeting, but..."

"This is it," I said. "I'm sure of it. I can feel it. Have you told your family yet?"

"Not going to do that until it's a sure thing, and even then, not sure what their reaction will be. Like I told ya, they're not too happy about the whole singing-in-a-band thing."

"Well, I'm deliriously happy for you."

"That's enough for me, babe."

Chapter 9

By the time Cillian returned to Austin, I'd decided our connection was more like a magician's trick than a miracle. Miracles defy explanation. They just are. Some explanation had to exist, some sleight of hand behind the feeling of insane joy that took control of my mind and body whenever we were together.

After hours in the club, Genevieve was cleaning the bar, the manager was mopping the disgustingly dirty floor—a futile exercise—and the guys were sitting on the edge of the stage, legs dangling, drinking beer and laughing at something Damian said as they shoved him to the floor. *Boys being boys.* Cillian and I were at a table in the corner, our foreheads pressed together.

"I've got some news," he said as he reached for my hand and intertwined his fingers with mine.

He hadn't said it was *good* news, and from the downtrodden look on his face, I was suddenly imagining the absolute worst of the worst—the meeting he'd been so excited about was a disaster, he was giving up the band and going back to Ireland, he was giving up on me. My heart thrashed against my rib cage.

"We signed with an agency, the one I told you about. They're helping us to sign a band manager and a tour manager."

I pulled back and looked at him, needing a second or two to process his words as good news.

"Oh my God! That's awesome!"

But he wasn't smiling. If anything, he looked sad—not the reaction I'd expected to such amazing news.

"What's wrong? I thought you'd be dancing on the tables."

He lifted my hand to his lips and held it there for several seconds before he said, "We're gonna be booked in bigger venues, more cities. There's even talk about a European/Asian tour."

"This is what you always wanted. Why the face?"

"Zee, I'm going to be gone for months at a time. I don't know when I'll be back, when I'll see you again."

In my excitement over the news of his impending success, that reality hadn't occurred to me.

"Oh."

He looked me in the eye and tightened his grip on my hand. "Unless you come with me."

I shook my head. "Cillian—"

"I know, I know. Your mam, uni, money. But what about *us*?"

He froze in anticipation of my answer, his emotions pummeling every inch of me. I let go of his hand and looked away. I could either fulfill my obligations and sign up for the life my mother had laid out for me—or for once do what my gut was telling me, no, screaming at me to do, and choose a new life full of passion and never-before-imagined adventure with someone I had come to love more deeply than I'd ever thought possible—and who, to my constant amazement, loved me back just as hard. If I said yes, I would be taking a step I couldn't take back.

His words tumbled out, his accent thickening the faster he spoke. "We'll get to travel the world together—Tokyo, Hong Kong, Barcelona, Rome—Paris! Just think, us together in Paris! I mean, I have to go with or without you, but I want you to—"

I was no longer listening. My thoughts were running record-breaking what-if marathons in my head. *If I said yes, would I come to regret it? If I said no, would I come to regret it even more?*

I had absorbed the urgency in his voice, but I was unable to take that trust fall.

His obvious disappointment in my lack of a response was already filling me with regret when he stated unenthusiastically, "I got us a hotel room for the night. Last night together before I leave for LA."

I nodded, leaving his life-altering question unanswered.

A couple of hours later, we unceremoniously checked into the motel. It wasn't a five-star accommodation, and the unbridled excitement of that first night at the Driskell was nowhere to be found, replaced with the weight of melancholy and dread as I made a down payment on a future regret. I had stupidly done this to myself—let myself fall in love so quickly, so blindly with someone on an entirely different life path than me. I remembered that Robert Frost poem about two roads diverging. Cillian was taking the one less traveled, while I was destined to take the well-trodden path that would send me in the opposite direction. He held tightly onto my hand as we silently rode the elevator up to our floor and entered the room, and when he kissed me softly, it felt like goodbye.

He tenderly undressed me, never unlocking his eyes from mine, and wiped a tear away from my cheek.

"Zee, let's just focus on here, on now. We're together now, yeah?"

I nodded, and he gently laid me on the bed, and we made love—slowly, sadly—neither of us sure if this would be the end as he went on to bask in his success and I went on to fulfill my obligations to my mother. I wanted to commit every touch, every scent, every sigh to memory.

As we lay together with only the sound of our slowing breath filling the silence, he said, "I promise not to go two weeks in between calls. I'll call you as often as I can."

I felt something building inside of me, ready to burst forth. I exhaled loudly before I said, "No, you won't have to do that."

"But I want to."

I propped myself up on my elbow, kissed him softly, and said, "You won't have to do that because... I'm coming with you."

Listening to the words effortlessly roll off my tongue was an out-of-body experience. Nothing in my life had ever felt so wrong yet so incredibly right.

He raised himself up, confused and slack-jawed.

"What about your mam, uni?"

"My mom will just have to deal, and I can always come back later and finish up school. Besides," I said, pausing for effect, "maybe I can transfer to a university in Dublin at some point." I breathed out the words, releasing my responsibilities and choosing my heart. "I choose you. I choose us."

Smiling, his dimple deepening, he said, "I love you, Zezelia Owens." Then he leaned down and whispered in my ear, "You won't regret it. It's going to be fuckin' brilliant!"

My announcement must have been an aphrodisiac because we had sex in the chair and against the door and ended up on the carpet, which left me with a major rug burn on my back.

He suddenly sat upright. "Let's go now and get tattoos!" he said as if that had already been a topic of discussion.

"What? Are you crazy? No way." Despite my insistence that my mother would just have to deal with my decision to go on tour with Cillian, all I could think of was how horrified she would be to see me inked up.

"Come on. It'll be fun."

"A needle repeatedly puncturing my skin isn't my definition of 'fun.' Anyway, it's after midnight. They're all closed."

His expression softened. "Okay, but I want to get one tomorrow. Something that reminds me of you every time I look at it until you join me."

The next afternoon, we stood outside Thoughtless Tattoos in downtown Austin.

"The name doesn't inspire confidence," I said.

"It's kind of ironic, don't you think?"

"I guess."

We walked in, and Cillian flipped through the three-ring binder of images.

"What are you thinking?" asked the guy with the sleeve tattoos, nose ring, and huge gauges in his ear lobes, which were stretched beyond recognition.

I was fascinated by the choices people made to pierce and paint their bodies.

I scooted closer to see the images on the pages. "Ooh, what about this one?"

It was a Celtic Serch Bythol, which stood for "everlasting love joined together forever in body, mind, and spirit," according to the binder. He pointed at that one in the book and had the tattooist add my initials, ZO. It was beautiful.

Despite my stance that a tattoo was not for me, two hours later, I walked out with a matching tattoo with the initials CB in micro letters on my left shoulder. We stood side by side to compare our permanent connection—more permanent than a wedding contract.

My mother was going to kill me.

Chapter 10

My to-do list before leaving with Cillian:
Get passport photos.

Apply for a passport (borrow fee from student loan).

Buy clothes worthy of a rock star's girlfriend (borrow from student loan).

Buy luggage (borrow from student loan).

Go to UT's registrar's office to put my education on hold.

Steel myself to reveal my plans to my mom.

Steel myself for her meltdown.

Cry. Cry some more.

Pack.

Fly to meet Cillian!

Be happy.

I wasn't sure who was more crushed—me or Cillian—to learn that my passport wouldn't arrive for at least a few weeks, and while there was an option to expedite the process for a fee, I had siphoned all I could from my student loan funds. Cillian might have been on the verge of greatness, but he was still just as broke as I was.

"Zee, but you're going to miss the first leg of the tour—and I'm going to be miserable without you."

"You'll have the tour and be dealing with all the logistics. I don't think you'll miss me as much as you think you will."

"You don't understand," he groaned. "I feel empty without you."

I wanted to jump through the phone line and take away his emptiness. But we would have to have patience, which was in short supply.

Dropping out of UT was anticlimactic. I had expected pushback when I showed up at the registrar's office to put everything on hold, maybe "Are you sure this is what you want to do?" I expected a lecture from the counselor about how I had only one more semester to go and the classes I had already started would be listed as incomplete. But nobody cared. Despite no longer being enrolled in classes, I kept up the ruse with my mom, rambling on about classes, instructors, and exams while I checked the other items off my to-do list.

Cillian called every few days, reinforcing our commitment and reconfirming our plans as we spoke dreamily about the future of The Swifters and our future together. Every part of me missed him. I was jealous of the band, who got to see him every day.

Three weeks into the passport waiting period, he called again.

"Zee, I can't wait any longer. We've got a couple of free days, and I need to see you naked."

"Well, I'm naked right now," I teased, despite being fully dressed in a sweatshirt and jeans.

"*Shit*, don't do that to me." He sighed. "I want you."

I laughed, but the image of the two of us, naked, touching, was making my heart pound.

"I want you too," I whispered. "When will you be here? Just hurry."

Whoever said, "Absence makes the heart grow fonder" was grossly understating the reality of it. Once we were alone, we would have willingly morphed into a single body if it were possible. He hungrily kissed every inch of me, and I met his passion with a version of myself I didn't know existed. But I couldn't stop my fatalistic thoughts. *What if everything—his band, my departure, our love—falls apart? How can I possibly survive without him?*

Or him without me?

Late into the second night, he rolled over and sat on the edge of the bed. I raised myself on my knees behind him, pressing my breasts against his back, and nuzzled his neck. He didn't move.

"What's wrong?"

He shook his head. "I don't wanna leave ya. What if everything goes to shite? What if your passport doesn't come? What if your mam convinces you to stay? What if you change your mind?" His last words were more a worry than a question.

I leaned over to breathe my words in his ear. "Cilly, nothing's going to keep me away. I want to go where you go. I'm so excited for what lies ahead for you, for us. It won't be long now."

He turned around and dropped me onto the bed, and we rolled over, falling onto the floor, laughing.

"I love your optimism. It's hot."

But the optimism I projected was an ill-fitting mask I wore to hide my deeply ingrained pessimism, developed over a lifetime of struggles and disappointment—both mine and my mother's. Maybe once I boarded that plane to be with Cillian for good, my optimism would become my reality.

After we showered and went over the logistics of me joining him on the road one more time, he was on his newly acquired cell, discussing the tour with his newly acquired tour manager. Things were changing. I wandered over to the window and stared out at the Austin skyline, wondering when I'd be back once I left.

I didn't want to love Cillian that much. It felt dangerous.

He came up behind me and waved a hand in front of my face. "Where'd ya go? I can tell something's on your mind."

"Nothing," I lied. "I'm just starving!"

"Me too! Let's order room service," he said as he handed me the folder with a menu.

I glanced at the offerings. "All this stuff is crazy expensive. Maybe we should just go down the street and grab a burger or a taco or something."

He cocked his head to the side. "Zee, darlin', those days are about to end. By the time the credit card bill comes, I'll have money in the bank."

"My mom always said, 'Don't count your chickens before they're hatched.'"

"I don't know about chickens, but I have a contract that spells out payment terms. Don't worry, luv. We can order whatever you want. We'll have a feast."

He called downstairs and ordered a ridiculous amount of food that neither of us would ever be able to eat. Room service later wheeled in a banquet of shrimp cocktail, pizza, steak fries, two hamburgers, a ham-and-cheese omelet, hash browns, Mexican vanilla ice cream, oatmeal cookies, and coffee.

"Oh my God!" I said.

We looked at the bounty then at each other and exploded with laughter. Cillian's laughter was like floating in still waters while basking in the sun. I would have the rest of my life to swim in it. I was bursting at the seams with happiness.

We never could have imagined that the feast would be our Last Supper.

Chapter 11

Cillian's cab idled outside the hotel, waiting to take him to the airport to catch his flight to Los Angeles and his rock star future—without me.

"My passport should be here soon," I said, tears welling up. Even though we would be together before too long, our parting left me feeling anxious and hollow.

"You alright, then?" he asked.

"I just miss you already."

"Me too. Counting the days," he said before caressing my face in his hands and giving me one last lingering kiss. As reassuring as it was to feel his warm lips on mine, it wasn't enough. I wanted more. I needed more.

"Let me know the minute your passport comes, and I'll make your reservations."

Now that he had some leverage, he had requested—demanded, actually—that my flight be paid for. I wondered if that was what my life was going to be like—infused with love, caring, support, and no more hand-to-mouth existence for me—or my mom.

After tossing his bag into the trunk and climbing into the back seat, he rolled down the window and blew me a kiss. I watched the cab head down the street, getting smaller and smaller until it turned left. Then he was gone. I stood in front of the hotel, staring down the street, where Cillian's departure had left a vapor trail of unease.

When I returned to the apartment, Sloane and Leah greeted me with empathetic hugs.

"Are you okay, girl?" Leah asked.

I simply shrugged. They knew I would need their support. But neither of them knew about my plans. Despite my excitement over my future with Cillian, an undercurrent of uncertainty and embarrassment over my rash decision had prevented me from sharing fully—until then. I had kept up the same ruse with them that I had with my mother, leaving for classes that I didn't attend and lugging books around that I no longer needed. While Sloane would likely be shocked, I was certain she would ultimately be supportive, like she always was, and that shored up my courage. The three of us were sitting at the kitchen table, and after Leah poured coffee in preparation for my debriefing of the previous night with Cillian, the phone rang.

The caller ID said Mom.

"Hey, Mom. What's up?"

She was asking me to come home for another visit. Unexpected, but I figured I owed it to her. I would be leaving soon, and once I was gone, she might not see me for several months at a time. An unplanned trip home would be the opportune time to reveal the extreme shift in my life plans—more like a shift in *her* plans for *my* life.

"Sure, I'll drive in tomorrow morning." I looked at Sloane, and she nodded permission to take her car.

My mother didn't ask about school, which had been a regular part of every conversation we'd ever had since I was five years old, but I figured she was saving up for an in-person interrogation.

"She sounds a bit needy, Zee," Sloane said after I hung up. "Maybe she's getting depressed, thinking about you graduating and us getting our own place instead of you going back home."

I cleared my throat. "That's something I wanted to talk to you about."

Her eyes widened. Leah sat straighter.

"I know you're both going to think I'm insane, that I'm not thinking straight, that I'll regret it, but I've already decided." I gave a single decisive nod as much to myself as to Sloane and Leah. "I'm going on tour with Cillian as soon as my passport comes in the mail."

Leah slapped her hand over her mouth to muffle a gasp, and Sloane pinched her lips. She looked like she was going to either punch me in the face or puke.

"Your *passport*?" Sloane asked, once she began to recover from the initial shock. "Where are you going, I—wait, what about school? What about our plans to rock this city after graduation?" I waited for her inevitable acceptance, for her support.

"I've already gone to the registrar's office and put school on hold."

"What the fuck, Zee? You can't be serious." Her face had turned an alarming shade of puce. She shoved her chair back, stood rod straight, and crossed her arms tightly across her chest. "What are you thinking? You just have to finish this semester to graduate!"

"I can always pick up school later. Right now, Cillian and I belong together. I'm not going to let this opportunity for my happiness slip through my fingers because of what I *should* be doing."

"This is fucking crazy! You couldn't wait a few more months?" She took a breath. "It's Cillian, isn't it? Is he pressuring you to do this?"

"No. This is my decision and my decision alone."

"Yeah, right."

I was unprepared for her deep disappointment and building anger. "How about you just be happy for me?"

"Well, that's a tall order." She grimaced. "You're not the only one affected by that decision, you know. I assume your mom doesn't know?"

My shoulders tensed. "No. I'll tell her tomorrow."

Leah hadn't said a word. I turned to her. "You don't have any-thing to say?"

She glanced at Sloane warily, and her face flushed. "You're fol-lowing your heart. I think that's a good thing."

With that, Sloane shot one last devastating glance in my direc-tion, huffed, and stomped out of the kitchen, and I heard the slam-ming of her bedroom door.

Chapter 12

I was sick with anxiety as I pulled into the driveway of my house—well, my mother's house. My decision to go on tour with Cillian suddenly seemed like an alternate reality that had nothing to do with me, with this house, with my mother. The thought of actually saying the words to her, "I dropped out of school, and I'm leaving to be with Cillian," left a stabbing pain in my chest.

Then I remembered Cillian's infectious smile, his laughter, and his childlike excitement over my decision to join him. Recalling the joy on his face and the passion that followed gave me the strength to reach for the car door handle. With a white-knuckled grip, I opened the door, stood, slammed it shut, and walked in slow motion to the house.

I took the concrete steps one at a time, sidestepping the hardy flowering weeds that had sprouted through the cracks, and I stood at the front door. I fumbled with the key until the lock clicked, and I pushed open the door.

The house was quiet. I yelled, "Mom? I'm home!"

She rose slowly from the sofa.

"Sorry, did I wake you?"

"It's fine. I was just taking a little catnap so I'd be fresh when you got here."

She had never been someone who napped, but she was getting older.

"You okay?"

"How about some coffee?" she asked.

"Uh, sure."

While the coffee brewed, she carried on a conversation as if we were mere acquaintances.

"How was the traffic? I know that construction is crazy on I-35. I think they're adding a lane. The weather is nice today. Did you stop at Dairy Queen?"

DQ had been a regular for us when I was a kid, and we would drive into Austin to shop at Goodwill.

She brought us both coffee and set the familiar mismatched ceramic mugs on the table.

"Thanks," I said, waiting for her to tell me why she had asked me to come, before I shocked her with my news.

She calmly sipped her coffee, sat back, and pulled an opened envelope out of the pocket of her housecoat and set it on the table.

"What's this?"

She simply nodded in the direction of the letter. "Read it."

I grabbed the envelope and turned it over. The return address was the UT Registrar's Office. I didn't have to read it. I knew what it said.

I opened my mouth to deflect, to ask what gave her the right to open mail that was clearly addressed to me, but now was not the time.

"I thought maybe it was a mistake, but I can tell by the look on your face that's it's not."

"I can explain, Mom."

"Okay, I'm waiting," she said as she crossed her arms tightly across her chest.

As much as I had tried to mentally psych myself up, I was ill-prepared.

I squirmed in my seat. "Please try to understand," I began, "but I'm putting school on hold for a while because... because I'm going on tour with Cillian."

Her face flushed, and she shook her head, never taking her eyes off me. I'd expected her to yell, to pound the table, to tell me how thoughtless, irresponsible, and reckless I was being. I was geared up to be defensive and argumentative. She grew still, and tears streaked her cheeks.

"Mom?"

"Zezelia, honey, I have to tell you something."

"What is it?"

She reached her open palms across the table, and I placed my hands in hers. Instead of worrying about what I had to tell her, the pain in my chest returned as I waited for what she had to tell me.

"So, I went to the doctor and..."

I barely heard her next words. I had to hit the replay button in my head to make sure I had heard right.

"Cancer? When did you find this out? What kind of cancer? What stage? Are you going to need chemo?" My throat closed before I could pepper her with any more questions.

"Pancreatic, stage four. Last week."

Shock didn't begin to describe the searing guilt, sorrow, and dread I experienced all at once.

"I don't understand," I said, my voice cracking. The truth was I didn't want to understand. My brain was unable to process the magnitude of what she was saying. Denial was the only way for me to cope with what sounded like a certain death sentence.

"So, what did the doctor say is the next step?"

"Chemo, but it would be a Hail Mary."

I pulled my hands back and curled them into fists. "But there's a chance, right? It happens all the time."

"Zee, honey, it actually *doesn't* happen all the time. There's only like a one to two percent survival rate."

"But you could be in that one to two percent!"

Her whole body curved into itself, and she sighed. "It's spreading fast. The doctor says I have only a few weeks without chemo, maybe a few months with it. And I would feel like crap the whole time."

I shot out of my chair and wrapped her in a hug. We had butted heads most of my life, but she was still my mom, my only family. Guilt hammered me for coming home to tell her I was leaving.

"Zezelia, I'm going to need your help. I'm sorry, honey, but I can't do this alone. I need you to put your plans on hold until I—"

I couldn't let her finish that sentence.

"Of course, Mom. I'm here. I won't leave you."

I was devastated for her, for me, for Cillian. A rush of confusion flooded the corners of my heart. I didn't know if I could do it, if I was even capable of setting aside my deepest desire to selflessly care for her, to watch her die, to be left motherless in the world.

Instead, I comforted myself with the certainty that when all the pain, the sorrow, and the grief had done their job, Cillian and I would be together.

Chapter 13

I stuffed my clothes, my books, my laptop, my lava lamp, my favorite mug, and all my school papers into Sloane's car before we headed out to Johnson City. We said little, the lingering tension between us palpable. *But really, what is there to say?* I wasn't leaving to be with Cillian after all, my mother was dying, and Sloane was struggling to reset her anger dial to supportive.

After half an hour of nothing but the Texas sun beating down through the windshield and the sound of tires singing on Highway 71, I broke the tension.

"Will you let me know when my passport comes in the mail?"

She took her eyes off the road for a second or two to look at me. "Have you told Cillian yet?"

"No."

"What are you going to say?"

"The truth. What else would I tell him?"

"Don't know. How do you think he'll take it?"

"He couldn't be any more disappointed than I am, but I mean, my mom is dying." I choked on the words. "He has to understand. If he doesn't, he's not who I thought he was. And it's not like our plans are cancelled, just postponed."

I was doing my best to focus on the "after"—after my mom would be gone. *Does that make me cold and calculating? Unfeeling? Does it make me a monster?* Knowing I had something amazing to look forward to would help me cope with the awful things that would soon be happening. I had often wished for her to disappear when she was criticizing me, pressuring me to be better, do more. But that was an adolescent, knee-jerk, I-hate-my-mom reaction. I couldn't process the fact that she would really be gone and I would have no family. I told myself that Cillian and I might be creating our own family someday.

We pulled up in the driveway, and I looked around the dirt yard, the peeling paint on the shutters, the carport that tilted to the left. I'd always understood that we didn't have much, but the stark contrast to my life in Austin and the new life that lay ahead of me with Cillian put my life growing up in high relief. I would eventually be stepping into a better life, but my mother would never get that chance.

I opened the front door and spotted her lying on the sofa. She didn't move when we walked in, and I had a hot flash of panic.

"Mom?"

"Zezelia?" she said groggily. "You're early. What time is it?"

I wasn't early. I was late.

"It's about five. Sloane's here. She going to help me bring in all my stuff, and then I'll fix us something to eat."

Sloane walked in, sat next to my mom on the sofa, and gave her a hug.

"I'm so sorry, Ms. Owens. If there's anything I can do…"

If it was possible, she looked thinner than she had just a few days earlier.

"Thank you, honey, but Zezelia's here now. I know she'll take good care of me."

She was revealing a softer, more vulnerable, needier side than I had been privy to growing up. *I guess a cancer diagnosis will do that.* The tangled hurt, resentment, and anger that had solidified over the years and weighed me down shapeshifted into an innocuous gas of slowly seeping forgiveness.

Sloane and I made several round trips to the car to unload and dump everything in my old room. When the final box was piled up against the wall, I looked around. I was moving back home, something I'd never, ever imagined myself doing. I had to keep reminding myself of why I was there and that it wouldn't be forever—a thought as depressing as it was uplifting.

Sloane hugged my mom goodbye, and as I walked her to her car, she stopped short and said, "I'm so sorry, Zee." She glanced back toward the house. "For everything. Seriously, let me know if you need me, and I can be here in an hour and a half."

"I'm not really sure what to expect, but whatever happens, I know it's going to be horrible. And I know I'll call you."

She wrapped her arms around me, and her body tensed as she exerted physical effort not to cry. She got in the car and blew me a kiss with trembling lips, then she was gone. I sat on the front porch steps, dropped my head in my hands, and I cried. That was going to be the hardest thing I would ever do, and I had no clue how to steel myself for any of it.

But I had to start by telling Cillian.

Chapter 14

Mom was napping—again. She had nodded off three times that morning. I tiptoed from her room, went to the kitchen, and took the receiver off the wall phone. Gripping it in my hand until my fingers ached, I readied myself to break the news to Cillian. I still wasn't sure I would be able to say the actual words "I can't join you anytime soon." I slowly dialed the hotel number he'd given me. I couldn't tell where it was, just that it was in a different country. When I was transferred to his room, the ring tone sounded like a ticking time bomb. Him answering would be the explosion.

"Zee, baby!"

I was nauseated, but then a numbness crept its way up from my toes.

"Cillian."

"It's so good to hear your voice. I hope you're calling to tell me your passport came. I can't wait for you to get here, wherever 'here' will be. We're not staying in the same place for too long. The crowds have been great, but it'll be so much better when you're with me. You're going to love it! I—"

"Cillian, wait... wait. I have some bad news." I was trying hard not to tear up, but my voice wobbled.

"What is it? What's wrong?"

There was no way to ease into the conversation, so I just blurted, "My mom's got cancer."

"Oh shit..."

"It's terminal, and she's too weak for chemo. So... I have to stay here to help her through this. She doesn't have anyone else. I... I can't come. At least not for a while."

"Zee, baby, I'm so, so sorry. I'd be a liar if I said I wasn't disappointed, but I understand. Is there anything I can do?"

"Not really. The doctor said it could be a matter of weeks. I've already ordered a hospital bed and called about home hospice care. There's a lot of medical stuff and arrangements for—after. It's kind of overwhelming right now."

"*Shit*. I feel fuckin' useless. I wish I could be there to help you. I know how hard it is. When my da passed, it was rough. But you're strong. You can do this. Just be there for her. Call me if you need to talk, and I'll call as often as I can." He lowered his voice to a whisper. "I miss you, and I love you."

"Me too." My future, which had seemed so certain, so beautiful, just a few days before was unraveling faster than I could stitch it back together.

"Where are you now?" I asked, trying to distract us both from the harsh reality of what was keeping us apart.

"Amsterdam. I'm meant to be in Paris in a couple of days."

Paris. That was the city we'd fantasized about experiencing together—the Left Bank, the Seine, the Tuileries, the bakeries, the sidewalk cafes.

"Zezelia!" My mother's fading voice sounded like a fog horn.

"Listen, my mom's calling me. I have to go. I love you, Cillian. So much."

"Me too. Just do whatever you have to do for you and your mam."

I disconnected and stared at the phone as if that would make me miss him less. I took a deep breath.

"I'm coming, Mom."

The doctor called me back after I'd left three desperate messages. "She's too weak to even come to her appointment, and she's in a lot of pain. What should we do?" I asked hopefully.

There was a long pause. It sounded like he was tapping his fingers on his desk. "Make her as comfortable as possible, manage her pain, and just be there for her. I'll call in stronger pain meds."

I knew what that meant.

The next few days were a blur of pain pills, visits from the hospice nurse, and hours and hours of sitting by my mother's bedside, watching her disappear before my eyes. The hospice nurse had told me that dying was an active process, and she wasn't actively dying—yet. Her body was shrinking, but her brain was still intact.

My mom patted the space next to her on the bed. "Zezelia, there's something I want to tell you before I can't think straight anymore."

I sat, took her hand, and kissed her palm.

"What is it, Mom?"

"This is really hard for me. So, I'm just gonna rip off the Band-Aid."

She's dying of cancer. I'm bathing her, brushing her teeth, wiping her butt, and changing her diaper. Whatever invisible wall existed between us before has been knocked down with a sledgehammer. What could possibly be so hard to discuss with me?

"It's about your father."

I blinked in confusion. In all my twenty-one years, she'd refused to touch on the subject of my father. I had long since come to think of him as nothing more than a sperm donor.

"My... father?"

"I never wanted to burden you with my mistake, but I won't be here much longer, and I just don't want you to make the same mistakes I did." She took a labored breath.

My interpretation of her words must have been written on my face, because she jumped in. "No, honey, you weren't a mistake. You were the one thing I've done right in my life. No, this is about the man who gave you to me."

"Okay…" My insides quivered. I wanted her to tell me before she would no longer be able to.

When I was a kid, I'd fantasized about who my father might be, what he might look like, and that he would walk through the door one day, swing me around, and say, "There's my girl! I'm sorry I haven't been here, but I'm here now."

By the time I turned thirteen, I'd given up on that fantasy, buried my anger and hurt feelings, and accepted that it was just me and my mom and always would be. But his unexplained absence was a chronic itch I couldn't scratch, and her refusal to tell me anything about him was the flint for the burning down of our relationship.

"I never told you about him because I didn't want to weigh you down with the knowledge of who he was or what he did. The man I was with, the man who was your father, was the love of my life, but"—she took another excruciating breath—"he eventually destroyed our relationship, destroyed himself, and he almost destroyed me in the process."

Chapter 15

My mother's first ever mention of my father and her offer to fill in the blanks of their story, of my story, left me stunned. She must have realized that it was now or never.

"Zezelia, I want to tell you so that you don't make the same mistakes I did—mistakes that I can see you're about to make."

"If you're talking about me and Cillian, I—"

"I know you don't want to hear it, but if I can prevent you from going down the same heartbreaking path I did, I can die knowing I did everything I could to save your future."

"Mom, it's okay. You don't have to—"

"Shush! Just listen. You can ask questions later if you want."

I felt my defenses go up before she even began. I was wavering between really, really wanting to know and really, really wanting to clasp my hands over my ears to block out her voice.

She took a labored breath and asked, "Can you hand me that glass of water, hon?"

I watched as she brought the straw to her trembling lips and took a single sip. I put the glass back on the nightstand next to her pills, a thermometer, and a magazine she hadn't opened. Then, I spotted a never-before-seen photograph of a guy about my age.

I picked it up, but before I could ask, she said, "That's your father."

She paused while I stared at the photograph, scanning it for any common features reflected in my mirror every day. His long blond, almost white hair framed big hazel eyes and long lashes evident even in the faded photograph. I could see that I was an unmistakable blend of him and my mother. My life's puzzle had always been missing a major piece, but now that I had that missing piece in my hand, I didn't know what to do with it.

"I met Daniel—that was his name—when I was younger than you. I thought he was the most beautiful man I'd ever seen. He was four years older than me, which at the time felt like a huge age gap, but I didn't care. He seemed so mature and together. It only added to the incredible attraction. Anyway, I was out with friends one night, drinking—we had fake IDs, of course."

A hint of a smile crossed her lips.

"He was a pharmaceutical salesman, mostly around Texas. Not as glamorous as a singer in a band, but there was just something about him. He was standing at the bar by himself. When he glanced my way and smiled, I was over the moon. What I saw was perfect boyfriend material. He had a good job, he was interested in what I had to say, and he just seemed really, genuinely nice. Something about his eyes. Anyway, that night, I did something I had never done before or since—I followed him back to his hotel, and we slept together." She paused. "Are you shocked?"

I shrugged. I didn't want to slow her pace of telling me the story.

"I felt guilty. I thought I had committed a mortal sin and was going to burn in hell. At least that's what my mother told me. But he had been so gentle with me, so loving. I convinced myself that it couldn't be wrong."

She closed her eyes, whether from fatigue or to replay her memory in the dark, I couldn't tell. When she opened them, she simply picked up where she left off.

"He traveled a lot, and I followed him whenever I could sneak away. Looking back, I believe Danny really did care for me in the beginning, but then he started doing drugs, and things quickly went south. By the time I realized I was pregnant, he was deep into his addiction, he was sleeping around, and he had been fired. He always had some ridiculous explanation for everything that was going wrong in his life. I wanted so badly to believe him that I did—for a time. In the end, I understood that he was a drug addict and a liar, and I was standing in the way of him getting what he needed. My parents kicked me out when they found out I was pregnant, and, well, I was on my own. And then you came. I never even told him I was pregnant."

I couldn't imagine. "Oh, Mom. I'm so sorry."

"I'm not telling you this for you to feel sorry for me, Zezelia. I'm telling this to you to warn you. That rock-and-roll lifestyle, all the touring, the drugs, the hangers-on, the women. It's abusive—physically and emotionally—to everyone in and around it."

I felt something in my chest contract.

"Before he left me, he asked for money, and when I said no, he hit me, called me every disgusting name in the book, and then he took what little I had. This was from a man who I thought was my one true love. A man who treated me with such tenderness in the beginning. A man who made me feel like I was the most beautiful creature on the planet. But when the drugs took over and he turned on me, it was even more painful than if he had been cruel from the beginning."

I leaned over and wrapped my arms around her frail frame and listened to the rattle in her chest. When I pulled back, I held her veiny hand in mine and raised it to my lips. "Do you know where he is now?"

"Six feet under somewhere, I suppose."

She didn't sound sad or resigned. She was simply stating something she assumed to be true.

"Mom, I know you think you're saving me from a similar fate, and I appreciate you finally telling me all this, but Cillian is nothing like that. He's a beautiful person, and he loves me."

"Zezelia, honey, when I first met him, your father was perfect, genuinely beautiful inside and out. But nothing that seems perfect and beautiful lasts. I want you to understand that. I'm begging you—I want you to promise me, really promise me, that when I'm gone, you won't follow this Cillian boy. I want you to stay here, finish your degree, get a good job, find a good man with a solid future, create a family, and live your life with as few regrets as possible."

I let go of her hand, stood, and paced the room. I stopped, arms crossed, and turned to her. "That's not fair. How can you ask me that and say it's your dying wish? I can't abandon Cillian. I love him! You don't understand—he *is* my future."

"I know you believe that, and you think he would be the exception. But no matter how you feel right now, when it all goes to hell—and it will—you'll be left behind to put the pieces of your life back together. I want more for you."

I could see her shoulders relax. She had said what she wanted to say then announced abruptly, "I want to sleep now."

She seemed to have expended all her mental and physical energy reserves to issue her warning. Her decline over the next few days was rapid as she drifted in and out of consciousness. She would open her eyes and ask me if she had been in a car accident then tell me she needed to get to work, and in a brief moment of lucidity, she looked at me and said, "I love you." I didn't have time to truly process what was happening. The hospice nurse came and informed me that Mom was actively dying.

Then, just like that, she was gone.

Sloane helped me with the arrangements. I wasn't thinking clearly enough to do it on my own. She came with me to the funeral home and did most of the talking. Each time I opened my mouth to say something, a sob erupted. Mom had told me she wanted to be cremated, and when I saw the prices for a regular burial with a casket, I understood why.

At one in the morning the night before the service, I was zigzagging between overwhelming anxiety and grief. My mother was gone, and I was stressing about how I could possibly pay for everything. I needed to hear Cillian's voice to calm me and remind me that there would be an "after" with the two of us.

Wherever he was in Europe, it was at least six to seven hours later. He had left me a voice mail with his number. I hated to wake him, but I needed to let him know what was happening and talk about what our next steps might be. Despite my deep sorrow, and despite my mother's dire warnings, I wanted to be with him, to begin our new life together. That thought was the only thing keeping me sane.

My anticipation expanded with each ring over the phone line. The sound of his voice would be the signal that my life was about to change direction, and it would be filled with love and happiness. He would smooth over the sharp edges of my grief.

The ringing stopped.

"Cillian? It's Zezelia."

I heard a cough and a huff. "Cilly, baby, it's for you!" she shouted. "A ZooZoo or something." The voice belonged to a woman with a thick French accent.

"Shit." He sounded furious.

A few seconds later, his voice was coming across loud and clear, but it wasn't having the soothing effect I'd hoped for. I had roused them both from sleep.

"Zee, baby, I'm so glad you called."

Is he serious?

"Who the hell was that?"

"Renee. She's a lighting tech on tour with us."

"What is she doing in your room so early in the morning, answering your phone... and calling you 'baby'? She sounds like she just woke up."

"What? No, wait, Zee, it's not what you think."

"Oh?" My heart was squeezed so tight that I didn't think it would take another beat.

"The hotel didn't have enough rooms, so she slept on the sofa in the parlor."

"And why is she answering the phone?"

"There's one by the sofa. Zee, we were just watching TV last night."

He said *we*.

"Okay. So tell me why is she calling you 'baby'?"

"She's French. She calls everyone either *mon chéri* or 'baby.'"

I couldn't swallow, much less breathe. "I don't believe you."

"You've got the wrong idea," he went on. "Zee, I would never... I love you. You know that."

My mother's prophecy was playing out more quickly than I ever could've imagined. Her words were a chorus in my head. It had been the score to her life, sung to the tune of struggle and disappointment. I wasn't going to let it be mine.

"Zee, you there? Zee?"

"My mother died," I growled.

"Oh, *shite*. I'm so sorry."

Then I heard what left no doubt that what my mother told me was excruciatingly, painfully playing out for me in real time.

"Cilly," the woman whined. "I'm hungry. I don't want to miss breakfast. Get dressed. You can talk to her later."

That was a hammer to my barely beating heart. They say the bigger the love, the harder the fall, and Cillian had just pushed me from a fifteen-story building to splat on the concrete sidewalk below. I ejected the receiver as if I were holding a hornet's nest, and it hit the floor with a crack. I heard Cillian's voice.

"Zee? Zee, baby, pick up the phone!"

My throat burned, and I felt as if every breath were going to be my last. I could still hear Cillian begging me to pick up the phone when I dropped the receiver back on its cradle, cutting him off mid-sentence and cutting him out of my life. *Was this how my mother felt?* I should have been more empathetic to her sadness. Up until a few days before, I had no idea what she'd been through because she never told me. I wished more than ever that she were still there with me. But I had to pull myself together. In less than eight hours after the door to my life with Cillian was slammed shut, I had to say goodbye to my mother.

The phone rang again and again and again.

I ran to the bathroom, dropped to my knees near the toilet, and vomited.

The phone continued to ring as I pushed the bathroom door shut with my foot to muffle the sound of the ringing.

Chapter 16

Elliott was one of a handful of people to show up at my mother's service. He looked the same as he had in high school. He looked *at me* the same. After the service—no eulogies, no prayers, just a simple goodbye—he approached me. Sloane had been glued to my side to keep me from collapsing under the weight of my life without my mother, without Cillian. Elliott said hello to Sloane, and when he reached out to give me a condolence hug, she stepped back to give us space.

"I'm so sorry, Zezelia," he whispered in my ear.

The utter sincerity of his words was like a bullet to my heart, and I hugged him back as hard as I could in my weakened state.

"If there's anything I can do, anything at all, just let me know."

"Thank you, Elliott," I said as I took a step back and he reluctantly let me go.

"Is it okay if I check in on you later to see how you're doing?"

I managed a weak smile. "Yeah, of course."

Once Sloane got me home, she placed me on the sofa and poured me a glass of cheap wine from the fridge, and I convinced her to leave. I had to figure out how to cope on my own, like my mother had been forced to do. I sat, staring into space, the glass of wine in my hand, but I hadn't taken a sip.

Sloane hadn't been gone five minutes when there was a knock at the door.

I set my glass on the coffee table, hoisted myself off the sofa, and slogged my way to the front door. I didn't need another casserole or flowers from neighbors or from people who were never friends but seemed to perversely enjoy offering condolences, grateful that they weren't on the receiving end.

I hesitated but opened the door, and there stood Elliott. He had changed from his funeral suit and tie into jeans and a T-shirt. His dark hair was still wet from a shower. When he asked if he could check on me *later*, I hadn't thought it would be only a few hours later.

"I hope it's okay that I just showed up. You looked so sad. I wanted to see if you were alright. Maybe you wanted company. Or wine?" He brought around a bottle of wine he'd been hiding behind his back.

His offer extracted a smile from me.

"I'm actually glad you're here. Come on in."

I left for the kitchen, emptied my cheap wine into the sink, and brought back two clean glasses and a corkscrew. We curled up on opposite ends of the sofa and reminisced about high school: about what mutual acquaintances were up to—who was already married, who was already divorced, who was in prison, who was super successful. Over better-tasting wine, we exchanged the basics—university, work, family (or lack of), and plans for the future. He finished off his glass of wine and looked sheepish when he confessed that he'd had a huge crush on me back then. We'd dated a couple of times in high school, and I always knew he had a debilitating crush on me. Seeing the way he looked at me had been painful.

I smiled and said, "I know."

"Ah, okay." He blushed and looked down into his wine glass. "And my seventeen-year-old self thought he was being so subtle."

"I don't think subtlety is standard issue for teenage boys," I said.

He smiled before reaching for the wine bottle. "True. More?" he asked, gesturing toward the bottle.

"Just a little." The wine was having a pleasant numbing effect.

"Seeing anyone?" he asked.

"No," I answered too emphatically. "What about you?"

"Nope. Haven't found the right person yet."

I winced. *The right person*. I thought I had found him, but I couldn't have been more wrong.

After a couple of hours and another glass of wine, we were winding down, and he said, "I've hung around too long. You must be totally wiped. I'll let you get some sleep."

I was exhausted, but I was genuinely glad he had dropped by. He made it possible for me to think about something else for a while, and for that I was grateful. We stood and walked together to the front door.

"You can keep the wine," he said, smiling.

"I should hope so," I said in mock indignation.

He leaned over to hug me goodbye. When he pulled back, he looked at me, and I could see it in his eyes—his feelings for me hadn't changed since high school. He leaned in slowly, assessing the situation, checking to see if it was appropriate, if he was out of bounds. Without debating with myself if it was the right thing to do, I let him kiss me. His unfamiliar lips against mine, the novelty of his smooth, just-shaved skin, and his almond-scented shampoo were having an unexpected, not unpleasant, effect on me. I wrapped my arms around his neck, and he responded like that seventeen-year-old boy finally getting to kiss his crush. I was suddenly verging on manic. I led him into my old bedroom and stripped as if my clothes were on fire, and with U2 looking down on us, we had frantic, grief-fueled sex.

The morning after with Elliott was awkward—not something I'd considered when I jumped into bed with him. When I opened my eyes and performed a self-check, the frantic need that had possessed me the night before was nowhere to be found and had been replaced with lead in my gut. Elliott rolled over in bed as though he'd been lying there, waiting for me to wake up, and he looked at me with such adoration and affection in his big brown eyes. I felt sick. He was a nice guy, objectively attractive, but he wasn't Cillian—at least not the version of Cillian that I had fallen in love with. I wanted Elliott to leave.

"How about we go get some breakfast later?" he asked as he lightly skimmed his fingers down my arm. His erection pressed against my thigh. He was expecting an encore before breakfast.

Shit!

I jerked upright in bed, covering my breasts with the sheet. "That's really sweet, but I have so much to do, stuff to figure out, you know?" I stood and grabbed my pile of clothes from the floor, using them as cover, and faced him. "Anyway, I think I'd be terrible company today," I said before I headed to the bathroom. I could feel him watching my nakedness from behind.

I showered, dressed, brushed my teeth, and stared at myself in the mirror. *What was I thinking?* I was a terrible person. *Cillian hurt me, and now I'm going to hurt Elliott?* I knew the situations were like night and day, but pain is pain, and I didn't want to be the one doling it out. Elliott was a good guy, and he didn't deserve to be summarily dismissed, but I didn't want to give him false hope either.

When I opened the bathroom door, he was dressed and putting on his shoes. I assumed he was getting ready to leave, and I was guilt-ridden over the degree of relief I felt.

"So, no breakfast?" he asked as he stood by the bed, his hands shoved in his jean pockets.

I glanced at the rumpled sheets. The memory of the night before, of me repeatedly asking for more, made me cringe with regret. That wasn't me. And it was certainly not an indication of any feelings I might have for Elliott. I'd used him, and I felt ashamed.

"Maybe another time?" Even as I said the words, I knew I had no intention of meeting Elliott for breakfast or anything else.

"Sure. I understand," he said.

Then he unexpectedly closed the distance between us and kissed me as passionately as he had the night before.

Clearly, he didn't understand at all. When I didn't respond in kind, he pulled back, looking confused.

"You sure you're okay? I can stay if you want."

"No, I'm good. I think I just need some time alone."

"Well, I'll call to check on you, okay?"

I smiled and nodded. It seemed like the right thing to do.

Before he left, he said, "You let me know if you need anything."

"I will," I said. But he couldn't help me with the one thing I needed—to turn back time.

In the weeks that followed, I seriously thought I might go insane. Cillian called constantly, but I stood my ground and refused to answer. In between his calls, Elliott called. Both must have had my number on speed dial. My voice mail was full, but I refused to listen to any of their messages. Waves of exhaustion and nausea had me sleeping fifteen hours a day.

When I was close to the breaking point, I called Sloane. I had cried on her shoulder about Cillian, and she was supportively pissed at him, telling me I deserved better, that he was a dick. She let me know that I was doing the right thing where he was concerned. But I needed to get my colossal misstep with Elliott off my chest.

I told her that I needed to talk but that it had nothing to do with me coping with my mother's death or Cillian's cheating—*unless me strangling my grief by banging Elliott's brains out was somehow related.*

Sloane arrived with a six-pack in one hand and chips and salsa in the other.

"Are we morning drinking now?" I asked.

"You sounded like this might be a beer-and-chips kind of situation. And I love the smell of beer and chips in the morning."

I reached out and hugged her tightly as she held her arms out to the sides so as not to drop her delivery.

"Thanks for coming so fast."

"But of course. What else are best friends for?"

She led the way to the kitchen, left two beers on the counter, and pulled down one bowl for the chips and another for the salsa. She twisted the top off a beer and handed it to me. The cold sweat of the chilled glass bottle offered instant relief from the heat of my regret and my anger at myself.

"Okay, so what happened?"

"So—well..." I cleared my throat. "The night of my mother's memorial... I was with Elliott. *All night.*"

She frowned deeply and cocked her head. "What?" she asked as though unsure she had heard me correctly.

I told her everything—Elliott's surprise appearance, the kiss, and my nymphomaniac metamorphosis. She listened, wordless, until I stopped talking.

"So, how do you feel about it?"

"Like shit!"

"Well, don't. It was clearly something you needed. And God knows it must have made Elliott insanely happy. He's had the hots for you since ninth grade. But you don't owe him anything. Guys do that shit all the time and walk away, feeling nothing but satisfied."

"I know, but—"

"Zee, so you went a little crazy. Given the circumstances, I think it's totally understandable."

"So, you don't think I should—"

"If you say you should apologize to Elliott, I'm going to throttle you. He's a guy. Granted, he's a nice guy, but he's a dude just the same. He'll be fine."

She gestured toward the bottle I'd set on the table. "Just drink your beer."

The phone rang, and I looked at the caller ID. It was Elliott.

"This has been going on for the past two weeks. If it's not him, it's Cillian, and I don't want to talk to either of them."

She calmly reached over and unplugged the phone.

"Come here," she said as she hugged me. She shoved a chip into my mouth and took one for herself. "Tortilla chips make everything better."

"Not everything."

She stopped chewing. "Oh? I sense there's something more."

"Could be. I'm not sure."

"Okay, continue...

"I'm probably overreacting. It's probably nothing."

"Jesus, Zee. What is it?"

"I think... I think I might be pregnant."

She plopped down in a chair and slammed her beer down on the table.

"Um, I'm thinking maybe you should have led with that?"

"I'm late. I bought a couple of pregnancy tests, but I've been too freaked out to do it."

"Okay. So, do it now," she said, shooing me to the bathroom. "I'll wait with you."

I closed the bathroom door, pulled out one of the tests, and stared at it before ripping it open. I peed on the stick and set it on the counter. *What if it's positive? How can I possibly have a baby, raise a child? If it's positive, maybe I should end the pregnancy and get on with my life.* Waiting for the result was the longest five minutes of my life.

The timer went off, and I looked at the stick. Too stunned to cry, I exited the bathroom, waving the stick with the double blue line around like a baton.

"Looks like I'm gonna have a baby," I said with forced enthusiasm.

"Fuck," she said. "Let me see."

She grabbed the stick from my hand, examined it, and let out a weighted sigh. "Shit! What now? Do you think you might want to keep it?"

"I... I don't know. I can't think right now."

"Are you going to tell him?"

Her question hit me with the shock of a stun gun. I didn't know who "him" might be—Elliott or Cillian.

I was even less sure of whom I would rather it be.

Fuck.

My passport arrived the next day, and I cried until I got the hiccups. I stared at my glossy passport photo, thinking back to how happy I'd been when it was taken. I held the useless passport in my hand. I wasn't going anywhere anytime soon, and I had no idea what I was going to do with my life.

Chapter 17

Cillian's calls decreased from several times a day to several times a week to a few times a month until he finally gave up and stopped calling. I'd read somewhere that not making a decision is in itself a decision. The result of me not making a decision was that I was five and a half months pregnant, and even after my due date revealed Cillian to be the father, I still had no idea what I was going to do. My feeling of betrayal clouded my judgment. I was far too hurt and angry to tell him he was going to be a father.

My mother had left behind a Mt. Everest–sized mountain of debt that I slowly discovered only after she was gone, and in the end, I was forced to sell the house to get creditors off my back. There was medical debt, but I couldn't deny that I was partly, if not mostly, to blame for the budget deficit she left behind. A good portion of that debt, even with my partial scholarship, was from my attending but not finishing UT.

At closing, when the lawyer shook my hand and handed me the check with the proceeds from the sale, I gasped. The little money that was left—and it was *very* little—would have to last me until I could get a job, and the chances of anyone hiring me in my condition were slim to none. I needed money for food, rent, and doctor and hospital bills, and as certain as the sun would come up the following day, I would need formula, baby food, baby clothes, diapers, and childcare—a must-have, assuming I would eventually land a job.

I felt like someone had put my head in a plastic bag and zip-tied it around my neck.

That was when Sloane stepped in. She'd graduated and scored a sweet job at a high-tech start-up and was more than happy to share her good fortune. I accepted with bottomless gratitude, knowing full well I would never be able to pay her back.

The Saturday after I closed on the house, I moved into a small apartment complex close to Sloane's sleek new condo. She offered to let me stay with her, promising to play the role of Auntie Sloane after the baby came, but I was stupidly determined to somehow make it on my own. I'd gotten myself into that mess, I was going to have to deal with it and figure it out myself.

She knocked on my door, and as soon as I opened it, she said, "How about we go baby shopping?"

I laughed and patted my swelling middle. "I already have a baby."

"Okay, smart ass. You know what I mean." She waved her newly minted platinum card in my face. "How about we pop the cherry on this thing?"

I shook my head and gestured for her to come in. "You're so gross."

"First on the list, maternity clothes. I think I can hear that shirt groaning," she said as she zeroed in on the fabric straining across my stomach and put a hand to her ear as if to hear better.

I had been in self-imposed solitary confinement since my mother died, but we were on our way to the people-packed mall that always smelled like popcorn, Cinnabon, and cheap perfume. Driving down Capital of Texas Highway, past the thick patches of cedar trees and the limestone-lined passages and over the Pennybacker bridge crossing Lake Austin felt like an adventure, a vacation.

"Where do you want to start?" Sloane asked as we parked close to the mall entrance.

"You're in charge of purchasing, so you pick."

"Macy's."

"Ah! *That's* why you wanted to come to the mall."

"They do have a maternity section, you know."

Once inside the mall, we stopped to get Dippin' Dots, enjoying some serious people watching and making up stories about them, like we'd always done in clubs.

"That one is maxing out her husband's credit card before she leaves him for a younger man. That guy is stressing over finding the perfect gift for his new girlfriend, who he's sure is already cheating on him. She's hoping her new Victoria's Secret purchase will recharge her sex life."

A couple walked by, and she was very pregnant. He was holding her hand and kissing her cheek.

As I felt tears welling up, Sloane nudged me. "Let's keep going."

On the way to the far end of the mall, a window display with beautiful bedding caught my eye. I pressed my hands to the glass, imagining how silky soft those sheets must be, how warm the comforter, how amazingly soothing that down pillow would feel. The scene brought me back to my night at the Driskell with Cillian on eight-hundred-thread-count sheets, but I quickly pushed back at the memory.

"Sloane, come here. Look at this. It's gorgeous!"

When she didn't answer, I turned around. "Sloane?"

She had abandoned me for a pair of platform shoes in a window display on the opposite side of the mall. "Sloane!"

She turned around. But she wasn't the only one responding to the sound of my voice. Just two stores away, Elliott stopped midstep, his mouth agape as his eyes zeroed in on my protruding belly, and I made a laughable attempt to suck it in.

Sloane rushed to my side as Elliott approached.

"Sloane, it's okay, really."

She hesitated before stepping aside. Elliott stood in front of me, his eyes full of questions—and hurt. He looked like he always did, neatly groomed, nicely dressed, and carrying a shopping bag from the Gap. He glanced at Sloane.

"Can we have a minute?"

She looked at me, and I nodded my okay. She retreated to a bench in the walkway but never took her eyes off the two of us.

He cleared his throat. "Well, I'd ask what you've been up to, but..." he said as he once again glanced at my stomach in what I could only describe as disbelief.

"Elliott, I..."

He cocked his head. "How far along...?" He stepped closer and lowered his voice. "Is it mine?"

There are moments in life where a simple yes or no can alter the trajectory of the rest of your life—job offers, marriage proposals, sex, an invitation to go on tour with your boyfriend. This was one of those moments. If I was honest and said no, Elliott could walk away, guilt- and consequence-free. If I said yes, I would be lying, but my yes would be a matter of survival for me and my baby. Elliott had always loved me, and I knew he would love this baby. Biology doesn't dictate love.

Still, I chose honesty.

"No, Elliott. It's not yours. I'm sorry."

His face fell like that of a child who'd just been told he couldn't have that candy so temptingly displayed at the checkout counter. I added that to the list of ways I'd unintentionally hurt Elliott over the years.

Once he composed himself, he said, "I'm sorry, I shouldn't have assumed. So, are you married?" He glanced at my ringless left hand.

"No."

"Where's the father? Is he helping you?"

"It's a long, boring story, and it's complicated, as these things tend to be."

He shoved his hands in his pockets and rocked back on his heels. "I'm really sorry, Zee."

"Don't be. It was my choice to go it alone."

"If you feel like talking, maybe we can get coffee somewhere—if you can still drink coffee?" He gestured toward my pregnant belly.

I chuckled. "I still drink coffee, but, well, I'm here with—"

Sloane quickly approached. "Hey, Elliott."

He cleared his throat and hesitated. "I was just asking Zee if she wanted to go get coffee or something. Um, maybe, you know, we can all go."

That was Elliott—always gracious, always inclusive, always so *nice*.

Sloane glanced at me to gauge my feelings about the invitation, and I gave her a subtle signal that I was okay, and she excused herself with a promise to call me later.

Elliott and I went out for dinner twice after that, and he came with me to my next ultrasound. It was awkward, but I couldn't say no to his hopeful request. So I was only a little surprised and certainly not shocked when he got down on one knee and opened a black velvet box with a beautiful diamond-and-ruby ring inside.

"We'll be a family," he said as he gently placed his palm on my stomach. "I love you so much. It can be a good life for us, Zee."

The following week, we had a quickie ceremony at the courthouse with Sloane as our witness. Elliott's parents were gone, and he was an only child, so just the three of us were there to make it official. Despite Elliott's excitement that I was about to be his wife, that we were going to be a family, to me it was a sad ceremony that officially marked my forever loss of Cillian. When the justice of the peace pronounced us husband and wife and Elliott kissed me, I burst into tears.

"Ignore me. It's just hormones," I said when he asked if I was okay.

But that was a lie. I was in denial—denial that I wasn't still desperately in love with Cillian, denial that I had made a rash decision that I was already regretting, and most of all, denial that I would be able to live with the consequences.

Chapter 18

I was surprised at how easily I slipped into the routine of married life with Elliott. Being with him allowed me to temporarily forget about love and lust and open myself up to a comforting relationship. The steady security he provided fulfilled a need that had nagged at me my whole life, and for the first time, I didn't have to worry about money. I spent my days playing house and nesting while Elliott went to work at his new job as a corporate tax accountant. He was happy, and his happiness was contagious. Sometimes, I could convince myself that my life, our life, the life for the soon-to-be three of us, would be just as good as he'd promised the day he proposed. Still, my brain had trouble processing the idea that this would be "till death do us part."

Two months, three weeks, two days, and ten hours after we said "I do," I woke up at one in the morning on a Tuesday, sat on the edge of the bed, and rocked back and forth, trying to decide if the twinges in my abdomen were the signal that I was about to have this baby—Cillian's baby. *No,* I told myself, *this is going to be Elliott's baby.* I had to believe that with all my heart if the life we were building together would work. I gently nudged him awake.

"Elliott, I think this is it."

He shot up, and his eyes popped open as if a siren had gone off in his ear. His dark hair was pointing in all directions. I couldn't help but smile.

"What? Now? Are you sure?"

"No, but this feels different. I think we should go to the hospital."

The words were still lingering on my tongue when a vise tightened around my stomach, which had become as hard as the linoleum on my mother's old kitchen floor. It felt like something was pulling me apart from the inside, something that didn't belong to me. I watched a documentary once about a rare condition where people felt like an arm or leg didn't belong to them, and they wanted it removed. That was what I felt like. I let out a deep animalistic groan.

As the pain began to ease, I said, "Okay, *now* I'm sure."

Elliott jumped out of bed and slipped into the clothes he'd placed over the back of a chair, almost as if he had practiced the drill. Maybe he had. I waddled to the bathroom to pee before we left, but when I sat on the toilet, water gushed out of me like a faucet.

"Elliott! My water broke. We need to hurry!"

He helped me get dressed and grabbed the prepacked overnight case as he tuned in to my every move, my every sound. But I couldn't stop thinking, *What would it feel like if it were Cillian holding my hand, doting over me, driving me to the hospital, anxious to meet his child?* The guilt that went along with those rogue thoughts made me even more nauseated than I already was.

We made it to the hospital with little time to spare. I was too far along for an epidural, and I screamed and grunted my way through labor with Elliott holding my hand. When the pain stopped suddenly, I had a beautifully serene seven-pound-eight-ounce baby girl in my arms. She looked around, blinked twice, and promptly fell asleep. Seeing the look of complete adoration on Elliott's face was like staring into the face of the sun. He was smitten. She was his baby girl.

He gingerly took her in his arms and made sweet cooing noises. "So, what should we name you?" he asked her.

We had tossed around several names but couldn't decide. I had secretly looked up Irish names, most of which were too hard to spell and pronounce, but then I found a list of American versions of Irish names. One clung to me. Maybe I was being stupidly selfish, unfair to Elliott, maybe I was holding onto something that had never been what I thought it was to begin with, but I couldn't ignore my desperate need to instill something of Cillian in her. An American version of an Irish name was the best I could do.

"I really like Ashlyn," I said.

He looked down at her in his arms. "So, is your name Ashlyn?"

"What did she say?" I teased.

"Well, she's a little hard to understand just yet, but I think she said yes."

As I looked at Elliott holding Ashlyn, already loving her, I truly believed that her birth might be a new beginning for us, that a love for him would grow alongside my deep love for Ashlyn.

We brought Ashlyn home to the nursery we had painstakingly decorated. The walls were a subtle shade of yellow, and we had ordered one of those frilly bassinets online, which had been delivered two days before. It was ridiculously expensive, but Elliott had insisted. A mobile of butterflies hung above, and next to the bassinet was a chest of drawers, a changing table, a diaper bin, a baby monitor, a collection of pacifiers, and a rocking chair, among a million other baby accessories. Maybe Elliott and I weren't perfect, but Ashlyn was, and so was her room. I thought of my mother. She would never get the chance to meet her first grandchild. I didn't know if she would've approved of my decision to turn to Elliott after I kicked Cillian to the curb. Her lifelong lesson to me was one of survival—do whatever it takes. I had learned it well.

Elliott immediately stepped into the role of a doting father. He was a natural. After work and on the weekends, he changed Ashlyn's diapers, no matter how disgusting. He cleaned her spit up. He pushed her in her stroller up and down the hallway when she was screaming like a banshee and it was pouring rain. He watched me breastfeed like it was the most beautiful thing he'd ever seen. When my breasts swelled and turned hard, he brought me warm compresses. And he made sure I had time to rest. He was everything a struggling new mom could ask for. *And yet...*

The weeks ran into one another like colors bleeding in the wash. They all turned the same shade of gray. When I went in for my six-week checkup, the obstetrician gave me the green light to have sex with my husband. Since I was no longer pregnant, I had hoped to recapture some of the grief-fueled passion that my mother's death had created. Maybe lust and love would reinforce one another and build something solid between us. The truth was I fell in and out of something akin to love with Elliott all the time. It was a warm, comforting feeling, like sitting back in a soft armchair in front of a wood-burning fireplace, a book in hand. My love for Cillian had been an out-of-control flash fire that, once ignited, couldn't be extinguished.

But despite my incredible gratitude and appreciation for everything Elliott had done for me and with me, his bottomless love for Ashlyn, and my deepest desire to truly love him and to want him body and soul, I would eventually come to accept the fact that I couldn't force my heart to feel something it didn't.

Chapter 19

The phone rang, and I answered on the first half ring to avoid waking Ashlyn. I had just gotten her down for a nap.

"Hello?" I whispered.

"Zee, baby, it's Cillian. I've been trying to get in touch with you for months."

My first impulse was to throw the phone across the room and hope Cillian would feel the pain. But the lilt of his voice and the sound of his breathing weakened my resolve. I closed my eyes.

"Zee, you there?"

I stood straighter. "Hello, Cillian." I heard my voice turn unnaturally formal.

"You've been avoiding my calls."

"And yet you keep calling."

"I get how hurt you were, but you have to let me explain. I swear the situation wasn't what it seemed."

Hearing from him again was almost as painful as the phone call that tore us apart.

"Seriously? I don't need you to explain anything to me, Cillian. The situation was crystal clear."

"Zee, I swear I didn't do anything wrong, and I think about you all the time. The truth is I'm shite without you. I love you. You have to give me a chance to explain."

My mother's words of warning were ringing in my ears, drowning out Cillian's pleas. I bit my lip so hard that it bled.

"I don't *have* to do anything. Anyway, it's too late."

"Not if you still love me. Just tell me you don't love me, and I'll disappear. Say the words, and I'll believe you."

I couldn't make myself say it, but he really was too late.

"Cillian, I'm married."

His gasp was followed by an airless silence.

"Jaysus! Are you fuckin' messin' with me?"

"No, I'm not *messin'* with you. I got married three months ago. His name is Elliott—he loves me, and he would never cheat on me."

I shocked myself with my capacity for such casual cruelty hurled at the man I had loved and still loved. I felt a cold weariness in every cell in my body.

"That makes no sense at all. Married? To someone you just met? Am I nothing to you now?"

"I've known him since high school. But that's really none of your business. You destroyed whatever it was we had, if it even ever really existed. It's time for you to go live your life and for you to let me live mine. Please don't call me anymore. Goodbye, Cillian."

I hung up and stared at the phone. Ashlyn began to wail as if on cue.

I went to her room, scooped her up in my arms, and cooed in her ear, "I love you, sweet girl. Your daddy loves you too. We'll be okay. I promise."

The years passed, and Ashlyn grew, along with my genuine affection for Elliott. I hadn't anticipated that, as Ashlyn matured, she would develop an uncanny resemblance to Cillian and that it would grow stronger with time. Elliott never commented on Ashlyn's unfamiliar features, but I wondered if he ever saw someone else in her face.

Her pediatrician commented once on Ashlyn's green eyes, sandy hair, and freckles, which neither Elliott nor I had. "Genes are funny that way," he said, and that became my canned response to whoever decided to point out the obvious to me.

Still, our little family flourished, and I decided to be happy or at least happy enough. Elliott changed jobs and was promoted, we bought a bigger house in a better school district and got a new car, we took Ashlyn to Disney World twice, and I was a full-time mom. Cillian didn't call me again—at least not for a very long time—but I masochistically followed his career online. All his dreams of being a rock star were becoming a reality as he toured the world, going to all the places we had talked about seeing together. Sometimes, while Ashlyn was at school, I found myself whiling away the hours daydreaming about what might have been then emotionally flogging myself for wasting so much time on a fantasy. I was living on the edge of my imagination.

I would occasionally hear one of Cillian's songs on the car radio, and it would split open a fresh wound. But with time, the sharp anger and hurt dulled and cut less deeply, and I chose to remember only the good things about him—his warmth, his sense of humor, the deep rumble of his voice when he said, "I love you," his beautiful body, and the incredible high I felt each time we made love. I was too ashamed to admit it, but sometimes, when Elliott made love to me, I would close my eyes and fantasize that I was feeling the warmth of Cillian's body, that his lips were pressed to mine, his breath whispering in my ear. More than once, Elliott said, breathless, "Look at me, Zee. I want you to really be here with me." But if I opened my eyes, any passion I felt vanished, and I was simply going through the motions.

Elliott wasn't stupid, just hopeful.

Ashlyn was twelve when Cillian left the voice mail that would, once again, send my life in an uncharted direction.

"Zee, it's Cillian. I know it's been donkey's years—I remember that expression made you laugh—and you might not be chuffed to hear from me, but I've been thinking about you a lot lately, about what happened between us. I'm coming to Austin next week, and I thought maybe enough time has gone by that... Anyway, if you'd like to meet me for a drink or for coffee... How about that place we used to go to with the strong espresso? I checked, and it's still in business. Can you meet me there on Wednesday? I would love to catch up, see how you're doing—if you want."

Later, thinking back to that meeting, I realized that it planted the seed that grew to a full understanding that I couldn't pretend with Elliott anymore.

Chapter 20

It took me six months after meeting Cillian at the coffee shop to muster the courage to tell Elliott how I felt or, more to the point, what I didn't feel. Maybe I couldn't be with Cillian, but I shouldn't have been with Elliott.

"Zee, I'm home!" he announced as he walked in the door at his usual 6:30 p.m.

I heard the click of the door closing and the familiar sound of his footfalls. My heart hiccupped. "I'm in the kitchen!"

He walked in and gave me a peck on the cheek, which was as intimate as we had been over the past six months, something he seemed to accept as a normal, temporary slump in our long-term relationship.

"What's the occasion?" he asked, smiling, as he gestured toward the bottle of wine and two glasses on the table.

"Elliott, we need to talk."

"That doesn't sound good," he said jokingly.

"I'm serious."

"Okay," he said, straight-faced. He took off his suit jacket and laid it over the back of one of the chairs. We had bought the set several years before at IKEA. That was a good day for us that had started off really bad. Ashlyn began to bawl the minute we walked into the store. Elliott swooped her up and put her on his shoulders to give her a bird's-eye view and got her ice cream, and all was right with her little world.

When we got the IKEA boxes home, I thought Elliott was going to turn into a crying toddler himself as he tried to figure out how to put the disparate pieces together. I sat on the floor next to him and tried to help decipher the instructions. We ended up drinking beer and laughing until we cried.

Are we now going to be fighting over who gets to keep those cheap chairs?

"What's up, Zee?" His casual question suggested he didn't have a clue what was about to happen. He poured himself a glass of wine from the bottle and took a sip.

"Elliott, are you happy?"

He almost spit out his wine. "What?"

"Are you happy with me, with us?"

"What kind of question is that? Of course I am."

"Really? You haven't noticed that I'm not?"

His expression shifted from curious to concerned.

"Where is Ashlyn?" he asked, his voice lowered.

"She's spending the night at Carolyn's."

He downed the rest of his wine and refilled his glass. "Why haven't you said anything?"

I picked up my glass and twirled the red liquid but set it back on the table without taking a sip.

"I'm saying something now."

"Have I done something? Do you want to go to counseling or maybe have a regular date night? Or I can come home earlier. What would it take to make you happy? I know I've been working a lot lately, and I can cut back on weekends if—"

He didn't get it. He thought the problem was something that, with a little effort, he could fix.

"I think we need time apart, to figure some things out."

He let that soak in. "I think you mean *you* need some time apart. Say what you really mean, Zezelia."

I lifted the glass to my dry lips and drank the wine in three gulps.

"Elliott, you've been such a good father to Ashlyn. You could have kicked me to the curb when I told you, but you didn't. But I—"

"But what, Zee?"

The panic in his face gutted me. I needed to rip off the Band-Aid, the same thing my mother did before she told me about my father.

"I can't pretend anymore. I care about you, Elliott. I do, but I don't love you in the way you deserve to be loved."

His panicked expression morphed into one of excruciating pain. He shook his head in disbelief.

"I believed in us. I thought you did too. When did you fall out of love with me?" he asked.

I stared at my lap. "Elliott, I…"

"Wow, did you ever really love me? Never mind. Don't answer that." He took a shaky breath. Then he said, "I'm not sure what I did to deserve this. I've tried my best to be a good husband and father, but obviously it wasn't good enough for you." He grabbed his glass of wine and downed half of it. "I hope you realize you're breaking my heart."

And his words broke mine.

He crossed his arms tightly across his chest. "But I don't want to hold you back if you want to go."

I was doing what was best not only for me, but for him. He just didn't know it yet. Still, it hurts when you hurt someone you care about. That was, in some ways, even more torturous than when I cut Cillian out of my life. My leaving Cillian was justified. Leaving Elliott was a judgment call, and I had judged that I couldn't spend the rest of my life with a man I didn't love, no matter how loving he might be toward me.

"I'm so, so sorry, Elliott. Really, I am."

After a prolonged and painful mediation process that dragged on for weeks leading up to the divorce, we agreed that Ashlyn and I would stay in the house until the divorce was final. Proceeds from the eventual sale would go into a college fund for Ashlyn. Elliott would then be responsible for court-ordered child support, and we agreed that he would get Ashlyn every other weekend. He threatened to file for full custody, but I offered up the matter of paternity as a veiled threat of my own. No way was he going to take my daughter away from me. She was the only thing I had left.

After the dust settled from the emotional wreckage, I had to figure out how to create a life for Ashlyn and me. My love-drunk decision to drop out of college years before was coming back to haunt me. That, along with my extended time as a stay-at-home mom, didn't exactly scream, "Hire me!" That was when I took a job at Nature's Trail. The position offered regular hours, health insurance, and along with Elliott's child support and Sloane's help, I managed to keep us afloat.

And that was how our lives chugged along for the next decade—until Cillian called me one more time.

Chapter 21

After I downed the last sip of my coffee before leaving for work, I realized I'd left my Nature's Trail apron in the bedroom. I was already running late, so I hurried back to the room and grabbed the apron, which I'd dropped on the floor in a state of exhaustion the night before. When I was pulling it over my head, I heard the muffled sound of my cell ringing in my purse in the kitchen. *It must be Ashlyn.* Sloane never called before ten in the morning. I ran to the kitchen, reached into my purse, and answered without looking.

"Ash?"

"No, it's Cillian."

The familiar tenor of his voice triggered a warm, visceral response.

"Cillian," I said softly as I collapsed in the chair. "Um, this is unexpected, to say the least." *Unexpected? It's surreal.* I couldn't think of anything deep or original to say, so I simply asked, "How are you?"

"Grand," he said, and it melted my heart. I closed my eyes. I wanted him to keep talking so that I could mentally record his lovely voice and replay it on demand.

"And you? You're well?" he asked.

"I'm good. You know, working. I'm divorced now."

That was a weird thing for me to say right out of the gate after a decade of not talking.

"I knew that."

I didn't bother to ask how he knew. It didn't matter.

"You know, I hear your songs on the radio sometimes. I remember that was always a dream of yours, and you did it. You've really made it big. You made your dreams come true. Are you still touring?"

"Not for about a year, but Damian and I are recording in the studio. Hoping for another album soon."

"How is Damian?"

"Same as always."

"Your family?"

"Good."

"Are you here in the States?"

"No, I'm calling from Dublin."

I heard a click on my end and pulled the phone away from my ear to look.

"Do you need to take that?"

"No, I'll call her back. It's my daughter."

Your daughter.

He paused. "Right, yeah."

Something in the regretful tenor of his voice put me on edge.

Our already weird, staccato conversation had taken a turn for the worse. I couldn't help recalling how our words had, at one time, flowed as easily as fresh water bubbling from a spring. I began to wonder if it was really him or some bizarre AI-generated voice.

"Okay, this is too weird. Is it really you?"

He chuckled, and the chill was gone. "Okay. Need proof? Remember when we were together and I was touring, how you would always ask me, 'Where are you now?' You had that map hanging in your room with push pins in all my gigs. It became a bit of a tradition, a way to start each call?"

"Of course I remember. So, is this your once-a-decade catch-up call?" I asked, my words infused with unintended resentment.

"No, I called for more than that."

"Okay."

"Zee..."

Speaking my name so softly brought on a tsunami of memories of the two of us when we were insanely in love. Since then, we had been pulled apart and separated by two decades and almost five thousand miles.

"I want to ask you something," he said. "Don't answer right away, but I want you to know that I'm completely serious."

"Serious about what?"

"I know this seems outrageous, but... what would you think about coming to Dublin to spend some time together, get reacquainted... see if there's still something there?"

A swell of emotion robbed me of my ability to speak. My feelings for him back then were like an intractable addiction. Whenever we were together, I wanted just one more soft touch, one more deep kiss, one more warm breath on my neck, one more whisper that he loved me. It took me years to kick the habit, though the craving never left. And there he was, asking me to sink into that addicted state again. Tears erupted with no warning. I was making little gasping sounds.

"Zee, please don't cry."

"Cillian, are you insane?" I managed to croak out the words. "You call me up almost ten years after we last spoke and want to know if I'll come to Ireland to be with you? I have a job. I have a daughter. I have an apartment. I have a life."

"You always were one to put responsibilities before pleasure. But I've been thinking about you a lot lately. Actually, not just lately. I miss what we had. I never forgot you. Did you forget about me?"

"No, of course not, but..."

"Just hear me out. I've reached a point in my life where I don't want to have any regrets, and the biggest regret of my life has been us not being together. I was hoping that if you felt the same, we could do something about it. I think we owe it to ourselves to give it another chance, to see where it might go. The last time we met, I asked you to be with me, but you were married, and I understood why you said no. But I guess, this time, I should ask you this first: are you in a relationship now?"

"No, but that's not even the point."

"Maybe it *is* the point. We're not in our twenties anymore, but I think the connection could still be there. Don't you want to find out? Maybe we could be happy, Zee."

His words pressed on the emotional bruises he'd caused all those years ago, which left my feelings tender to the touch. Dread and desire were battling it out in my head and in my heart.

"Cillian, this is really too much. Maybe if you had come to me with this five or six years ago, but it's too late. I mean, this is crazy. And I don't do crazy. Not anymore."

"But is it? Is it crazy? We can do this, Zee. *You* can do this. Say the word, and I'll buy you a first-class ticket to Dublin. I can finally show you Ireland, and you can meet my family. They'll love you. I promise."

I drew in a sudden breath. This was what I'd been dreaming about and praying for over the last twenty years, but now that he was offering it up on a silver platter, I was scared. Starting over is one thing, but starting up again is something else. I could easily envision our reunion falling apart and me returning home with no job, no apartment, and no self-esteem.

I wasn't sure I had the fortitude to start again and lug all that overweight emotional baggage along with me.

"Cillian, I don't know what to say."

"Say yes."

When I didn't respond, he said, "Or if you need to take a wee bit of time, have a think—that's fine. Just let me know. Zee, this could be a real chance for us to make up for all those lost years."

That was the Cillian I used to know, full of optimism and hope. Still, I thought maybe those years should stay lost—maybe they were better kept as gossamer memories. *But what if we could create new memories, even better memories?*

"You have to understand this would be a life-changing decision for me, for my daughter. What if what we had isn't there anymore? And I don't know if I've ever completely forgiven you." I let my words hang in the air for a few seconds before I said, "I have to think about it."

I had somehow shifted from "This is insane" to "Let me think about it."

"Sure. You're right. That's probably smart. I just hope I'm not too late for forgiveness and that," he said.

I heard the disappointment in his voice. *But does he really expect me to drop everything and hop on a plane to Ireland?*

Even if his invitation went against everything I knew I *should* do, I couldn't deny that it was what I really, really *wanted* to do.

Chapter 22

In the days that followed Cillian's jaw-dropping invitation to join him in Ireland, my conflicted feelings were intertwined like thick vines, choking out any clarity of thought.

Sloane patiently listened to my repeated ramblings. In a rare move, she offered no hardcore advice. Instead, she played the role of a therapist, following up my imagined scenarios with the question, *How would that make you feel?* The problem was, all I felt was confused.

My cell rang. *Not now, Elliott.* It rang again. And again.

I let out a bone-tired sigh before answering. "Hey, Elliott, what's up?"

"I believe it's somebody's birthday."

"Who?... Oh."

"Happy birthday, Zee Zee."

He hadn't called me that in years.

"Thanks, Elliott. I've just been so busy I totally forgot. Who wants to remember they're turning forty-two? Fifty is the next stop."

"I think you're jumping the gun a bit. That's eight years away."

"Yeah, I counted."

"You sound down," he said. "Is it the birthday, or is it something else?"

"I'm fine. Really. Just got a lot on my mind."

"Look, if you don't have any birthday plans, why don't you and Ashlyn go out for dinner? My treat."

Moments like that sometimes made me question my decision to leave Elliott. More than once, I'd wondered, "What if?" *If I'd never met Cillian, would I have believed myself happy with Elliott?* But once you've held the gold in your hands, bronze is never good enough. Maybe he wasn't *my* Prince Charming, but he could be charming enough.

"That's sweet, Elliott. Thank you."

Forty-two. When I met Cillian, I was twenty-one and I felt like I would be young forever. Back then, I viewed the land of forty-two as a place other people were forced to inhabit. I guess I thought that, short of dying, I could somehow escape stepping into that place and beyond. But there I was at forty-two and counting—two years older than my mother had been when she died.

As soon as I hung up with Elliott, my phone rang again.

"Morning, Ash."

She proceeded to sing her rendition of "Happy Birthday" to me, a tradition we'd held for each other over the years. While I was always gratingly off-key when I sang "Happy Birthday" to her, she had apparently inherited her father's vocal cords.

"It wouldn't be a birthday without you serenading me," I said after she sang the last note. "Listen, Dad offered for you and me to go out to a birthday dinner. His treat. Are you free tonight?"

"That's so Dad. Sounds good. Where do you want to go?"

"How about you choose?"

"But it's *your* birthday."

"Choosing the restaurant can be your present to me. You know I hate having to make a choice."

"Okay, let me check if it's okay with Jason, and I'll pick you up at seven?"

I hated that she felt like she needed her husband's permission to take her mother out for a birthday dinner. She seemed to need Jason's permission for pretty much everything lately.

"Can't wait," I said in the perkiest voice I could muster.

My effort to be perky paid off. I hung up feeling lighter. A birthday dinner with Ashlyn would be a much-needed distraction from my mental machinations.

She chose a new ramen place close to downtown, to satisfy my well-established ramen cravings. The place was small and cozy. Ashlyn knew my favorite dish, so I sat down at the tiny table, and she went to the counter to order.

When she joined me, she said, "So, a year older. How does it feel?"

I shrugged. "Same."

"Well, you look great, Mom. You don't look old enough to have a twenty-one-year-old daughter."

"Thank you, Ash. You're my one-person fan club."

If I say yes to Cillian and he sees me again, will he think the same, or will he see that his hot young girlfriend has morphed into a middle-aged woman?

Enough of that.

I was not going to let myself fall down the Cillian rabbit hole.

A very young, very cute waiter brought over our bowls of ramen and set them on the table.

"Can I get you ladies anythin' else?"

"Love your accent," Ashlyn said in a surprisingly flirty tone.

"Thanks," he said, which came out as a familiar "tanks."

"Where are you from?"

"Dublin, Ireland. Going to UT. This is my last year, then headin' home."

Okay, either this is a sign from God, or the universe is playing a cruel trick on me. I decided to take it as a sign.

"Cool. Good luck," she said.

We devoured our spicy noodles in silence, aside from the indelicate slurping sounds.

When I was about halfway through, I asked, "So, how are things with Jason?"

She shook her head slowly. "I don't want to talk about him tonight. It's your birthday! Tell me something fun."

"How about I'm having a birthday dinner with my favorite daughter."

"Mom, seriously? I'm glad you think this is fun, but there's nothing else?"

"Let me think."

I thought hard, but I honestly couldn't remember the last time I'd truly had fun.

When I answered with a shrug, she said, "Mom, that's sad."

The words were barely out of her mouth when our Irish waiter brought over a bowl of mochi ice cream with a birthday candle in the middle. Ashlyn was smiling like she did when she was six years old and brought me a handful of wildflowers from the backyard for my birthday.

"Thank you, Ash. That's so sweet. This looks really good."

After I filled my lungs, ready to blow out the single candle, she said, "Wait, Mom. First, you have to make a wish, and promise me you'll make it something fun."

"Okay. I promise."

I took another breath and blew out the single candle. The hot wax dripped and immediately hardened atop the melting ice cream.

A week later, Cillian called me back.
"Hello?"

He jumped right in with no greeting. "So, Zee, should I buy that ticket now?"

"Cillian," I said, my voice infused with apologetic indecision. Despite my desire to jump in feet first, my birthday wish no longer felt quite so hopeful.

"Ah, right. You're not comin'."

"I didn't say that. There was a time when I would have done anything for this to happen. But things are different now. It's not like I can just pack a bag and hop on a plane."

The truth was I was in a dead-end job, my daughter was grown, and I was on my own, free as a bird to do as I wished. But I couldn't help worrying that I might be setting myself up for yet another colossal Cillian-related trauma. I no longer had the emotional reserves to deal with it.

"I get it, yeah," he said, shades of disappointment and frustration in his voice.

Clearly, he didn't get it at all.

"Don't be like that. I'd be dislodging my current life for the unknown."

"I'm an unknown?"

"Well, yeah. We've been unknown to each other for a long time now. Maybe it would be a mistake to think we could just fall back into place and pick up where we left off. And if we didn't? Then what?"

I was presenting a case that I didn't have the heart to defend. I couldn't let him know that I was leaning toward a yes, because I didn't want to make promises that I might not be able to keep.

"I'd say, 'Take all the time you need,' but that's not how I feel."

"Cillian, I..."

"It's okay. You haven't said no. We can do this, Zee. What we had is still there. I know it. I can feel it. With a little tending, it could be even better than it was before. But don't take too long to decide. I'm not that strong."

"Okay, I see what you did there." I couldn't help but smile as his song played on a loop in my head.

"Come on. Let's make the most of the time we have left. We're not getting any younger."

As if I need a reminder.

Chapter 23

Iopened the door to the closet in my bedroom, hesitated, then stood on my tiptoes to peer over the top shelf, but I couldn't see the box. I dragged the chair from my desk to the closet, stood on it, and carefully pulled a green shoebox down from its perch in the back, atop other shoeboxes that actually contained shoes. When Ashlyn and I moved into the apartment, I'd ceremoniously placed the box up in an unreachable hidden spot, vowing never to look at it again. I wasn't sure why I kept it, if the plan was never to break it open. I guess in the back of my mind, I knew that was unrealistic, and the day would come when I couldn't resist the urge to revisit our past together.

I held the box close to my chest so the contents wouldn't spill out, gingerly stepped off the chair, set the box on the bed, and stared at it. I hadn't had the courage to acknowledge the box or its contents for years, but the time had come. Maybe reminiscing about what Cillian and I once had would give me permission to say yes to him, to a second chance, to a new life, a better life, in Dublin with him.

Before I had time to convince myself to put it back on the shelf, I flipped the top off. My heart pounded as I peered inside. Sitting atop the collection of matchbooks, postcards, and handwritten notes was a single photo of the two of us as we stood outside the club where we first met. Cillian had his arms around me, our bodies pressed together, and we were about to kiss. Someone, maybe it was Damian, had captured that sweet moment. *My God, we were beautiful.* We were young and in love and so, so hopeful. Love like that makes you feel bulletproof. As I look at the photo, the intensity of that moment washed over me. I could almost smell the club, inhale Cillian's scent, and feel the heat of our love. I desperately wished I could jump into the photo, be twenty-one again, and have Cillian's lips a hair's breadth from mine and hear him whisper into my neck, "God, I want you right now." He always made me feel impossibly beautiful.

I shook my head to break loose the memory, set the photo aside, and reached into the box to pick up a scrap piece of paper with Cillian's handwriting on it. It read, "This is for you, for us, my gorgeous girl." Underneath that were song lyrics that I recognized as words I now sometimes heard on the radio. I closed my eyes as the song played over and over in my head, then I gently placed the paper alongside the photo and pulled out a matchbook from a motel where we stayed a few times. I used to strike a match and light his after-sex cigarette, all the while pestering him to quit. *I wonder if he ever did.* Below the matchbox were more souvenirs, more photos, more memories. *A lock of his hair?* I didn't remember taking that. I pressed it to my nose, but no scent of him remained.

At the bottom of the box were postcards he sent while touring in the States before he made it big. There were postcards from Baltimore, Scranton, New Paltz, Texarkana, and Monroe, each with the simple message, "Miss you, love Cillian." The last postcard was the one from Berlin, which I received just a few days after the phone call that tore us apart: "Zee, the wait is killing me. I can't enjoy everything that's happening without you. I need you here with me. Love, Cillian."

"He *still* needs me," I said out loud.

And I needed him too.

I couldn't deny it anymore.

I began creating my "I'm leaving to be with Cillian" to-do list, and while the items on the list were vastly different from twenty years before, the déjà vu was dizzying. I fervently hoped I would be able to check everything off the list this time and board that flight to a new life with the only man I'd ever truly loved. I intended to frame the photo of my almost-kiss with Cillian, and if doubts started creeping in, I would focus on that image of the two of us and remember that perfect ache of love.

I had read stories about high school sweethearts who broke up and got back together decades later. After the breakup, they had gone on to live their lives, have other relationships, have children, but in the end, they found each other again and were living out their happily ever after. Maybe that would be Cillian and me, and I would have a new framed photo of the two of us to create a then-and-now gallery of our love's journey.

The top two items on my growing list were "plan family meeting with Elliott and Ashlyn" and "tell Sloane." They were easy to jot down, but I was fabulously unprepared to deal with either one. I needed more time, but I also needed to set a date, a deadline, so I wouldn't have the option of backing out or postponing the inevitable. In the meantime, I had plenty of other things to check off my list—a scary but incredibly satisfying prospect.

When I was on the phone with the management company for my apartment—number three on my list—I heard Ashlyn unlock the front door, and Maple's nails *click-click-clicked* in the entryway. They must have been at the dog park. She'd been dropping by more frequently for moral support as she tried to shore up her strength to leave Jason.

"I'll have to get back to you with the dates," I blurted and hung up.

"Dates about what?" she asked as she and Maple stood in the doorway to my bedroom.

"It's nothing. Just dealing with the credit card company about a charge that isn't mine. You know, the usual aggravations."

Maple jumped onto the bed and curled up next to me, and Ashlyn sat next to her, stroking the snow-white fur on her back.

"So, what's up, Ash?"

"Not much," she said with a dismissive shrug.

Maple jumped down and headed to the kitchen, where I always had a full water bowl waiting for her.

Ashlyn was staring at her hands, clasped tightly in her lap. Misery radiated off her. "Mom, can I ask you something?"

"Sure, what is it?"

She turned to look at me.

"When did you know that you wanted to leave Dad?"

I had expected her to share with me how she was wrestling with a major life decision, not ask about *my* life decisions. I didn't know how to answer without revealing more than I was ready to.

"Oh, Ash."

"You've never talked about it, and I've never completely understood. Was there someone else—for you or for Dad?"

"I told you before neither of us had an affair, if that's what you're asking."

How can I explain a decision I made only after navigating the twists and turns of a complex emotional maze that had no clear exit sign?

"Then why?"

"Ashlyn, honey, if you're asking because you believe my answer might help you decide if you want to leave Jason, I can promise you it won't help. Every relationship is unique, with its own hardships, its own hurdles, its own issues with love and happiness. My relationship with your father was just that—my relationship with your father. Only you can decide if staying with Jason is what you want. What I can say, from the outside looking in, is that you seem very unhappy right now. Do you think that Jason is at the root of that unhappiness?"

She hammered out her answer in a single blow. "Yes."

She clearly didn't need my input. Her mind was made up. She just didn't know it yet. My wish for my precious daughter was to find happiness, to find someone who would make her feel everything—someone who valued her, someone who laughed and cried with her, someone whose touch made her forget the outside world, someone she would love beyond all reason and who would love her back just as much.

Once upon a time, I'd found that with Cillian, and I was hoping to find it again.

I still hadn't given Cillian my answer though a yes was forming in my heart and on my lips. I no longer cared if I was being impulsive, acting like a lovesick teenager. I had to know if the emotional seeds we planted all those years ago were lying dormant, waiting for just the right circumstances to rebloom. Or maybe I was simply recalling being in love with the boy I used to know, not the man he was now.

When I was in college, I'd taken an elective in Greek mythology and learned that Plato believed humans once had four arms, four legs and two faces, but then Zeus ripped us apart as a punishment for pride, so we were all destined to walk the Earth, searching for our other half.

Before I met Cillian, I had poo-pooed that idea of soul mates, that there was only one person out there who was a perfect match. But after our first night together, I knew, more than I'd ever known anything, that there would never be anyone else who could come close to the way Cillian made me feel. I knew I could stop searching. Now, I was on the threshold of entering the life I'd always wanted, the one I'd been pining for over the last twenty years, for *my* other half.

I'd once read a quote from Susan Sontag that stuck with me: "It's easier to endure than to change." I'd been enduring most of my life. If I were to stop enduring and take a bold step to change things up,

I had to wrap my doubts in a straitjacket. Paralyzing doubt was what changed the course of my life for the worse all those years before. And I was counting on the truth of the second half of that quote to hold true: "But once one has changed, what was endured is hard to recall."

Once I gave myself permission to take that jump, I hoped for a soft landing, and I was giddy with anticipation. But before I could tell Cillian of my decision and hop on the next plane to Ireland, I needed to get all the ducks in my life lined up. If he was still the same Cillian, he would be anxious for my arrival and would be calling every few days to ask when I was coming. I wanted to take care of everything, from my apartment lease, my job, my car, to putting my mail on hold before I shared my decision with him. All that was just a matter of checking things off my list. The hardest task would be breaking the news to Ashlyn and Sloane. Ashlyn would have the most questions. She had no clue about my connection to Ireland or—more to the point—*her* connection to Ireland. And it worked both ways. Cillian had no clue about his connection to Ashlyn. I guessed the time had finally come to tell them both the truth. Sloane was another matter. She thought of Cillian as the antichrist. As far as she was concerned, he was to blame for everything. Once I told her of my plans, she would probably want to have me committed. *And Elliott... What can I say to Elliott?* He would probably feel like I was abandoning Ashlyn, but I knew he would feel like I was abandoning him as well. His feelings for me refused to fade, much like my feelings for Cillian. Elliott's hope sprang eternal.

My giddiness slid into panic at the thought of having those tough conversations. Until Cillian's call, I'd thought I had my life figured out, more or less. I was enjoying my beautiful daughter, grateful for having Sloane in my life, accepting my life circumstances, and making do. I had a place for everything and everything in its place, whether or not it was a perfect fit.

I hoped—no, I had to believe—that once I landed in Ireland, this shiny new piece of my life's puzzle would slip perfectly into place.

Chapter 24

The next morning, as I made my breakfast, I was twenty-one again, full of possibilities for the future. My stomach fluttered with excitement at the thought of actually saying the words to him, "Yes, I want to be with you." I glanced at the time: early afternoon in Ireland. I still had time. As my coffee brewed, I opened my laptop to skim the news. The usual—the planet was still spinning, people were still fighting over land, and inflation was still rising. But then, there was this headline so casually tossed in front of me: "Cillian Byrne, 43-Year-Old Lead Singer of the Irish Rock Group, The Swifters, Found Dead."

Our story's ending had been suddenly, shockingly rewritten. I struggled to absorb the words, but my emotional sponge was saturated. I lacked the stamina to deal with such personally apocalyptic news. I reread the headline. Surely, I had misunderstood. *I just talked to him a few days ago. He sounded tired, but there was the time difference, and—*

I fought the urge to throw my aging laptop across the room. But then the full article came into view.

And there he was, under the bold headline, in pixelated black and white, looking just as beautiful as the night we met.

So young.

We both were.

"Byrne, lead singer for The Swifters, was found dead at his home in Dublin, Ireland, yesterday morning, following a brief illness."

It didn't feel remotely real, yet my first thought was that I should have sensed something was wrong. It was a crazy, stupid thought that at the same time felt absolute. We had once been connected in every way—physically, emotionally, intellectually—until we weren't.

My mind flipped through the stored images I'd kept of him. The Cillian I knew and fell in love with had been a boyish twenty-four-year-old freckle-faced Irishman with a beautiful voice and eyes a shade of green rarely found in nature. As I conjured up his image, I could almost feel his warm breath as he whispered an invitation in my ear, the invitation that changed everything.

My thoughts then flickered to the future, a future that had been altered in an instant, a future I had allowed myself to believe in but could no longer imagine. My decades-long fantasy of a reunion with Cillian had come so tantalizingly close to becoming a reality, but the bold headline declaring Cillian's death cut short what I thought was our never-ending love story. Cillian and I were never meant to end like this.

I had to call Sloane.

PART 2: AFTER

Chapter 25

I step into a scalding shower to divert my thoughts from the past and my black hole of a future, which has now become even darker. I review everything I have—and haven't—found in my search for Damian. He lives in Dublin. Divorced several years ago, no kids. He and Cillian were still collaborating when Cillian—even thinking the word triggers a tsunami of grief. I need to know what happened. Maybe Damian can offer a much-needed sense of closure, a final acceptance of what will never be. If anyone knows Cillian's story, it's Damian.

Out of the shower, I wrap a towel around my body and follow Sloane's ring tone to my bed. I sit down, water droplets from my hair spotting the beige duvet. I grab the phone, and my throat seizes because I know the conversation that's about to take place.

"You saw it?" I answer without a "hello," my voice raspy.

"Oh my God, Zee, do you know what happened?"

I feel the blood leave my lips. "No. The article didn't say." I can't catch my breath but manage to eke out the words "I want to see if I can contact Damian. He can tell me what happened."

"Damian," she repeats, drawing out the syllables. "God, I haven't thought of him in ages. You remember that night at that club when... Shit, sorry. Of course you do."

She stopped herself just in time.

"You want me to come over?"

"Maybe tonight? I'm having lunch with Ashlyn."

"Okay. I'll do some googling in the meantime. And there's a tech guy at the office who can pretty much find out anything about anybody. I'll text him. He loves a challenge." She hesitates. "What was Damian's last name again?"

"O'Leary. Damian O'Leary. All I know right now is he lives in Dublin and he's divorced."

"I guess it's a place to start. Oh, and tell Ashlyn I said hi." I can almost hear her concern before she speaks it. "How's she doing? You know, with Jason."

"Things are okay, I think."

I'm a terrible liar despite years of practice.

"**M**om, over here!" Ashlyn shouts as she waves me over before I've even lowered my sandaled foot onto the asphalt, softened by the unusually warm fall day. Sun rays slip through the trees, highlighting the auburn streaks in her thick sandy hair. As always, she flashes a dimpled smile. It simultaneously warms my heart and shatters it. *Never more than today.*

She's sitting at one of the weather-beaten picnic tables outside the tiny, century-old frame house, a favorite of ours for lunch and some mother-daughter time. Jason hates it. He came with us once but refused to stay. He took one look at the old house, glanced at the menu, and pronounced, "Not for me" before tossing some cash on the table for Ashlyn. That was the first time I witnessed the disdainful gesture, but it wouldn't be the last. The money was welcome but not nearly as much as his departure.

"I figured you'd want your usual, so I went ahead and ordered. Hope that's okay."

"Of course," I say as I reach for her hand, and I kiss her cheek while scrutinizing her expression, searching for any new hints of emotional upheaval and hoping she isn't scrutinizing mine. I'm hiding the hurt and sadness as best I can, and I can't help but wonder if she's doing the same.

By the time I settle on the bench, opposite Ashlyn, our veggie sandwiches are being served along with sodas made with real sugar. The place makes a point of advertising "no high-fructose corn syrup."

She looks at me then down.

There it is. "Is everything okay?"

Her face flushes, and my heart stutters in response. *Has Jason finally crossed the line from domineering to dangerous? Is she scared?* I couldn't let my daughter face the same fate as Leah. She fell in love and followed her heart despite all the red flags waving frantically, and she's now living in a battered women's shelter, trying to create a new life for herself and her daughter. I scan Ashlyn's neck, her bare arms, her hands for telltale signs of abuse.

"I... I... know what you think of Jason—"

"Ashlyn, I would never—"

"Let me get this out."

I push my plate aside and lean in.

Her voice quivers. "I don't know what to do."

My crying threshold is already at an all-time low. It's all I can do not to slump into a mess of heaving sobs.

"Tell me what it is, and I'll help you however I can."

"I think I may want to leave... Jason."

I feel giddy. She can come and live with me. I'll help her to distance herself, to heal, to move past that horrible mistake of a marriage. She's still so young. It would be a fresh start.

I stand and sit next to Ashlyn on her side of the picnic bench. "What brought this on?"

"I... I've been thinking about it for a while."

"Ashlyn, listen to me. If it's truly come to that, if that's what you really want to do, you know I'll help you with whatever you need to make the transition easier."

"Mom, I know you would help if you could, but a divorce can cost thousands of dollars, and Jason would fight it with everything in him—hire the best lawyers." She sighs. "How could I afford even a single crappy lawyer?"

"I'll take out a loan," I say. *An unlikely event, given my subterranean credit score.*

"Another loan? No way. I wouldn't put you in that position."

The defeated look in her eyes flattens me. She rests her head on my shoulder.

"If you divorce and get half, you could always pay me back."

She sits up, looks at me again, and cocks her head as if to say, *Seriously?* "I know how Jason operates. I wouldn't be surprised if, in the end, the courts ended up saying I owed *him* money."

"We'll figure something out," I say with far more conviction than I feel.

"Anyway," she says, "it's more complicated than that. I may not have the right to get half."

"Why complicated? The law says that—"

She leans forward and whispers, "Mom, I've met someone." Her face brightens as she utters the words.

How can that possibly be? Jason rarely lets Ashlyn out of his sight. "Where, when, how?"

"In the park when I was walking Maple. Mom, he's made me feel—I don't know—like me again."

Her path to leaving Jason, to getting a divorce, to walking away with enough money to start over, has been made more treacherous by her revelation.

"Are you having an affair?"

She blushes hard. We talk about almost everything, but sex is one topic we have always tiptoed around.

"Is there such a thing as an emotional affair? If yes, that's what we're having."

"Okaaay." I'm trying to wrap my head around this. "How often do you see him? Where do you go together? Are you worried about Jason finding out?"

"Mom, whoa. We haven't even kissed yet."

Relief washes over me as I make note of her choice of words. *Not yet.*

"We meet in the park a couple of times a week, and we just talk. We held hands once. I don't know what it means, but we had this strong connection, like, right away. Anyway, the first time we met, he was walking his dog, Gretchen, and Maple tugged us over to where he stood and started sniffing Gretchen's butt. We laughed, wandered over to a bench, sat down, and started talking." She takes a breath. "His name is Dax, and he's a web designer and videographer. He's divorced, has a four-year-old son, and—anyway, there's no way Jason would know unless he followed me, and you know he hates the dog park."

We sit in silence for a while, shooing hungry flies away from our uneaten sandwiches.

Finally, I ask, "If you're not sleeping with him, why would it affect your position in a divorce? Ash, you need to do what's best for you."

She gives a dismissive wave in the air. A heavy sigh signals she's switching tracks, changing directions, already changing her mind.

"You know what?" she says with a snort and a shake of her head. "Forget I said anything. It's a fantasy, wishful thinking on my part. It's okay. I'll be okay. So Jason is not the perfect husband." She shrugs. "It's not like he drinks or beats me or gambles. Jason's not a monster."

"Ash, Jason doesn't have to be a monster for him to treat you badly or make you miserable. I want you to be happy. You deserve to be happy."

"I think I'm just expecting an emotional connection with him that he isn't capable of. And the connection I seem to feel with this guy, Dax? I don't know. Maybe it'll fade. I remember feeling an incredible pull toward Jason in the beginning. I thought I had married my fantasy."

That, I understand. But while Ashlyn's marriage to Jason is a mistake that could still be rectified, my lost opportunity with Cillian can't be undone. It is, as of the morning's news, devastatingly irrevocable.

"Anyway," she continues, sounding even wearier, "if I did divorce Jason, what if he walked away with everything? He could hide his money, sue me for emotional distress. I'm sure of it. Then what? I don't have a clue how much he has or where it's invested. Since he won't let me work, I don't have any work experience or any money of my own. At all."

Roiling rage at Jason, at the system—at life—hollows me.

She gives me a wan smile. "Let's eat before the focaccia gets soggy. I'll be fine. Everything will be fine. Really."

If she stays with Jason, she has about as much chance of being fine as I do of being fine in a world without Cillian in it.

Chapter 26

I take the scenic route home, the road by the lake, to give myself time to process the news—hers and mine. I walk into my apartment, collapse on the sofa, and release the tears that have been building and that I've been holding back with a Herculean effort. Once they're unleashed, I cry until I think I might lose my lunch on the garage sale rug beneath my feet. I've made such a mess of my life, following in my mother's footsteps. *Is Ashlyn starting on the same self-destructive path?*

When Jason asked Ashlyn to marry him, I thought well, at least now she'll be financially secure. Jason was a big deal in a well-known venture capital firm in town. Even I had heard of it. While I never completely understood the inner workings of venture capitalists, I just knew he drove a nice car, he wore what looked like expensive clothes, and he treated Ashlyn to extravagant dinners and luxurious island getaways. At the age of thirty-two, he owned his own condo in downtown Austin. At the age of forty-two, I could barely afford my rent. I couldn't help but be impressed by his accomplishments at such a young age. That made me hopeful for my daughter's future. When he made their relationship official with that gorgeous two-carat yellow diamond engagement ring, I breathed a sigh of relief that she wouldn't have to squeeze every single penny like I had, like my mother had. I couldn't have predicted that after they married, Jason would hoard his money, keep Ashlyn under his thumb, and make my beautiful, sweet girl feel less than.

Her situation has left another deep bruise on my already black-and-blue heart.

I don't know how long I've been stuck in the same position on the sofa when there is a knock at the door along with the ping of a text message. I dig my phone out of my purse. It's Sloane: *I'm here.* I forgot she said she was coming over. I look at the time. *How can it already be six o'clock?* I grab a tissue, wipe my eyes, and blow my nose before I open the door and fall into Sloane's open arms. Her hair smells of a spring rain and lavender, and it soothes me like it always does.

I sink further into her embrace. "Oh, Sloane. I can't believe it."

"I know, hon. I know." She pulls a tissue from her purse and wipes away my fresh tears. "Let's go inside."

We haltingly walk arm in arm to the sofa.

"Whenever you want to talk..." she says as she sits back on the sofa she bought for me when Elliott left and hauled off half the furniture in an uncharacteristically petty act. He was hurting, and I couldn't muster the appropriate amount of anger at him. Sloane also gave me a microwave, a TV, a mattress and sheets, a washer and dryer, and a shitload of clothes for Ashlyn that I couldn't afford.

"I... I... I'm not sure where to start." My hands tremble.

"Got any wine? Let's start there."

"There's some red in the fridge."

She turns toward me, tilts her head, and raises her eyebrows in mock disapproval. Her reaction elicits a forced chuckle and a shrug. She returns with two glasses of red wine and cozies up next to me, our knees touching.

"We can just sit here and drink your refrigerated red wine if you want."

That is exactly what we do for a time. After a comfortable silence, the words spew from my tongue with shocking force.

"He's gone, Sloane! He's fucking gone!" I gulp the last of my wine, stand, and pace the room. I stop and lock eyes with her. "He didn't sound sick."

"What? You talked to him? When? Why am I just now hearing about this? What the fuck, Zee!" She ends her barrage of questions with her mouth agape, her face layered with disappointment, betrayal, and confusion.

My reconnection with Cillian was so new, so tenuous, so strange that I didn't want to believe it, much less share it, at least not right away—even with Sloane. Cillian and I had a sweet history that soured all those years ago. He lit my heart on fire, and I have never completely come to terms with the way it burned to ashes from a single phone call.

I return to the sofa, this time at a distance. "Sloane, don't be mad. It was just weird. You know that aside from a few texts and voice messages, it's been years since Cillian and I actually spoke."

"So, he called you?"

"Yeah, out of the blue." I shift my focus to my bare feet and my self-pedicure, which is starting to chip away. "Hearing his voice was like walking into the past. He just said, 'Zee, it's me, Cillian,' and I freaked out."

"What did he want?"

"*What did he want?* He wanted *me*."

"Whoa, whoa, whoa... Like, what, after all these years, he dials your number, and it's 'Let's forget about what I did to you and live happily ever after'? I mean, I'm not one to speak ill of the dead, but please."

Her words echo in the empty chambers of my heart.

She takes one look at my face. "Sorry," she says.

"I had decided to go to Ireland to be with him. I was making arrangements. I was going to tell you, I swear."

I didn't have to look her in the eyes to know what she was thinking—that I've lost my mind.

"It was all my fault. I did everything wrong."

I can barely recall the logic behind my life-altering decisions back then. *How can I possibly lay them out for Sloane now and make her understand when I don't fully understand, myself? Who or what was I trying to protect back then—Cillian, my mother, my heart?* None of us emerged unscathed. Everyone around me ended up hating Cillian. And I ended up deeply resenting my mother—long after she was reduced to ashes and placed in a wooden box.

"What do you mean it was all your fault?" The naked, accusatory tone of Sloane's voice rattles me. "Nothing that happened back then was your fault. Don't start rewriting your history together now that he's gone." She's not upset with me. She's releasing her residual, if misplaced, anger at Cillian.

I look at the ceiling and sigh. "You're right. You're right. Forget it."

I don't have the emotional bandwidth to untangle the whole thing for Sloane right now. My sigh is heavy with resignation, and she deftly follows my cue, letting me change the subject.

"So, did you find out anything about Damian?"

"Yeah," she says, her mood lifting as she pulls out her phone and starts scrolling. "My little techie friend found some trade publications with stories about him, but it was mostly fluff. You know, pics of him in concerts, at his beautiful, overpriced home in Dublin. However," she says, "he did find some contact information. At least I think you'll be able to track Damian down from there."

My stomach is on the edge of a steep cliff, about to take that final step. If I talk to Damian, it would be only one degree of separation from Cillian and the worst decisions of my life.

"I'm texting it to you. It's the name of his record label, his manager, his agent and the name, phone number, and social media accounts of his ex-wife."

"Oh, geez! Damian's ex-wife?" My phone dings with Sloane's text.

"I'm thinking that while you'll probably have trouble getting through the gatekeepers, you might have more luck reaching out to his ex."

"That would be really awkward—don't you think?"

"It's not like you had a relationship with Damian. She might be your best shot. I'm not sure how to pronounce her name." She stumbles over it twice. "Seriously, the Irish don't know how to spell."

I open the text and glance at the name and the list. I swallow hard. "Are you serious?"

"What is it?"

"Sloane, Aislinn is the Irish spelling of Ashlyn."

"Are you shitting me? Okay, that's really weird. But you claimed it long before Damian got involved with her. Evidently, they were married for only five years."

"Okay, well, thank you for this."

"Speaking of Ashlyn, how is she?"

"Oh, you know."

"What's going on?"

I release a sigh weighted down with concern, fear, and resignation, then I tell Sloane everything: Ashlyn's growing desire to leave Jason, her "emotional affair," her money worries, her backtracking on her thoughts, and my growing concern for her safety.

She places her warm hand on mine and gives an empathetic squeeze as her stacked silver rings click together. "Look, if money is the biggest obstacle, I'll give her the money for the divorce. Hell, I'll pay for the rent on a new apartment and help her get set up. She needs to kick Jason to the curb."

Sloane to the rescue? Again? I hug her and whisper in her ear, "You've done enough. More than enough."

Sloane got her first job out of college at Triple T Protection, a data security startup in Austin. She majored in computer science in college, which I thought was weird and so not Sloane, but the programming language made sense to her. When I asked her what the Triple T stood for, she informed me it was Tic Tac Toe, something about how you have to fill in the spaces with the right combination of *x*'s and *o*'s or you lose. She said programming was a lot like that.

Every year she's worked there, she's received hefty raises, bonuses, and stock options. When the company went public, she became an instant multimillionaire. And she's been generous to a fault with her newfound wealth. Ashlyn and I would have been out on the street years ago without Sloane's help. Now, here she is, enthusiastically offering, yet again, to share her good fortune.

We pull apart, but she holds tight to my hand. "Zee, there's no such thing as enough. Just think about it and tell Ashlyn. I know I've only met Jason a few times, but he gives off an unsavory vibe, and from everything you've told me about the way he treats Ashlyn..."

"She says Jason hasn't been physically abusive, but emotional abuse is still abuse."

She pauses, letting the thought register, and slips into silence. She closes her eyes, and I know she's thinking about the other pillar in our triad, Leah. She draws a long breath and opens her eyes. "Have you heard from Leah lately?"

"No, but I know things can't be good."

Sloane has had her own brush with men who tried—unsuccessfully, I might add—to control her. She left the hole that Zach punched in the sheetrock of her bedroom as a reminder to never go down that path again. A Banksy print hangs over it. She likes knowing the damage is there, hidden from view.

Sloane is with Peter now. He's a nerdy sweetheart six years her junior, and he adores Sloane. And she adores him right back. They met at work. He's not the guy I would've pegged as the one to win Sloane's love and trust, but they've been together seven years, and they just fit. I assume he has his own treasure chest of stock options from his time at the company. Together, they could probably bankroll a small country. But I shrink away from Sloane bankrolling Ashlyn's divorce. She's been subsidizing my life for far too long.

Sloane left, but not before her generous offer shifted to an unwavering insistence that she help Ashlyn make the break from Jason, help her get on her feet, and help her find a job. I still have a hard time seeing Sloane as she is: a forty-two-year-old grown-ass responsible woman. In college, she was crazy Sloane, wild Sloane, irresponsible Sloane, slutty Sloane. I never would have guessed she would be the one to save my life, inject me with love and hope—and cash—and bring me back from the brink more than once.

A text dings my phone. *What's going on with Ashlyn?*

Terrible timing, as always. Elliott's simple question makes my heart hurt. Our relationship belongs in the dictionary under "dysfunctional." I haven't heard from him since last New Year's Eve, when he drunk dialed me.

Maudlin and slurring his words, this forty-three-year-old corporate accountant in charge of billion-dollar businesses cried like a toddler in the midst of a temper tantrum. I couldn't decipher what he was saying. Then, as if he had suddenly been slapped sober, his voice steadied.

"Zezelia," he said.

I held my breath, knowing what he was going to say—again. This was a regular event. I just never knew when it would come.

"Zee, let's give it another try." He took a shaky breath. "I still fucking love you. Please."

Sweet, gentle Elliott never used the F word. I'd once thought he was the answer to my prayers. I tried, but I never felt that spark with Elliott that I so desperately wanted to feel, that I had felt in spades with Cillian. So, after twelve years of trying hard to convince myself that being with Elliott was where I belonged, I moved on.

But Elliott couldn't.

My phone rings. He couldn't wait for me to text back.

"Hello, Elliott. How are you?"

"Bigger question. How's Ashlyn?"

"Why do you ask?"

He snorts. "Seriously, Zezelia? I worry about Ashlyn. You know that. Don't make this weird."

"So, you talked to her?"

"Yeah, and she sounded off. Did that dick, Jason, do something?"

Elliot gave her away at their wedding. But he doesn't like Jason any more than I do.

"Elliot, I don't think it's my place to tell you what's happening with Ashlyn. She should be the one to tell you."

"So, something *is* going on with her?"

"Elliot, please."

His voice gains momentum. "Zezelia, I'm her father!" He clears his throat and falls silent then says, "I'm worried about her."

"Elliott, call Ashlyn again, and ask her directly. If she's free to talk, she'll tell you. I don't want it to come secondhand from me. Besides, she's unsure herself."

"Unsure about what?" he shouts into the phone.

"I think you know. Just call her."

I hang up the phone, make myself a cup of chamomile tea, and sit at the kitchen table, occupying the same spot I did when I read the devastating news about Cillian. I take a sip, and the liquid scalds my tongue. *How appropriate.* My thoughts are scalding my brain as I review everything from Cillian's death to Sloane's visit to Elliott's call. I should be grateful for Sloane's offer to finance Ashlyn's potential divorce, for Elliott's desire to be involved in Ashlyn's life, but they're just reminders of where my life is, where it will always be—dogpaddling and barely keeping my head above water and only with the help of my best friend and my ex. I go upstairs, lie on the bed, and completely drained, I instantly fall asleep.

Chapter 27

Mondays are always hard—starting a new work week, going through the motions, trying my best to appreciate the things I have and not focus on the things I've let pass me by. My recent birthday is a chained anvil dragging behind me as I wait for my future to be hammered into shape. It's a very different future from what I envisioned twenty years ago, even from what I imagined just a few weeks ago. But I do what I always do—I don my Nature's Trail cap and apron and head to the store, where I've been working as assistant manager for the past decade. The hourly pay is pitiful, but it's regular. I get overtime on holidays, but none of that is enough to keep me from drowning in debt. Or I would be drowning if not for Sloane. Despite her constant insistence that I accept her help without protestation, I know I can never repay her, not without winning the lottery first.

"Morning, Zezelia! How was your weekend?"

That's Clyde, the manager—nice guy. His happy meter is always set on high. Despite having worked with him for the past five years, I know little about his personal life. I'm not sure if being perniciously happy is his baseline or if he's putting up a front to hide some unbearable pain. That, I can relate to.

"Morning, Clyde. It was good." It's not like I'm going to share with him that the love of my life has died, my daughter is having an almost affair while contemplating leaving her emotionally abusive husband, and I'm about to sink deeper into financial quicksand. "How was yours?"

"Great! Sandy and I went to the lake, rented a paddleboat, ate lunch at Torchy's Tacos, and came home and took a nap. We're ready to face the new week."

It was always Sandy this and Sandy that. It took me a while to realize that he was talking about his dog, not a woman in his life. He got me thinking that maybe that was what I needed—go to the shelter and bring home a dog to fill the empty spaces in my life with unconditional love and affection. I've made it as far as the parking lot of the shelter a couple of times. But that would've meant another mouth to feed, vet bills, and monthly medications to keep fleas and heartworms at bay. So I wisely put my car in reverse and came home each time, dogless.

"So, what's going on today?" I ask.

"I need you at customer service. Kyle called out. I know it's not your favorite station, but I really need your help." He pushes his glasses up on his nose and looks at the schedule on his clipboard.

I have the urge to take a razor to that remaining tuft of hair left on his almost bald head.

"Sure. No problem." *People. I'm going to have to deal with people. Complaining people. Disgruntled people.* I'm not a "people person" although I can usually fake it. But the news of Cillian's death and Ashlyn's wavering decision about Jason are going to turn this day into the ultimate test of endurance.

Once behind the customer service desk, I close my eyes and take a deep cleansing breath before I turn on the lights, clock in, and unlock the cash register. The time slogs by as a customer wants to return milk with an expiration date that has passed, one wants a refund on a half-eaten snack bar that "didn't taste right," and others want to buy lottery tickets, get money orders, or pay their gas and electric bills.

My interaction with customers consists mainly of "Yes, ma'am," "I understand," "I'll take care of that right away," "Here's your receipt," and "Have a nice day." Normally, I manage to take it all in stride. But this is not a normal day.

I glance at the clock—almost lunchtime. I've made it this far, so I just have to survive the second half of the day. I'm checking the cash register receipts, my mind wandering, when I feel him approach the counter.

"I wasn't expecting you to be here," he says.

It's Elliott. He made it clear long ago that he wasn't going to stop coming to his favorite store just because I work here. Between his calls declaring his undying love for me, we'd reached something of a detente. Over the years, we would pass each other in the aisles, or he would spot me in the office through the glass panel and nod. Now, we're being forced to interact face-to-face.

"You work customer service now?"

I can feel him weighing his options—run or face his fears.

"I'm just filling in for someone who called out today." I will a pleasant smile to cross my lips. "What can I help you with?"

He takes a step back, and for a second, I think he really is going to make a run for it. I wonder if this will be the last straw or if he'll tough it out and risk a face-to-face with his ex-wife, whom he's still in love with and who has always been in love with someone else.

He reaches into a pocket, pulls out some cash, and without making eye contact says, "I need a three-hundred-dollar money order, please."

I want to be filled with helium so I can rise up and float above the fray, but the atmosphere there is too thin. I would explode and crash back down to my rock-hard reality.

"Sure thing." I reach out for the money, and despite my best efforts, our fingers brush.

He takes in a breath in response to my touch, and I empathize. How many times had I had the same reaction whenever my skin came in contact with Cillian's?

I turn my back to him to create his money order. It's supposed to be a no-brainer process, but my neurons are short circuiting, and I fear I might make a mistake, further extending our encounter. I feel him staring at me. I want this cringeworthy interaction to be over.

It's true that Elliott is one of the good ones. Sloane thought he was my golden ticket, but I couldn't make myself feel for him what I knew I should, what I wanted to feel, what I knew he felt for me. I tried. I really did. I wanted a better life for myself and for Ashlyn, and Elliott was more than willing to provide that. He wanted to rescue me when I desperately needed rescuing. He did nothing wrong. He was patient, understanding, and loving. He was crazy about me. He was crazy about Ashlyn. But he wasn't Cillian.

In the end, I came to the impossible conclusion that it wasn't fair to me or to Ashlyn and least of all to Elliott, to commit myself to a relationship that wasn't real. His skin turned sallow the day I told him how I felt. There was no way to convey the depth of my self-loathing as I put my real feelings into words for him.

And his anguished response was "Tell me what I can do to fix this."

I had no answer. It seems that honesty isn't always the best policy when it ties a stone to the heart of someone you care about and tosses it into a bottomless well.

Nothing about custody was specified in the divorce papers, but he was always there for her. He came to her school plays, bought her toys and ice cream, and took her hiking, bowling, and to the movies on weekends. He let her bring along a friend, which made him Superdad in her eyes. When she was a teenager, they stayed close, and he gave her money and bought her clothes, shoes, schoolbooks, an iPhone or two, and even a used car when she got her license.

I'm so lost in my thoughts that I barely notice him calling my name.

"Zezelia, you okay?"

I've stopped moving and am gripping the money order. Waves of acid crash against the lining of my stomach, creating an undertow of nausea. I turn around.

"Sorry. Guess I checked out there for a minute. Here ya go." I set the wrinkled money order on the counter and smooth it out. I clear my throat. "I can cancel this one and make another one if you want."

"It's okay. This is fine."

His head tilts in sympathy. Maybe he thinks my reaction is because of residual feelings I have for him, despite my repeated rejections. I guess hope springs eternal where love is concerned.

"Okay, well, have a good one, Elliott."

He hesitates, nods, and walks away, money order in hand. Just before he disappears around the corner aisle, he turns to glance at me one last time.

All I could think about was how Cillian turned around and gave me that same look the last time we met.

Buoyed by a promise from Clyde that he'll get someone else to man the customer service booth tomorrow, I survive my shift.

"Thank you, Clyde," I say, utterly sincere in my undying gratitude.

I grab my purse and head to the exit faster than usual. I've put in my eight dreary hours, and I'm ready to go home, shift gears, listen to some Nora Jones, and maybe watch *When Harry Met Sally* for the fiftieth time. The automatic doors slide open, and I'm ready to welcome a breath of crisp fresh air. Instead, a storm has rolled in and is at full throttle. Fall storms in Texas typically bring in a sudden, crazy drop in temperature and pelting rain and ice. True to form, the temperature has plummeted, hovering just above freezing. Tiny ice pellets ping off windshields. Having spent my day in windowless isolation, I didn't think to check the forecast. So here I am in short sleeves, arms sheathed in goose bumps, and no umbrella.

"Shit."

I hold my purse over my head, run to my car, and fumble with my keys, getting wetter and colder by the second as ice needles prick my naked arms. I get in, slam the car door, and switch on the heat as soon as the motor turns over. The DJ on the radio promises a string of top-forty hits. While I wait for warmth to spread through the small interior of my compact Kia, I listen impatiently to a string of local ads for laser hair removal, a used car dealership—*No credit? No problem!*—and a discount on a "home, pest, and lawn" service.

"And now, here's a half hour of uninterrupted hits to carry you through this winter storm. It's a whopper! Hope everyone is staying warm and dry."

It takes only a couple of beats for me to recognize the song. It's Cillian's first hit, born of the words scribbled on tiny pieces of paper at the Driskell Hotel, the words that he said I inspired. Of course they would be playing his music in memoriam. I had convinced myself that the sting from that initial slap of grief was already lessening—that this grief was finding its proper place and would soon settle in. But the sound of him singing his heart out chops mine into tiny, bite-sized pieces. Being more of a masochist than I realized, I turn up the volume, lay my head back on the headrest, close my eyes, and let the words drift over me. He's here with me. I feel the rhythm of his heartbeat in the song. I can sense his breath on my lips when he kissed me that morning. I reach my hand out, almost expecting him to take hold of it.

The song ends abruptly, jarring me back to my reality—a cold, wet day with me sitting in the parking lot of Nature's Trail. The ice has morphed to rain crashing against the windshield, the heat in the car is now stifling, and Britney Spears is belting out "Hit Me, Baby, One More Time."

And Cillian is still dead.

I turn the windshield wipers on high and slowly make my way home. I feel like I've won the parking place lottery when I'm able to position the car on the street right in front of my apartment building. I make a mad dash for the door. I am soaked from head to toe, and my hair is a conduit for the water dripping in my eyes. My teeth chatter uncontrollably. The rain and wind have bested me. Normally, each day after work, I check the mail before climbing the stairs to my apartment, but today, the short trip to the community mailbox would mean a second—no, a third—drenching as I run to my building. It likely contains nothing but bills and offers of credit cards with twenty-five percent interest, along with a couple of late notices.

As I unlock my door and step in, the dry warmth of my apartment feels as if I've entered a five-star spa with fluffy white towels, a juice bar, and a masseuse. For the first time today, I feel grateful. I head straight to the shower and drop my leaden jeans on the floor. Under the spray of hot water, nothing has to be done, no calls have to be answered, no bills have to be juggled, and no clothes have to be washed. I want to stay under the steaming hot spray and never leave. But my mind wanders, this time landing on Damian's ex-wife, Aislinn. *What time is it in Ireland?* I'll look up the time difference and call when it's a decent hour. Or maybe email would be better instead of catching her off guard with an American voice on the other end. An email would give her time to process who I am and the reason for my call. *Or maybe WhatsApp.* Everyone in Europe uses WhatsApp.

What should I say? "Aislinn, you don't know me, but I used to be friends with Cillian Byrne, and—" Friends?

I step out of the shower, slip into my soft gray yoga pants and my worn Swifters T-shirt. It isn't a maudlin choice. After hundreds, if not thousands, of washings, it's the softest, most comfortable item of clothing I own. Barefoot, I head to the kitchen to make myself something to eat and indulge in a late-day cup of coffee as I scroll through the news on my phone.

I zero in on another article, this one with quotes from Damian. He's reminiscing in sound bites for the *Irish Times*. "I'm gutted. Cillian was not just my bandmate and collaborator—he was my best mate."

As I read the words, they come out in a distinctive Irish accent in my head. And I'm suddenly desperately homesick for a place I've never been.

Chapter 28

I t's Saturday morning, and I'm holding my cell phone in my hand, dizzy with anticipation. Not the good kind—no, I'm wading through a swamp of dread, unsure if I can slog through or if I'll be swallowed with no chance of resurfacing. An overreaction? Maybe, but reaching out to Damian's ex-wife so soon after Cillian's death strikes me as unseemly.

Sloane's IT guy provided not only Aislinn's cell number but her work history, where she went to school, her office number, the names and numbers of her immediate family—more than I need or want. I clutch the phone tighter, still debating whether this is a good idea or a really, really bad one. It's 7:00 p.m. in Dublin. She's likely home from work, a public relations firm. *Will she hang up on me before I have a chance to explain? Will any residual resentment she might have for Damian prevent her from helping me?* But Aislinn is my best connection to reach Damian, and Damian is the only person who can tell me the things I need to know about Cillian's life—and death. I can't *not* call her. I slowly dial her number and listen to that distinctly European ring.

The first time I tried to call Cillian in Ireland, the double ring on the other end sounded to me like a busy signal, and I kept hanging up after the first couple of rings. When he finally answered on the first ring, he said, "Playing games with me, are ya?" I wonder if he ever told Damian about that and if they had a good laugh at my expense.

"Hello?" Her voice brings me back.

"Is this Aislinn O'Leary?"

"It's Doyle now, but yes. Who's this?"

My heart pounds. "Um, my name is Zezelia Owens. You don't know me, but—"

"Cillian's Zezelia?"

I'm dumbstruck. I swallow hard before muttering, "You know about me?"

"Cillian spoke of you often." She pauses and takes a breath, and the tenor of her voice drops. "So, you heard."

"I read it online. The news didn't really provide any details. What happened?" I ask even though I'm still not sure I want to know.

"Oh, so you didn't know about Cillian's condition?"

"His condition?"

"I'm not sure if it's my place to say, and I don't know the details, but Damian told me that he got really sick really fast. He lost a lot of weight, and... anyway, Damian is having a hard time of it."

Damian. I almost forgot why I was calling. Aislinn saying his name makes it easier for me to ask.

"So, you're still in touch with Damian?"

"I guess you know that we're divorced, yeah? But it was a good divorce, if there's ever such a thing. We... Wait, if you haven't spoken to Damian, how did you find me?"

"A friend of a friend is good at online sleuthing, and he found your name and number and passed it on. I was hoping you could put me in touch with him—if you don't mind. I have so many questions, and I thought maybe if I went through you first... you could tell me if it was a bad idea to contact Damian."

"Oh no, luv, I'm sure he'll want to talk to you, and he'll answer any questions you might have. I'm happy to give you his mobile number." She takes a breath. "I have to say... Cillian so idealized you there was a time when I thought maybe he made you up. But Damian assured me that you were indeed real."

"Oh." Her words somehow lift me while simultaneously pushing me deeper into a dark place that threatens to swallow me whole. I read once about a material called Vantablack, the world's darkest man-made substance, used by the military to keep satellites and jets from being detected. That's where I find myself, in the Vantablack.

"I'll text you the details of the funeral, along with Damian's number. It'll be in Cillian's hometown, on Tuesday."

Funeral. That seven-letter word bludgeons me. Of course there will be a funeral, but the mental image of Cillian being lowered into the hard earth, leaving me for good, is more than I can bear.

"I know it's short notice, and I understand if you can't make it, but it would give you a chance to talk to Damian in person. He'll be there, of course."

I thank her profusely before hanging up and proceed to stare at her text. All this new information is more than my weary brain can process—Cillian's death, his being sick, Aislinn knowing exactly who I am, her casual mention of how much Cillian talked about me over the years, and now his funeral.

I sit on the edge of the bed, forcing myself to breathe in, breathe out. My brain is churning out random, crazy thoughts faster than I can process them. I should be there. I *need* to be there. I have to say one last goodbye even if he can't hear me. And I would be able to talk to Damian—in person—if he's willing to talk to me.

Before I can begin to rationally weigh the pros and cons, where the cons would surely win out, I find myself entering my credit card information and booking a round-trip ticket to Ireland, a ticket I can't possibly afford.

What the hell am I doing? That's my only thought as I click Buy for an insanely expensive ticket to Ireland that's leaving in four hours. I have no plan, no itinerary. *Will I arrive and want more than anything to take the next return flight to Austin? Or will Ireland seduce me, just as Cillian had, and I'll find myself compelled to experience first-*

hand everything he shared with me about his place of birth? Will I feel an irresistible pull to walk where he walked, have a pint or two in his favorite pub, and sit and think about his music where he did the same? Despite my doubts, I'm diving in headfirst, not knowing how deep the water is. The trouble is I never learned to swim.

I tell Clyde that I have a family emergency and that I need to use my vacation days, which I'd let idly accumulate for years. I don't even tell Sloane that I'm leaving, but I text her right before takeoff. She'll be freaking out, calling and texting me repeatedly. I tell Ashlyn that I won a stay at a wellness yoga retreat in Greece from a company contest and will be gone for a few days.

"Oh, Mom, that's so great! You deserve it. Send me pictures!"

I'll deal with the picture problem later.

I pull my suitcase from the storage unit downstairs, dust it off, and begin throwing things in, most of it reclaimed from the dirty clothes hamper—no time to wash and dry a single load. I dig out my never-used passport from the bottom of my underwear drawer and run my fingers over the embossed silver emblem of the American eagle, reliving the promise it held when new. I renewed it last year when Ashlyn wanted us to take a trip to Europe. She hoped Jason would foot the bill, but that never happened. A trip to Ireland for Cillian's funeral is not how I thought my passport would be broken in.

The Uber app says Terry will arrive in a blue Prius in ten minutes. I sprint through the house, turning off lights, unplugging the coffee maker, and double-checking the locks on the doors and windows. Remnants of Elliott's concern—bordering on obsession—for safety and security didn't leave when I showed him the door.

"How's it going?" Terry is a nice enough thirtysomething guy with a thick Boston accent and a sweet smile. I open my mouth several times to tell him to turn around and go back home. The words are right there on my tongue. I can taste them. This isn't like me. But dead or alive, Cillian has been at the root of the most impulsive decisions of my life.

S itting in the middle seat of the very last row on a 757 bound for New York—the only seat available on such short notice—I'm doing my best to block out the insistent roar of the engines and ignore the passengers trekking to the bathroom right behind me. Instead, I focus on my mental list of all the questions I want—no, that I need—to ask Damian. I have no idea what Cillian told him about me over the years, about us. That puts me at a distinct disadvantage.

When Damian finds out I'm coming, will he wonder what right I have to be at Cillian's funeral? Will he be angry with me, want me to leave? Or maybe he'll be pleased to see me and welcome a chance to reminisce about our shared connection to Cillian. Either reaction is equally possible.

As I wait out my layover at my gate at JFK, the seats are beginning to fill, and the sprinkling of Irish accents from fellow passengers simultaneously soothes me and yanks at my heart. I put my phone on silent and vow not to glance at it until I've landed in Ireland.

" C hicken or beef?" the flight attendant asks.
I shake my head and gently wave away the foil-wrapped meal he's offering. I'm too busy obsessing over how I'm going to rein in my grief in front of Cillian's family. Midthought, my eyelids close without warning, and when I awake, we've begun our descent. My ears pop, I roll my neck to knock out the kinks, and I look out the window. I'm in Irish airspace. Cillian and I talked often about how I would move here and we would make a home in Dublin and raise our children here. We both grew up in small towns and villages, but

we craved the pulse of the city. I can barely remember the pleasant tingle of anticipation, looking ahead to a future that held so much promise.

The moment the wheels touch the tarmac, I turn on my phone—very little juice left. I have tons of texts from Sloane, of course. One is from Clyde, expressing concern about my family emergency. One is from Ashlyn, asking me if the place for the yoga retreat is nice. *I hope I can keep my stories straight.* Then I see a voice message from an unknown number. I press Play.

"Zee, this is Damian. Aislinn says you're coming for the funeral. I hope we'll have time to chat. I know you have questions. I have questions too."

His warm Irish brogue is a salve. I'm incredibly relieved that he's willing to meet with me and more than a little anxious over the prospect of reminiscing with Cillian's best friend.

As we taxi to the gate, the recycled air fills with the sound of seat belts being unbuckled, phones dinging with messages accumulated over the last seven hours, and excited conversations about plans while in Dublin. I wait in my seat as the rest of the passengers shuffle their way to the front exit, my anxiety swelling by the minute as I ruminate about meeting Damian for the first time in twenty years, meeting Cillian's family for the first time, and recycling all the heartbreak from back then—Cillian's and mine. When it's finally my turn to stand and grab my bag from the overhead bin, no one is left to help with the heft of my overstuffed carry-on. A flight attendant comes to my rescue.

"Can I help ya there, luv?"

"Please. I think I overpacked."

He reaches up and effortlessly lowers my bag and smiles. "First time in Ireland?"

"Can you tell?" I chuckle.

"I meet a lot of first-timers. Business or pleasure?"

Blurting, *"I'm here for the funeral of the love of my life,"* would be incredibly awkward for us both, so I say, "Neither."

"Well, you have a lovely time."

"Thank you." I'm appreciating what I think could be the last smiling Irish face I encounter.

Chapter 29

The Dublin airport isn't that different from most airports in the States, except for the signs that are written in impossible-to-pronounce Irish as well as English. Cillian told me once that learning Irish was mandatory when he was in school though he spoke it only with his family and with his bandmates when they wanted to talk in code.

"Say something in Irish to me," I said in my most sultry voice.

"*Mo grá*," he said as he pulled me closer.

"What does it mean?"

"It means 'my love,'" he answered and followed up with a kiss.

Those were the only two words I learned in Irish. My heart swelled each time he uttered them. There had been no one to call me "my love" in twenty years, at least no one whom I loved back with such ferocity.

I pass a sea of suitcases abandoned in the baggage claim area and congratulate myself for bringing only a carry-on, even if it is full of dirty clothes. As I walk toward the exit to grab a cab, I spot a gray-bearded middle-aged man with thick glasses, wearing a black suit and tie and holding a neatly printed sign to his chest that says, "Zezelia." I'm completely taken aback. *What are the odds that another Zezelia would be landing in Dublin at the same time?*

"Zero" is the answer to my rhetorical question.

I tentatively approach the man and stand in front of him for a few seconds as the crowd parts around us. "Excuse me. Um, I'm Zezelia."

"Zezelia Owens?"

"That's me." I hesitate. "I wasn't expecting a ride. Who hired you?"

He pulls his phone out of his jacket pocket and scrolls for a few seconds. "That would be one Damian O'Leary, ma'am."

"And he paid for it?"

"All paid, including tip, ma'am."

"So, you know where I'm going?"

"Yes, ma'am, I do."

I had texted Aislinn the address of the Airbnb I booked. She must have shared it with Damian, along with the news of my arrival.

"Thank you, um…"

"It's Colin, ma'am."

"Thank you, Colin."

"You can thank Mr. O'Leary, ma'am."

I place my carry-on into his outreached hand. "Just call me Zezelia, or Zee is fine."

He smiles and nods once, and I follow him out into the drizzling rain, to my—*Mercedes stretch limo*? That is so unnecessary. Damian is either trying to impress me or intimidate me. Either option makes me like him a little less. Maybe all that success over the years has gone to his head, and he isn't accustomed to interacting with plebeians like me.

I climb into the back of the impossibly roomy limousine, and Colin shuts my door, hermetically sealing the space. The interior is outfitted with a bar, a television screen, speakers, and tinted windows.

"Comfortable?"

His voice startles me.

"Press the speaker button if you want me to hear you."

I look around and press the button. "Yes, very."

"Let me know if you need anything. It should be half an hour or so."

My phone dings with a message. This time, I recognize the number. It's Damian.

Colin says he found you, no problem. I would have come myself, but I had a meeting I couldn't get out of. Sorry about the over-the-top ride. It was all I could get on such short notice. But it's nice, yeah?

So, I was wrong on both counts.

Thank you. That was really thoughtful.

Colin will be able to take you to and from the funeral as well.

There's that obscene word again—the same number of letters as goodbye.

The ride to my destination is nerve-wracking, not because of Colin's driving skills but because of Irish driving rules that dictate driving on the left side of the road. Each time he makes a left turn, I tense in anticipation of the crash from oncoming cars. The signs reminding drivers to Keep Left don't ease my anxiety. I consider turning on the TV to give my eyes someplace to go besides the road, but then I would miss everything I've waited years—decades, really—to see. As we come closer to the city center, the buildings become a generational mix of the old and the new, and several side streets that we turn onto are old cobblestone, making the ride briefly bumpy. I'm surprised, though I'm not sure why, to find a river running through the city center.

"It's the River Liffey," Colin tells me when I ask.

Turns out, several rivers run through Dublin, which to my mind quadruples the city's charm. On the main roads, people—who looked like they could have been dropped into almost any city in the US and blend in—crowd the wide sidewalks.

"Yer place is up here," Colin says right before we pull to a stop.

I look at the front door then at the address I have on my phone.

"Colin, I think maybe there's been a miscommunication. This isn't the address of the place I booked."

My phone dings with a message.

I hope you don't mind. It's a wee upgrade. I want you to be as comfortable as possible while in Dublin.

Wee? I booked a studio. This is a townhouse and a historical building from the looks of it.

I dial Damian's number. He answers right away.

"Damian, this is too much. The limo was over the top, but this place... It's really unnecessary!"

"It's more space than you need, but please, just accept it and make yourself at home."

Make myself at home. The irony of those words slices through my already-bleeding heart.

Colin brings my bag inside, sets it at the foot of the stairs, and hands me a business card with his phone number on it. "Call if you need to go anywhere. It's all taken care of, luv."

"Thank you," I say, distracted by the incredible charm of the place.

Colin quietly closes the door, and I start down the wainscot-walled entryway. The stained-glass light fixture overhead provides a fractured rainbow effect on the walls, like a bit of magic welcoming me to Ireland. I wander from room to room on the first floor, taking in the wide-planked knotted wood floors and curved archways, each room more ridiculously charming than the one before. Paintings, sculptures, Indian rugs, and pottery are displayed throughout. Despite the overcast day, light pours in through vintage paned windows. A cast-iron fireplace from a time long ago serves as the centerpiece of the living room. I venture up the curved staircase—wide wooden plank steps match the floors and are accented by white decorative spindles beneath the banister. Upstairs, I have my choice of three beautiful bedrooms—an embarrassment of riches, as my mother used to say. When I push open the door to the bathroom, my jaw drops—a blue claw-foot tub and a fireplace. I'm already imagining myself sinking into a tub of steaming hot water, a roaring fire in the fireplace. I'm unaccustomed to such luxury, and for a moment, I forget why I'm here, and I'm happy.

I go back downstairs to grab my suitcase and bring it up to the bedroom with the four-poster bed, but before settling in, I need to let Ashlyn and Sloane know that I've arrived safely at my destination. I pull my dead phone from my purse. I packed my charger, but I don't own an adapter for European plugs. *Shit! Why would I?* I stand in the entryway, considering my options. I could call Colin, but I seriously doubt that taking me shopping for an adapter is in his job description. Maybe an electronics store is within walking distance, but I can't even search Google for the nearest store. The ringing of a phone startles me. I stupidly glance at my cell phone, still in my hand. It's dark. I run through the house, following the sound, and am shocked to find a black wall phone in the kitchen. I hesitate before answering.

"Hello?"

"Zee, it's Damian."

"Oh, hi." My brain is scrambled. "I forget people still have land lines and—wait, how do you even know this number?"

"It's my place. I thought Colin told you. I tried your mobile several times, but—"

"You *live* here?" *I absolutely refuse to stay with Damian. I'll find another Airbnb, and Colin can take me there.*

He chuckles. "No, that would be a wee bit awkward, don't you think? I usually let it out, but it was free, and I thought you might find it a nice place to escape to after—everything."

"Oh, well, thank you."

"I just called to see if you're comfortable, if you need anything else."

"You don't happen to have an adapter for American plugs, do you?"

"Yeah. There are several in the stand in the entryway. Quite a few Americans visit Ireland, you know."

The teasing in his voice makes me feel sheepish.

"Thank you, Damian—for everything."

"No worries, luv. Listen, why don't you help yourself to the wine cellar? The door is to the left of the staircase. A glass'll help you relax, and you can get some rest. Jet lag is a killer."

Of course he has a wine cellar.

We hang up, and I beeline to the collection of conveniently labeled adapters filling the drawer of the stand in the entryway. I pull out two labeled "US," return to the kitchen, and plug in my phone. It immediately begins dinging with dozens of missed calls and messages. Most of them are from Sloane. I resist the urge to deal with them right away and instead decide to check out the wine cellar. It might not be happy hour in Austin, but it's wine o'clock in Dublin.

I go downstairs and scan the impressive racks of bottle after bottle of wine, but knowing nothing about vineyards or vintages, I make a random choice based on the lovely label. With the bottle in hand, I return to the main floor. I don't want to pop the top on some thousand-dollar bottle of wine by mistake, so I figure I should check with Damian to see if my choice is okay. I set the dusty bottle on the kitchen counter, take a picture of it, and text it to Damian.

Is this okay?

He answers right away. *Excellent choice! Enjoy!*

I'm on a scavenger hunt for a corkscrew and a wine glass, opening drawers and cabinets and slamming them shut. Once I have both and the cork is pulled, I pour the scarlet liquid into the crystal wine glass and indulge. I didn't know wine could taste this good. I vow to never again refrigerate my red wine. After the first couple of sips, I set the glass down and pick up my phone. Attached by a cord, I rest my hip against the counter. I'm not sure who I should respond to first.

While I mull that over, a message from Elliott pops up. *Crap.* There's even a message from Clyde with a picture of him and Sandy attached. He's probably already wanting to know when his most reliable employee will be back on the job.

I need to grab a photo of my "yoga retreat" from the internet before I message Ashlyn. Sloane will require an extended conversation, an in-depth explanation and analysis. I have no idea what to say to Elliott. He knows my history with Cillian. We may have been divorced years ago, but anything related to Cillian pricks Elliott's heart. I try to muster empathy for his feelings. He's never gotten over me, just like I never got over Cillian.

I opt to first text Clyde and tell him that I'll let him know ASAP about my return date, and I add, *Cute pic of you and Sandy!*

I send Ashlyn multiple images of a yoga retreat in Greece I found online, complete with a zero-entry pool looking out onto the sea. The website promises the retreat to be inspiring, enriching, and transformative, something I could use right about now.

Lying about my whereabouts is shamefully easy. *The place is lovely. I'm a little tired, but it's going to be great. I'll call you tomorrow. Wish you were here! Love you. Mom.*

I take another sip of wine and take a deep breath before dialing Sloane's number. She picks up on the first half ring. She must've been clutching the phone, waiting for my call.

"What the hell, Zee?"

"Yeah, I know."

"Are you actually in fucking Ireland right now?" Her voice has reached a squeaky pitch of panic.

"Dublin, to be exact."

"And you're going to Cillian's funeral? I know you didn't ask for my advice, but I think that's a colossally bad idea."

"Why?" I ask though I could think of a million reasons why.

"Zee, hon, don't you think that man caused you enough heartache when he was alive?"

"It's something I feel like I need to do. For closure, I guess."

She sighs. "So, I guess that means you were able to get in touch with Damian's ex?"

"Yeah, and Damian."

I fill her in on the details—Aislinn's open invitation, the limo waiting for me at the airport, the beautiful townhouse, and Damian's call—and my lie to Ashlyn, in case they speak. I've already added that one to my seemingly endless list of lies.

"Are you okay? I mean, do you think you'll be okay, you know, with the funeral and meeting Damian—in person?"

"That remains to be seen," I say though I'm pretty sure I'll be the opposite of okay.

"Do you need me to come? Seriously, I can be on a flight tonight."

Sloane to the rescue? Again?

"That is so incredibly sweet of you, but no. I need to deal with this on my own."

I know that if I don't face Damian and say a final goodbye to Cillian—and do it alone—I'll never be able to close that chapter of my life and truly move on.

Chapter 30

Anxiety overpowers my jet lag and the two glasses of wine that I've downed. I can't turn my head off, and it keeps me from sleeping. After tossing and turning in my four-poster bed, I finally climb out around two in the morning, grab my laptop, go downstairs, and make myself a cup of tea. I leave my laptop on the kitchen table and, using the mug as a hand warmer, roam the townhouse, stopping to stare out of a living room window into the dark, quiet street. Memories that Cillian and I never got to make in Dublin form against my will. The effort to suppress them makes my ribs ache.

In that alternate reality, our children would have grown up here, worn uniforms to school, had the same accent as their father, and called me "Mam" instead of "Mom." This was supposed to be our forever home. Instead, I'm here for the single saddest day of my life. I want to snap my fingers and send those almost memories packing.

But right now, I have to wash clothes if I have any hope of being presentable tomorrow. I make a quick study of the washing machine in the kitchen. None of the settings are familiar, and I can't find an instruction booklet tucked away in any of the drawers. I have no idea how to convert Celsius to Fahrenheit. I'm not even sure of the temperatures on the settings I use at home, which are offered up in much simpler terms—cold, warm, hot, delicates, and hand wash. The way things are going, I can see me unwittingly setting the machine on super hot and shrinking to unwearable the few items of clothing I've brought. Overwhelmed with yet another thing to figure out, to deal with, I give up.

My tea is cold. I zap the last few sips in the microwave and plant myself in front of my laptop. I figure I should learn more about Damian's life over the last twenty years before coming face to face with him at the funeral. We're basically strangers, after all. He was always nice to me when Cillian and I were together, but girlfriend-of-his-best-friend was the extent of our relationship. I wake up my laptop and jump down a Damian rabbit hole.

If I'm to believe everything I'm reading, Damian has lived more than a few lifetimes over the last two decades. In his twenties and early thirties, he drank, he dallied in drugs, and he was evidently a frequent customer of tattoo parlors. He had a well-oiled revolving door to accommodate the women in his life—I find photos of him with a blonde, a brunette, a redhead, the one with the blue hair, the one with the nose rings and a tongue piercing, and the stick figure with the huge boobs. Then he married Aislinn, and the gossip seemed to stop. Surprisingly, I don't find any rumors of infidelity.

I read an interview with Aislinn in which she candidly said, "Damian and me, we're better suited as friends than husband and wife. But he's a good man, that one." In my brief conversation with her before I left Austin, I hadn't detected any residual resentment from their divorce.

I come across hundreds of photos of Damian and Cillian on stage with the band, in recording studios, candid shots of them living their lives in the streets of Dublin, Paris, New York, Rome—all the places I was supposed to go with Cillian. As I scroll through the photos, I can almost convince myself that Cillian is alive and well—that he'll be calling any minute.

It feels like only minutes have passed instead of hours, but the sunlight peering through the kitchen window tells me otherwise. My impulse to run away, to avoid what lies ahead, is almost as strong as my impulse had been to hop on a plane to Ireland, but I know I'll never find peace if I take the coward's way out. When the sun has fully risen, it's just after one in the morning in Austin, and I switch from tea to coffee, to create the illusion of morning. My phone pings with a message from Sloane.

Are you up? How are you doing? When is the funeral? Call me if you need emotional support, no matter the time.

You're up late. It's morning here. The wake is in just a few hours. Funeral tomorrow. To be honest, I feel like I'm going to be sick. I'll call if things go south. Hugs and kisses.

Soaking in the claw-foot tub helps me relax as I mentally gird myself for what lies ahead. *What do I say to his family? What do I say to Damian, to Aislinn?* Obviously, I've never been to an Irish wake or any wake, for that matter. *Are there customs I should know?* I have no idea what to wear because I have no idea what I threw into my suitcase in my haste to leave. There's no time to shop for appropriate attire, but I think I remember grabbing a couple of clean things from my closet. *Shoes!* I didn't pack dress shoes. Hopefully, no one will notice the strange woman in the wrinkled dress and worn sneakers—or care.

I step out of the tub, dry off, and hovering over my suitcase in the bedroom, consider my clothing options: limited at best, dirty and wrinkled at worst. However, at the bottom of the suitcase, which I still haven't fully unpacked, I find a black knit dress rolled up in a ball. I shake it out, sniff under the arms, and say out loud, "This will have to do."

My cell rings.

"Hello?"

"Hey, did ya sleep?" I recognize Damian's voice now.

"Not so great. The bed is super comfortable, but jet lag and... you know."

"Me either." A couple of silent seconds pass. "So, I was thinking you can ride with me instead of calling Colin. I can fill you in on what to expect and such."

"Oh, okay. That's a good idea."

"So, in about an hour?"

"I'll be ready."

That's perhaps the biggest lie of all.

Chapter 31

I slip on the black dress and run my hands down the front to smooth out a few stubborn wrinkles. If there was ever a time I wanted to be dressed properly for the occasion, this is it. I'm not trying to dress to impress. I simply want to be dressed appropriately out of respect for Cillian and his family. My muscles tense as I once again consider the reality of coming face-to-face with his family. My heart races. *What am I doing here?* My breathing becomes shallow, and my chest tightens. *Am I having a panic attack?* I lie on the bed, close my eyes, and try to remember those anxiety-reducing breathing exercises—the ones from my brief post-Cillian stint with a therapist at the free clinic. She was trying her best to help me cope with the dual loss of my mother and of Cillian's love within days of each other. *Breathe in for four seconds, hold for seven seconds, exhale for eight seconds. Repeat. And again.* It's helping, but I'm on the verge of texting Damian to say I'm not feeling well and can't make it to the wake. But the thought of backing out now makes me more anxious than the thought of being there.

I take one last deep breath, stand, step into my sneakers, and glance at myself in the mirror. The sneakers are the *coup de grâce* of my fashion disaster, and I laugh at my appearance. My laugh turns into sudden tears, and I sit back down on the edge of the bed, questioning everything about my life up to this point. I don't think I'm going to walk away from all this with the feeling of closure I've been hoping for since the moment I made the wrong-headed decision to buy the ticket. But here I am, and Damian will be here—I glance at the time on my phone—in forty-five minutes. Our meeting for the first time in twenty years is yet another source of my ballooning anxiety. We were never close, but we had that one degree of separation from Cillian, which created an intangible, nameless connection between us.

I grab a tissue, swipe away tears, and head to the bathroom for some much-needed makeup repair, and staring at my reflection, I vow out loud to hold back more tears, at least until Damian arrives.

I use the remaining time to finish unpacking and hang up the few clean clothes I had packed, and I set aside a pile of things I'll need to wash—as soon as I figure out the washing machine.

I go downstairs and mindlessly wander from room to room before deciding that another cup of coffee is in order. While some people find coffee to be a stimulant, it relaxes me, or maybe it's the ritual of making it, holding the warm mug in my hand, and taking one slow sip after the other. I pop a pod into the machine, fill the tank with water, and impatiently wait for the mug to fill. I can still hear Cillian's voice: *"You Yanks' idea of coffee is shite."* It makes me smile. I grab the coffee-filled mug and go to the living room. Aside from the four-poster bed in the bedroom and the blue claw-foot tub in the bathroom, this is my favorite room in the house.

The wait for Damian feels akin to emotional waterboarding. I'm not sure how much more I can take before I break. I peer out from behind the curtains and focus on the rivulets of rain streaking the window panes—a meditation of sorts. The thought occurs to me—or maybe it's more of a hope—that this might be a *Waiting for Godot* situation: Damian won't show, and I'll sidestep the trauma of facing Cillian's mortality as well as my own.

I turn around and catch sight of a small bookshelf hiding in a living room nook. I wander over and glance at the titles. Some are in Irish, which of course, I can't read. But the titles in English range from *1984* to *Pride and Prejudice*. Then I notice a copy of *Gulliv-*

er's Travels by Jonathan Swift, the band's namesake. I pull the worn paperback off the shelf and open the cover. Cillian's signature and a date are written on the title page—it must be his book from high school. I turn the page. The entire band signed it, and underneath their signatures is written, "The Swifters." I close the book and press it to my chest. I can still feel the same butterflies as when he leaned in close that first night, our lips almost touching—until Damian interrupted us. My thoughts are cut short when I hear a car door slam outside.

I go to the window and spot Damian outside. He's early. He's not in a limo with a driver or some outrageously expensive sports model, as I expected, but behind the wheel of an almost comical subcompact.

He walks up the cobblestone path and rings the doorbell. I set my unfinished coffee on a side table and grab my purse and the keys as I brace myself for what's sure to be an incredibly awkward reunion.

I open the door.

"Zezelia," he says softly. He steps forward, and we share a tentative embrace. When he pulls back, he looks at me and says, "Yer just as I remembered. The years have been good to ya."

"You're a sweet liar."

He, on the other hand, doesn't look the same. His floppy hair is shorn and highlighted with streaks of gray, but longer strands fall stylishly onto his forehead. He's dressed in black jeans, a white T-shirt, an expensive-looking black leather jacket, and black boots. Small gauges are displayed in his ears, and tattoos peek out from the collar of his shirt. The multiple rings on his fingers are lingering reminders of the Damian from twenty-plus years ago. In contrast to my memory, he's clean-shaven, revealing a surprising cleft in his chin. Beyond the superficial, he exudes an air of maturity and experience. *And pain?* The years have evidently taught him a hard lesson or two.

But his eyes are the same cobalt blue, his eyelashes still cast shadows each time he blinks, and his voice has the same rich, raspy tone.

"Can I come in? We have time for a cuppa if you like. I thought we could talk for few minutes before we head to Cillian's mam's."

"I thought we were going to a church."

He gives me a grim smile.

"I need to let you know what to expect. Cillian's mother is more than a wee bit traditional. It won't be anything like in the States." He holds out a book. "I brought this for you. It'll give you a wee glimpse of what the wake and the funeral will be like. I highlighted some sections for ya."

I take the book and glance at the title: *My Father's Wake*, by Kevin Toolis.

"What is this, a guidebook?"

"Not exactly. It's the author's experience with a very traditional wake after his da passed. Very few people hold wakes like that anymore, but Cillian's parents live in a small village and are from the older generation. Cillian was the youngest in the family."

"I know," I mumbled.

"You won't have time to read the whole thing, but I thought it might help. You can skim the marked pages on the drive there. It'll be about three hours."

"Well, now you've got me nervous."

"I'm not gonna lie. It may be intense. It helps if you know what to expect from his family, yeah?"

Although I never got to meet his family, I feel like I know them—their names at least—his mom, Sadie, and his late father, Hugh; his brothers, Declan, Kieran, Dermot, and Niall; and his sisters, Margaret, Fiona, and Noreen. I can't believe I remember their names, but back in the day, I practiced saying them over and over again, like a nursery rhyme, so I wouldn't forget or mispronounce them when we finally met. That never happened, of course, but their names are imprinted on my brain. *What do they know about me, if anything?* My brain gets stuck on the thought.

The keys slip from my hand and land on the floor.

"You okay, luv?"

"I think so."

He picks them up and hands them to me. I'd been gripping the keys so tightly that I have a key imprint in my palm.

"Sorry. Didn't mean to leave you standing there. Come on in," I say.

Once in the kitchen, I flip the switch on the electric kettle and grab a couple of tea bags and cups. "Milk? Sugar?" I ask. A memory flashes—Cillian asking me the same question that morning at the Driskell after our first night together.

"A wee bit of both."

We sit at the kitchen table, hands wrapped around our porcelain tea cups, the steam rising. We take a sip in unison.

"So, how are you doing, Damian? I know this all must be so hard."

He sighs the universal sigh of people in mourning. "My head is in bits. I knew he was sick, of course, but we were still working. We were in his home studio right the day before. I thought he'd have months, maybe years left, not hours. It's all shite."

His face torques as he tries to hold back tears. I reach out and place my hand on his. I want to ask about Cillian's illness. *How long was he sick? Did he suffer? Is it genetic?*

"I'm so sorry, Damian."

He takes another deep, shaky breath before regaining his composure, and I withdraw my hand.

"What about you?" he asks. "To be honest, I was shocked when Aislinn told me you were coming."

"It's surreal. I haven't really processed it all, you know? I—"

"Cillian always loved you, but you know that, yeah?"

I can't decide if I should tell him, but I can see by the look in his eyes that he's hungry for anything Cillian related.

"Actually, he called me just a few weeks ago and wanted me to come to Ireland. Said he would buy me a ticket."

He jerks back. "What? Are you bloody serious? I can't believe he didn't tell me."

"I didn't know... I didn't know he was sick. Now I realize he must have known he didn't have long, and—"

"And he wanted to spend the time he had left with you."

I stare down at my tea and nod. "I mean, his call came out of nowhere. I was so taken aback at first... I told him I needed to think about it."

Those were the same words I said to him back when he asked me to go on tour with him.

I cover my eyes with my hands. I can't let Damian see my pain. His must be so much worse. He stands and comes around to where I'm sitting, pulls me up, and wraps his arms around me. The scent of leather blends with his freshly showered scent, and it comforts me.

"You couldn't've known. It's okay, luv. We're both hurting."

Chapter 32

The rain has slacked off—a slight concession from the heavens—and we run from the house and squeeze into Damian's car.

"I have to admit this is not what I thought you'd be driving."

"So what, you thought a Lamborghini, a Maserati?"

"Well, yeah, maybe."

He chuckles and shakes his head. "That's very American of you."

"If you saw my 2008 Kia, you wouldn't say that."

He glances at me and frowns as if recalibrating his notion of who I am and what my life is like back in the States.

As I open the car door, I'm somehow surprised by the spotless interior.

"Here," he says, handing me a black umbrella. "In case it starts lashing again. Do you have any other questions about, you know…?"

I'm sure the book he's given me will help. But it all sounds a bit much.

"You say his family knows who I am? They know what I look like—what I used to look like, anyway."

"Cillian had lots of photos of the two of you together. They'll know who you are."

God help me. It would have been better if they thought I was just some strange woman crying in the back of the room. I may have his siblings' names memorized, but I'm not sure I'll be able to match the names with the celluloid images of faces from twenty years ago to the present-day real thing. Maybe if I make myself small, no one will no-tice me in my less-than-white sneakers.

I skim the pages of the book he's shared with me, but I read the same paragraphs over and over again, unable to focus. When we pull up to Cillian's parents' home, I'm pretty sure I could have picked it out myself from Cillian's loving description. I so clearly remember his words as we sat at a coffee shop near the lake, sipping the coffee I found too bitter but he loved.

"My mam and da have lived in that old cottage all their married lives and raised all eight of us there." He looked off in the distance and chuckled. "I guess it looks like something you'd see in a tourist booklet of old Ireland—built from stone, the bright-red door, the slate roof, shuttered windows, a garden, and a worn picket fence."

The red door, he told me, was said to ward off ghosts and evil spirits.

"They don't really believe that, at least I don't think they do. It's kind of like knocking on wood? A wee bit of luck, just in case." I had detected a thread of homesickness woven into his words. He may have been on the verge of becoming a rock star, but he was still an Irish boy at heart who missed his mam and da.

And now I'm at his home—without him.

"We're here. You ready?"

I'm still staring at the cottage when Damian comes around to my side and opens the door, a gentlemanly gesture that belies his jaded rock star appearance.

Cars are parked everywhere in a tangle of congestion. Voices and music burst from inside the cottage as if grief is an unwelcome guest at this boisterous gathering. Damian gently guides me to the door. A woman greets us and immediately wraps her arms around Damian.

"Oh, Damian, you're here. Aislinn said you were on your way."

I'm stunned. She's a shocking age-progressed image of Ashlyn. I try not to stare as she squeezes Damian tightly, sharing their disbelief at what has happened, what is happening.

When she lets go, she takes a step back and turns her questioning eyes to me.

"Zee, this is Margaret, Cillian's sister. Margaret, this is Zezelia."

She lets out a tiny gasp and, with a tilt of her head, reaches for my hand and says, "Cillian's Zezelia."

I don't deserve the warmth infused into those two words. I turn to look at Damian, and he gives a subtle nod. I follow her into the main room with Damian trailing behind. Despite his attempt to let me know what's in store, I am spectacularly unprepared—unprepared for the open casket, unprepared for the crowds milling around, and unprepared for the loud bagpipe music and all the open windows, despite the chill in the air. My knees go weak when Margaret pulls me in front of Cillian's mother, who looks as if her pale skin is melting from the gravity of sorrow.

"Mam, this is Zezelia."

She looks at me through Cillian's green eyes, which alone is enough to fell me, and she says, "He wanted you with him in his last days. Why didn't you come, lass?"

I swear my heart stops for a few seconds before I blurt, "I was going to come, but I... I didn't know he was sick. If I had known... I'm so, so sorry."

I open my mouth to say more, but the words are lodged in my throat. I have no business being here. I abruptly turn to run away but crash into Damian, who's standing right behind me. He puts his arm around me and says something to Cillian's mom in Irish before guiding me to another room. I'm certain all eyes are on us. I have to will myself not to vomit.

He gently pushes me into the next room and closes the door behind us.

"Zee, you okay?"

I look up at him and press myself into his chest. "No," I mumble, not caring if I leave mascara stains on his white T-shirt. "I shouldn't be here. I don't belong here. I missed my chance to be a part of Cillian's life. I don't deserve to be a part of his death."

I have no claim to grief. But there it is, burrowing beneath my skin.

He pulls me back and looks at me with unfeigned concern and says, "Yes, you do. Cillian would've wanted you here." He pauses. "I want you here."

Now, I'm sobbing, unable to catch my breath. He hands me a box of tissues from the nightstand, and I noisily blow my nose, wipe my eyes dry, and exhale my sorrow. I stare at my dirty sneakers. I don't belong here any more than they do.

"Better?" he asks.

"A bit."

"Come on, luv," he says as he motions toward the room we just escaped. "It's time to say a proper goodbye to Cillian."

As Damian and I approach the open casket, I'm physically unable to take the last few steps. The line of communication between my brain and my feet has been severed, and I stand frozen in place.

He peers into the casket and makes the sign of the cross. I lower my head and mumble, "Damian, wait. I don't think I can do this."

He turns to look at me. "Yes, you can, luv." He steps back, leans in close, and lowers his voice. "It's thought to be rude not to view the body."

The body.

He tightly clasps my hand in his and coaxes me over. I hold my breath and close my eyes. I brace myself before slowly opening them, and something cold cracks my chest open. My frozen heart shatters. Bile rises in my throat. The still body lying in the casket is Cillian, but it isn't. His illness has stolen everything that made Cillian who he was. He's older, of course, but far thinner than I could have imagined. His cheeks are hollowed, erasing the dimple that melted my heart all those years ago. His slender fingers are wrapped tightly around a rosary, and a crucifix lies on his chest, neither of which he would have clung to when I knew him. But the copper coins covering his eyes are, to me, the most horrifying detail of all. I indiscreetly point a trembling finger at them.

Damian gently lowers my hand and whispers, "I'll explain later."

A chorus of prayer from a group of elderly women imbues an otherworldly feel to the room.

"I can't breathe. I need air," I growl at Damian before abruptly turning and propelling myself through the crowded room. I catch bits and pieces of conversation as I make my way through the throngs of people: "It's going to be a lovely Mass." "Shame he never found himself a wife, never had children." "His mam doesn't look good." And I hear the constant refrain of "Sorry for your troubles" to Cillian's family.

I run out the front door and collapse on the stone wall outside. The scent of honeysuckle that I hadn't noticed before is pleasantly distracting for a second or two. My heart stomps around in my chest as I desperately try to catch my breath. I guess this is what I do, what I've always done—I run away and check out when things get hard.

Damian follows me outside, sits beside me, and begins rubbing circles on my back.

"Breathe slow. In. Out. In. Out."

I try to focus on the heady scent of honeysuckle and Damian's warm hand on my back. When my heart finally settles and my breath slows, I look at him.

"What's wrong with me? I thought I had to come here to say goodbye, but I can't even stand to look at him. Not like that. That's not the Cillian I remember. He looks like a wax likeness of Cillian."

Damian sighs heavily. "That he does. Have you never seen a dead body before, luv?"

"My mom. But that was over twenty years ago, and I watched her gradually get sicker and sicker. Seeing Cillian like that is such a shock."

"Well, you don't have to see him again, but you should meet the rest of his family. And Aislinn wants to say hello."

I huff a breath. I have to pull myself together even while guilt and regret are tearing me apart.

As he opens the front door for me, we're met by Aislinn. She's casually beautiful, her auburn hair tied up in a topknot, her skin almost translucent, just like in the pictures I had scrolled through online. Without saying a word, she embraces me.

Then she says, "I'm so glad you decided to come. It couldn't have been an easy decision. I know Damian is helping you, but please call or text if you need anything—anything at all."

"I wouldn't be here if it weren't for you," I say, trying to sound like I feel only gratitude for making the trip.

Damian plays funeral host and, one by one, tracks down Cillian's siblings and introduces me. An uncanny family resemblance runs through them all, but the strongest belongs to his oldest brother, Niall, the priest.

I can't help but stare at him as he extends his hand. "I'm so sorry to meet under these circumstances," I say.

He takes my hand, and instead of offering a handshake, he gently sandwiches my hand between his. "So, you're Zezelia."

There's no suppressed resentment in his words. No, his voice is warm and comforting. His genuine welcome touches me, and all I can muster is a wobbly smile and a nod.

Damian nudges me away. "Niall, we'll see you tomorrow at the Mass," Damian says.

I'm tethered to him like a dog on a leash. Without him to guide me through what's happening, I would be running away again, not knowing where I'm going or where I would end up.

"I think we need a bleedin' drink," Damian says.

"I second that."

I watch him walk across the room, and I feel like my safety net has been pulled out from under me. I cling to the wall as if I actually might fall without him here to support me. I've never felt so ill at ease in my life.

He quickly returns with two glasses of amber-colored liquid and hands one to me. I take a sizable gulp. The burn triggers a coughing fit.

"Not a whiskey drinker, eh?" he says as he downs his glass with a satisfied sigh.

I take another gulp and manage not to cough as it burns its way down my throat and into my stomach.

"Another?" he asks.

I feel the knot in my chest loosen. "Sure."

I've always been a lightweight when it comes to alcohol. Cillian used to tease me about it.

But today, I'm going to ignore my inability to handle liquor and hope that this Irish whiskey offers me a temporary reprieve from the grief ripping my heart apart.

Chapter 33

Damian and I say little on the drive back from the wake. Nothing we could say will make either of us feel any less sad. I stare out the window as the lush green pastures fly by and paint over my darker thoughts. When he pulls up in front of the house, the thought of being alone fills my chest with a sticky panic.

"Want to come in for coffee or tea or something?" I say, trying not to convey how desperate I am for company.

He simply nods, gets out, and comes around and opens my door. When I stand, I feel woozy, and I sit back down in the car.

"You okay, luv?"

"I guess I'm not used to drinking Irish whiskey."

He smiles, offers me his hand, and we walk, elbows linked, up the path and into the house.

"Coffee?" I ask.

"Yeah, go on."

In the kitchen, I grab the coffee maker as he pulls up a chair to the table.

"Maybe I should make it?" he asks before he sits down.

"I'm not *that* drunk," I say, and we both chuckle—the first light moment since he picked me up this morning.

As we settle in with our coffee mugs, a fresh awkwardness takes over, and we avoid eye contact. But I want him to feel at ease enough to stay.

I look up from my coffee cup and really see him for the first time—not as my lost love's best friend, not as a rock star, but as a man with expressive eyes and a warm smile, who has done everything in his power to put me at ease in such a sad and stressful situation.

"Can I ask you a question?"

"Sure," he says.

"Did he still have that tattoo on his arm with my initials in it, or did he have it removed... you know, after what happened?"

"Still there."

I simply nod. Something of me will be with Cillian for all eternity.

"So," I say, pausing to consider if there would ever be a right time to ask, "what's the deal with the coins, you know, over his eyes?"

He looks up, blinks twice, and takes a deep breath. "Right. It's an old tradition based on a Greek myth, I think. No one really does it anymore, but Cillian's mom is old-fashioned, big on tradition, and she's never left the village, so... it's what's done."

"It just seemed ghoulish to me."

"Yeah, I guess it does."

"So, what does this myth say?"

He hesitates. "It's odd, for sure. Something about the coins being a bribe for an underworld lord to escort you to the other side or some shite like that."

"Okaaay. That doesn't seem very Catholic," I say.

"I know. I know. It's a bizarre contradiction."

"Well, if it helps his mom better cope with the fact that her son is dead, who am I to judge?"

"Right. It's a random business, this."

I frown.

"Death," he says. "It feels random, yeah?"

My thoughts drift to my mom. Only after several years had passed did I fully grasp just how random, how unfair, how untimely her death really was. I couldn't help but wonder, if she hadn't gotten sick, hadn't died, whether Cillian and I would've built a life—a good life, a happy life—raised Ashlyn together, and ultimately provided a better life for my mother?

"I still don't know what happened. The news said that he died 'after a brief illness.' Was it a heart attack?"

"Well, it wasn't brief. I can tell you that."

"Oh God. Was it cancer? Please tell me it wasn't cancer."

"Not cancer. He had a lung disease. Alpha something. The name is a mouthful. I can never remember. Hold on."

He pulls his phone from his jacket pocket and begins typing. He looks up. "I can't pronounce it."

He turns his phone around so I can see.

"Alpha-1 antitrypsin deficiency," I read, recalling some of the medical jargon in Leah's textbooks from back in the day. I keep reading. "It says it's some sort of enzyme deficiency and it's... it's hereditary?"

"None of his brothers and sisters has it. They were all tested. He was the only unlucky one that inherited the defective gene from both his parents."

My phone rings, and I dig it out of my purse. My hand is shaking, and I glance at Damian.

"Sorry, I need to take this."

I muster a strained falsetto. "Hey, sweetie, how's my favorite daughter?" Looking back over my shoulder, I catch the surprised expression on Damian's face.

"So, how's the retreat going? The classes good?" Ashlyn asks.

"Everything's great. Yeah, the classes are wonderful. I'm a little sore, but you know..." I lower my voice to a whisper. "Anything new with Jason that you want to talk about?" Even though I don't think I can manage that particular conversation right now, I have to ask.

She hesitates. "Not really. Anyway, I'd rather talk in person."

"Okay, that's fine," I say. "It can wait until I get back."

"When is that?"

"I'm not sure."

"I thought it was like a three-day package or something."

"I need to check." I force a laugh. "I'm not sure when my return flight is."

"Really? What about work?"

"It's all good. I'll check with Clyde."

"Well, just enjoy whatever time is left. I love you, Mom."

"Love you too. Bye, sweetie."

Hearing her voice, so full of life, eases my anxiety.

Damian cocks his head and leans across the table.

"You have a daughter?"

"Yes."

"Everything okay?"

"Yeah. Jason is her husband, and they're having... problems."

Before I can answer, he follows up with "What classes?"

"Sorry. I know that sounded weird."

I take a deep breath and proceed to tell him why I'm lying to my daughter. When I'm done telling Damian my version of what's happening, he shakes his head.

"Not sure I understand the secrecy about your trip to Ireland, but that's your business."

"It's complicated," I say.

"Isn't everything? I can't believe you have a grown, married daughter." He pauses. "You married?"

"Divorced."

"Sorry."

"Don't be. He's a good man, but the marriage was a mistake."

"Do you have a picture of her—your daughter?"

I scroll through the photos on my phone and choose one with the two of us together—the one everyone says makes her look like me. I hand my phone to Damian, and he stares at her image.

"She's beautiful. She looks like you. What's her name?"

"You're not going to believe this, but her name is Ashlyn. It's just spelled differently than your Aislinn."

"Really? Wow, that's unexpected."

He gives the phone back to me, and I look at her picture again. I miss her. I feel like I've been gone forever.

"It seems the two of you are close. You know, sometimes I regret not having kids. Maybe if Aislinn and I had stayed together..."

"It's not too late, you know. I'm sure there are lots of young women who would love nothing more than to have your babies."

As soon as I say it, I realize how wrong it sounded: too personal, too intimate, too sexual.

"Sorry."

He chuckles. "Believe me, I've had enough of women who want to have a rock star's babies, even a fading rock star. It's hard to find a woman who looks at me and sees Damian O'Leary from Killgantry Village, not Damian O'Leary of the Swifters, who's lived a fast and furious life."

A beat of quiet follows. Then I click my tongue and say, "Poor Damian. Must be tough. Too many women wanting you."

He waves his hand in a dismissive gesture and laughs. "Okay. Alright."

"Aislinn was right about you."

He raises his eyebrows but doesn't pursue it.

"You've been so kind to me since I got here. More than kind. I don't think I could've made it through today without you."

"Well, we've still got the Mass and the cemetery tomorrow to get through."

"Yeah, there's that," I say.

He shifts in his seat. "Zee, I don't think you realize how much you being here has helped me as well. No one else from the band could make it in time. You're the only one here who was around for that part of Cillian's life back then. Of *my* life back then. It's really lovely to have you here."

I stand and turn away before my tears spill over. "More coffee?"

"No thanks. I'm away there."

His "thanks" comes out as "tanks," and I half expect to turn around and find Cillian standing there. While I still have my back to Damian, the legs of his chair scrape across the wood floor. I try to breathe through the lump in my throat and discreetly wipe away my tears. I feel him come up behind me. I turn around and look up at him, and he wraps his arms around me and gently kisses my forehead.

"I just wish... things were different, you know?" I say into his chest. "I wish I had come when he asked. I wish—" I swallow my words. I feel awful, like something sour is beginning to rot inside me. "If I had known..." I huffed a tired breath. "I know it doesn't seem like it, but I really am trying to keep it together."

"You don't have to hide your feelings from me, luv."

For the second time that day, I dissolve into sobs with Damian's arms around me.

After he leaves, I go upstairs and fall asleep before my head hits the pillow.

Chapter 34

"Where's Cillian? Has he left me? I need Cillian." I'm in the house that I lived in with Elliott, and I'm dashing from room to room, looking for Cillian. I'm now in my mother's house, and I run to the window of my old room, and I spot Cillian walking away. My voice is strangled as I try to call out to him. Elliott pulls me away from the window and tells me that I'm where I belong. He tries to kiss me, but it feels wrong, like being kissed by a stranger. I break free from Elliott, run to the open door, and call to Cillian. He turns around. He's emaciated, his spotty beard is fully gray, and he has a rosary clutched in his left hand. I wave at him, but he can't see me—copper coins cover his eyes. The most disturbing—he's holding baby Ashlyn close to his chest. He turns and walks away again, taking Ashlyn with him.

I wake up screaming Ashlyn's name. The events of the dream have always been the same. But this time, my subconscious added the horror of Cillian's emaciated form and the funereal details.

My pillowcase is damp with tears. Saliva floods my mouth. I throw back the covers, run to the bathroom, and retch. Physically and emotionally drained, I ease down onto the cool tile floor, trying to reorient myself to the place, the day, the hour. I slowly stand, and after splashing water on my face, I look in the mirror. Dark circles under my eyes accent my nascent crow's feet. An extra layer of concealer could remedy my dark circles, but I can't turn back time.

Sleep is a nonstarter, so I grab my phone, go downstairs, and make coffee. The coffee mug in one hand, I unlock my phone with the other. I have a text from Sloane checking on me, asking how I'm doing, asking about the wake, and wanting to know when would be a good time to call. It's early evening in Austin. I'll call later and bring her up to speed on yesterday's drama.

Years ago, when I told her I was dropping out of school and leaving to be with Cillian, she was livid, judgmental, unforgiving. But in time, she realized her anger was mostly due to her hurt feelings. She had been looking forward to us moving ahead with our lives, together. Her anger was also generated by her concern for me and my future. When my mother got sick and Cillian cheated on me, it became clear I wasn't going anywhere, so we called a truce.

Her words back then meant a lot to me: "Zee, I'm so, so sorry. I'm not just saying that because you're not leaving with Cillian now. I would have eventually said the same thing even if you had gone with him. I swear," she said, crossing her heart and pledging a Scout's honor.

Although I doubt she'd have been so quick to apologize and offer her support if I'd actually gone with Cillian, she meant it when she offered to help. Just like she means it now.

I read her text.

Elliott called. He's worried that you haven't texted him back. He went by your apartment, and when there was no answer, he texted me. He said he didn't want to call Ashlyn and have her worry. What should I tell him?

Maybe it's finally time to start telling everyone the truth.

By the time Damian knocks on the door, I've already texted Sloane about the wake and the Mass and about Damian's soothing presence, and I've told Ashlyn about my "yoga retreat" and how wonderful it is. I've switched from coffee to tea, and I've slipped on the same black dress I wore to the wake. I step into my sneakers, which are less gray after I figured out the machine settings and tossed them in the dryer last night. I look at myself in the mirror. *Good enough.* Today isn't about me.

I open the door. Damian is dressed in a midnight-blue suit clearly tailored to trace the lines of his still-slim body, a white shirt, and a black tie I wouldn't have thought would work, but it does. He could easily be mistaken for a corporate lawyer. The only giveaways to the rocker beneath the suit are the gauges in his ears and the rings on his fingers.

"You look really nice," I say.

"You too."

I snort a laugh. "You think anyone'll notice that I'm wearing the same dress as yesterday?"

"Black is black," he says, "but you still look lovely."

I grab my purse and my keys.

"Shall we?" he says, gesturing to his car.

Most of the conversation we have over the next three hours on the drive to the church is rote, forced, forgettable. When we're about half an hour away, he unexpectedly begins regaling me with stories about Cillian's life, all the things I didn't realize I wanted to hear—Cillian's reaction to their first sold-out concert, their first Asian tour, their first gold record, their first appearance on a late-night show—how Cillian took it all in stride and never changed from who he was from the night I met him in that club in Austin.

"He was always just Cillian from Killgantry Village," he said as he held the steering wheel in a choke hold.

"I remember how badly he wanted to make it big. He—and you—exceeded his wildest dreams. The day he called me to tell me the band had gotten an agent, he sounded like a kid at Christmas who'd gotten the shiny new bike they'd hoped for but didn't expect. I was so happy for him, and I..."

I don't have the emotional fortitude to take this trip down memory lane, not now, when we're on the way to Cillian's funeral. I clear my throat and swipe the tears away. "I'm sorry Sean and Ronan couldn't make it. It would have been nice to see them after all these years."

"They were gutted, but, ya know, contracted gigs and all."

I nod. The stark realization of all the years that had passed—that I had allowed to drift by, dormant, unfulfilled, without Cillian—pushed me to a new level of sadness, and I hear a disembodied gasp, unsure of its source.

"You okay, luv?"

"Sorry, yeah, no, not really."

He reaches across and brushes my cheek, keeping one eye on the road. "Me either."

When my breathing returns to normal, I say, "Damian, can I ask you something?"

"Yeah."

"Was he happy? I mean before he got sick."

"As happy as he could be, I guess."

I hesitate before asking the next question, but I need to know. "Was there ever anyone, you know, special in his life?"

He slowly shakes his head. "Nah. There were women, of course, but none of them could live up to what he remembered feeling for you."

His answer is somehow what I want to hear and what I had hoped wasn't true. I had wanted Cillian to be happy. Always.

"What about you?" he asks.

"What about me?"

"You said you're divorced, but was there ever anyone else?"

"No. After Cillian and then my divorce, I figured I was better off with just me and Ashlyn. I dated a bit, but I think the memories kept me from moving on. I didn't have the emotional space for anyone else in my life."

"Zee, you loved him. Still do, as far as I can tell, even after all this time. Why didn't you ever tell him that?"

"Oh, Damian." I heave a jagged sigh. Damian might be the one person who would understand without judging me—or at least try to—but now is not the time. "I did everything wrong. It's a far more complicated story than we have time for right now."

"Another time, then," he says.

"Yes, another time."

We pull into the "car park," as he calls it. My stomach churns as I watch people filing into the church.

"Zee, look at me."

I turn to face him.

"Don't let regret cast an ugly shadow over your life, over your future. Whatever happened between you and Cillian back then, I'm sure you did what you believed was for the best. Right now, in this life, you have a beautiful daughter who clearly cares about your happiness. Don't lose sight of that."

It's never too late for regrets, I think to myself. I risk choking on my tears if I speak, so I say nothing.

We enter the ancient-looking stone church—the pews are packed, standing room only. A local boy who made it big is about to be put to his eternal rest. The Dalai Lama once said that grief is a reminder of the depth of our love. Right now, this church is bursting at the seams with love.

Damian whispers, "I'm to sit up front with the family. I'll see you after." He gently places his hand on my shoulder before making his way up the aisle. I take several steps back, trying to blend in with the crowd as best I can. Just when I feel comfortably invisible, I spot Margaret heading my way. She's zeroed in on me and motioning for me to step forward.

Does she really expect me to sit with the family?

That's the last thing Cillian's mother would want.

Her hand reaches through the crowd, searching for mine. I repeatedly shake my head and mouth "no," but she ignores my protestations. Before I can register what's happening, she's dragging me to the front of the church. My face burns with humiliation. Sitting in the second row, Damian scoots over to make room for me, and I squeeze in between him and Margaret. Cillian's mother is sitting in the front row. She turns to look at me. I tense, expecting daggers, but she gives me a subtle nod, and I realize she has given her approval for me to be there. Damian smiles at me, and I know he was behind the invitation.

The service is as painful as I knew it would be. The priest speaks, two of Cillian's siblings get up and say a few words, a friend who is a stranger to me talks about their lifelong friendship. I'll be eulogizing Cillian in silence. Then Damian stands and makes his way to the dais. I'm sure his will be the words that break me.

He adjusts the mic and clears his throat, the rumble amplified.

"If you don't know me, my name is Damian O'Leary, and Cillian and I made beautiful music together for more than twenty years. I've lost not only a collaborator but my best friend. There's a hard-to-duplicate intimacy that comes from writing songs together, putting emotions on the page, touring together, doing business deals together. Cillian worked hard, played hard, and loved hard." He looks directly at me when he says those words, and I have to look away.

"We've been through a lot together. A whole lot." He stops, bows his head, and huffs a breath. "It's no secret that I went through a rough patch several years back. You might have read about it in the tabloids. Almost everyone had written me off, but his love, support, and belief in me never wavered. Not for a second. I wouldn't have made it to the other side without him." He clears his throat again and brings his fist to his mouth as he tries to short-circuit a sob. "So, I'm going to share a story that I've never told anyone, never made it to the celebrity gossip columns, but it feels right to share it with you now as we send him off.

"I was off the rails, in the thick of it. It was the night before a booking in a huge venue, with thousands of fans expected. Our biggest yet. The tour manager and the label were ready to cancel our contract because of me, because of my... problems. Cillian knew the shape I was in, and he was checking on me every hour on the hour, all night, even though he needed his sleep for the next gig. He had a key to my room, and he would just walk in. His invasion pissed me off, and we argued. I tossed a few ugly insults his way—almost got physical—but in an hour, he was back, checking on me, making sure I was still alive. I have no memory of the last time he checked on me, but I woke up in hospital, an IV in my arm and Cillian dozing in the lumpy chair next to my bed. He literally saved my life." He pauses and shakes his head. "I just wish I could've saved his."

The silence that follows echoes off the stained-glass windows.

He bows his head toward the microphone and, with a raspy whisper, says, "That's all I have to say."

He returns to his seat next to me, and I glance at him. He's staring straight ahead, seemingly at nothing. His chin trembles ever so slightly. It's clearly taking everything in him not to cry. I want to comfort him, to wrap my arms around him like he did for me and tell him I understand his pain. Instead, I discreetly take his hand and squeeze.

He squeezes back so hard I want to cry out in pain.

Chapter 35

I've made it through the wake and the Mass. Now, I have to hold the fragile pieces of my heart together for the burial. Just as everyone piled into the church, they're now piling into cars to make their way to the cemetery. When I sit in the passenger seat of Damian's car and fasten my seat belt, I feel as if that buckle is the only thing holding me together.

"You okay?"

I give Damian a what-do-*you*-think look. If I answer, I'll crumble. But I'm touched that he keeps checking on me, making sure I haven't shattered under the stress.

"Yeah, shite question. Listen, if you don't want to go to the cemetery, I'll understand. I can drop you off at a cafe or the shops and come and get you after."

"No, I have to be there. I *need* to be there."

He gives a subtle nod and starts the car. The electric car is too quiet for my noisy emotions. I crave the constant growl of a gas guzzler.

The cemetery isn't far from the church, and we arrive sooner than I'm prepared for. We pull up close to the entrance, and I know that if I don't immediately unfasten my seat belt and step out of the car, I'll need the jaws of life to extract me.

A light drizzle has started, and water droplets crawl down the windshield, adding to the somber scene. Damian comes around to my side of the car and, like a magic trick, pulls out a black umbrella and hands it to me.

"Thanks."

He gestures toward the crowd gathering around the six-foot-deep hole in the ground. Cillian's casket is propped up, ready to be lowered. As we come closer, I can see his mother silently weeping. All his brothers and sisters sit stiffly in folding chairs, staring at the casket as if they expect Cillian to pop out at any minute. One of his brothers, I think it's Declan, signals to the priest to get started despite several still-empty chairs. I guess most everyone has reached their limit of grief. The priest says a few words and a quick prayer about Cillian's eternal reward. I want to laugh. *Reward?* Not a single person here views Cillian's death as a reward—certainly not me, not his family, not Damian. I glance over at him. He looks to be in physical pain. Aislinn wanders over and puts her arms around him. That simple gesture is all it takes for him to finally erupt into sobs. I step back to give them space.

Each of Cillian's siblings tosses a handful of dirt from their land onto the casket before it's lowered into the ground. The agonizingly slow motion of the descent feels designed to prolong the misery of mourners. Afterward, there are more condolences and hugs.

Then it's over. Cillian is gone for good.

Umbrellas spring open, as the drizzle turns into a stinging gray assault. After debating if it's the right thing to do, I make my way to Cillian's mom.

"Mrs. Byrne, thank you for allowing me to be here, to say goodbye. Cillian... he meant a lot to me." The look in her eyes is something I hope to never witness again. "I'm so sorry for your loss." Such a trite, hollow phrase. This was her son, her baby boy. My thoughts leap to Ashlyn. If I had to attend the funeral of my baby girl, I don't think I would be able to go on.

Without any forethought, I accost her with a hug so tight I push the air from her lungs, and our umbrellas collide. I linger, and within seconds, she's wrapped her arms around me just as tightly. We pull apart as if on cue and wipe away tears. One of Cillian's sisters approaches, her eyes red and swollen, and wraps her arm around her mother's shoulders and gives a subtle nod. No words are spoken, but we communicated volumes. I turn away and scan the remaining mourners to seek out Damian. I spot him leaning against his car, his head bowed. He's removed his jacket, rolled up his shirt sleeves, exposing his many tattoos, and loosened his tie. He's talking to Aislinn, their umbrellas overlapping. Sadness is etched on both of their faces. Aislinn hugs Damian, and I hesitate, but she turns, acknowledging my presence, and walks away.

As soon as I'm within earshot, he says, "I need a fuckin' pint."

"Excellent idea."

Despite the pain, the grief, and the nagging regret, I feel incredible relief that Damian isn't judging me for my decisions of the past. He knows how Cillian felt about me, and he's beginning to understand that I felt the same. But he's curious. I'll tell him the whole story when it feels right.

In less than ten minutes, Damian pulls into the gravel parking lot of the pub. The bright-blue exterior looks exactly like what I always imagined a traditional Irish pub would look like. Wood benches worn to an ashen color sit outside, waiting for warmer weather. I can envision them full of people drinking their pints, enjoying the not-often-seen sunshine. Damian opens the door for me, and I enter the darkened space lined with mahogany wood. The smell of beer and cigarettes is as much a part of the pub as the people who frequent it. A roaring fireplace in the corner provides warmth, and the hearty laughter of the people adds to the welcoming atmosphere. The bar is lined with dozens of beer taps and bottles of whisky. Damian points to a table in the corner, and I sit while he gets two Guinness on tap and sets a glass in front of me.

I look at it and hesitate. "I've never had dark beer."

"Nah, you're lyin.'"

"Nope, never."

Eyebrows raised, he says, "Okay, well, I hope you're hungry. We've got shepherd's pie comin.'"

My stomach rumbles in response. "Never had that either."

He shrugs. "Makes sense since you've never been in an Irish pub before."

His words are a painful reminder of the life I haven't lived. "But I'm here now." I raise my mug in a toast. "This is for Cillian."

He clinks his mug against mine, creating a false note of celebration. "Sláinte! To Cillian."

We drink our beer in silence for a while, but I know questions are swirling in his brain.

"If you really want to know, I can tell you pretty much what happened back then," I say.

He was staring into his already empty mug, but in response to my offer, he looks up. "Yeah, I would like that. He filled me in there, but never made sense to me. Fuck, it never made sense to him."

I huff a breath. "I think another pint might make it easier," I say.

He jumps up, heads to the bar, returns with two more dark beers, and sets them on the table.

"I hope you don't hate me after."

"Never."

I take another sip then another before sharing with Damian what led me to the worst decision of my life.

Chapter 36

After I've shared with Damian my mother's dire warning and the devastation I experienced after hearing that woman's voice in Cillian's room, he drains the last of his second draft. He looks over at me with—understanding? sympathy? sorrow?

"I remember that day like it was yesterday," he says, staring into his empty mug. "It tore him up."

"Tore *him* up? I felt like I was going to burst into flames. I actually hoped I would, to put me out of my misery."

"I remember Renee. She—"

"What? *Shit, Damian.* I don't want to hear about her. Even after all these years, and with Cillian gone, it still makes me sick to think about it."

He leans forward and grimaces, hanging his head before he looks at me again. "Zee, he didn't sleep with her. He was telling you the truth. She slept in the other room. She was always sleeping on someone's extra bed or couch."

I down the rest of my draft in three big gulps. I shake my head in denial. "No, that's not true. I heard her. She was cooing at him and calling him 'baby.' I woke them up, for fuck's sake! He was doing *exactly* what my mother warned me he would."

"I know it must have seemed that way. I'm not gonna lie. She fancied him, came on to him like crazy. But he didn't want her." Damian looks me in the eye, daring me to disbelieve him. Then he says, "Up to that phone call, Cillian never slept with anyone else. He was crazy in love with you. He couldn't wait for you to join him."

I'm hit with a blast of retroactive shock. My head is swimming, and I'm about to go under for the third time. *Have I done this to myself?* I drop my head into my hands. I feel as sick as I did the day I cut Cillian out of my life. If I let myself believe Damien's version of the truth, that would mean I tossed my one chance at true happiness in the trash and hermetically sealed it shut.

And I'd hurt Cillian.

"Zee, you alright, then?"

I've always had my anger, my hurt, and my insane jealousy to keep me warm. Now, I'm left out in the cold with no protection. I clench my hands on the tabletop, and Damian's tattooed arms reach out, but I jerk my fists back into my lap before he makes contact.

"I only knew Cillian's side of the story," he says, "at least what he was willing to tell me. I thought there might be something more to it, but he shut down for a time after that."

"Why are you telling me this now?"

He runs his ringed fingers through his hair, and stubborn strands fall back onto his forehead. "Now that I know the other side of the story, your side, I don't want you to walk away and go home believing that he chose to hurt you like that—I don't want you to remember him that way."

"So, you're saying it was all my fault. I... I'm to blame."

"Nah, Zee, no one's to blame. Your mother wanted to protect you, and when you called Cillian, it was just a shite situation. I understand why you thought what you did."

My heart is beating double time, and I take a couple of deep breaths to slow it.

"He tried to talk to me several times after that," I say. "Did you know we met for coffee in Austin once?"

"What? When?"

"That was several years ago. We didn't talk about that day. It was mostly an awkward sort of catching up. He told me he was sorry, and I thought he was apologizing for what he had done to me. But now—after what you told me— I'm thinking he was saying he was sorry for the way things turned out. I remember the hurt in his face.

"We were at a coffee shop downtown, filled with a crowd about the same age we were when we met. We kept being interrupted by people who recognized him and wanted a picture, an autograph. It was surreal. To me, he was just Cillian, the boy I had loved all those years ago. But he—and you—were famous by then. We moved from our table to a booth in the corner, away from stares. He sat close to me, and we talked for a while. He told me about your latest tour, and I told him about my life without mentioning Elliott. He took me totally by surprise when he asked me if I was happy. I didn't have to answer. I've never been good at hiding my feelings."

I'm no longer sharing with Damian—I'm lost in the memory. As I sit here in this Irish pub, across the table from his best friend, I'm yanked back in time—I feel Cillian's lips on mine and the tingle down my spine as he inched closer to me and gently swept my hair behind my ear. It was like all those years without him hadn't passed.

I wanted to tell him that without him, everything seemed wrong. A voice in my head was screaming at me, *Tell him! Tell him that you still love him!*

He took my hands, kissed my palms, and whispered with that accent I'd missed so much as an essential part of him, "You're still crazy beautiful." He cupped my chin in his hand, kissed me on the lips, and whispered, "Come back to my hotel with me, Zee."

I wanted to. God, I wanted to. Memories of our sweaty bodies melded together flooded my brain. The sex was wild, sometimes reckless, and deeply emotional. Sex with Elliott was only mildly satisfying. But then I thought of Elliott sweetly walking through the door at the end of the workday. How he doted on Ashlyn. How much he loved me.

I looked down at the tabletop and shook my head. "I can't," I croaked.

He lifted my face to meet his, and he kissed me again, harder, and I thought my heart was going to be ripped from my chest.

"You sure?" he asked.

"Yes," I said in barely a whisper.

"I understand," he said as he pulled back. He looked the saddest I'd ever seen him. Then, as if he hadn't just kissed me twice, he said, "You know, I always thought you'd come back to me. But I want you to be happy, Zee, whether or not it's with me."

He slid out of the booth, stood, and looked over his shoulder at me one last time. I wanted to devour that look, devour him. As I watched him walk away, I had the barely contained urge to yell at him not to leave. I wanted to follow him, tell him all was forgiven. In that millisecond of confused indecision, I was fully prepared to leave Elliott, start over with Cillian, and face the consequences. But I just sat there frozen, my fingers resting on my lips where he'd kissed me, my feet glued to the floor.

The memory still has the power to leave me breathless.

"So, you ever talk to him or see him again?" Damian's question yanks me back to Ireland, to the pub, to our conversation.

"No. He didn't try to contact me after that. Well, not until a couple of months ago. The irony is my marriage to Elliott began to collapse shortly after Cillian and I met that day. And—well, maybe it wasn't ironic. The truth of the matter is, I couldn't make myself love Elliott the way I had loved Cillian. And I couldn't stop loving Cillian the way I did. Seeing him again that day just set things in motion."

Damian looks at me as if trying to read my mind, then he nods in the direction of my empty mug and asks, "Another?"

I nod in response. I never drink this much, but I want to numb the encroaching pain of my past mistakes.

When he sets my third and last draft on the table, I say, "Just tell me if it's none of my business, but what you said at the funeral, was that the reason you and Aislinn split back then?"

"Nah, I fucked up after that. When we split, I felt like I lost my anchor. The band was traveling, flying to a new town, a new city, a new country every couple days. It was insane. Drugs were everywhere. The cliché about drugs, sex, and rock and roll is spot on. I thought it was helping me cope, but it was fuckin' me up." He rubs his hands over his stubbly cheeks and groans. "Yeah, it was a real shit show."

"So, how long has it been...? I mean, are you...?"

"Am I clean? Fifteen years since I touched the stuff."

This time, I reach out to him, and our hands link on the table.

"Is it okay if I ask you something about Cillian's... condition?"

We break apart, and he takes a gulp of his beer before he says, "Go on."

"Was... was he sick for a long time?"

"Define 'sick.' He seemed to be doing okay for a long time after he was diagnosed, but then he got a couple of lung infections, one right after the other, and he couldn't bounce back."

"Do you remember when he was diagnosed?"

"If you're wondering if he knew he was sick when he came to see you that day, the answer is no. He was only diagnosed five years ago."

"Did he suffer much?" I don't know why the hell I'm asking that. I figure I already know the answer, and confirmation would create a fresh wound and a new worry about Ashlyn.

"It was sudden and unexpected, but at the end, yeah. Breathing was hard, especially while we were trying to record..." He shakes his head as if he can dislodge the memory. "Okay, can we talk about something else?"

"Of course. Sorry."

He nods, sits back, and crosses his arms across his chest.

"So, you got married, had a daughter. She's lovely. How old is she?"

"Twenty-one." That information escapes my lips without any forethought.

"How long after everything blew up with Cillian did you get married?"

Is he doing the math?

"Not long. I was in a really bad place, you know, and Elliott was there for me. He was a good guy. Still is. Despite our failed marriage, he's been a good father to Ashlyn."

Exhausted, a tad tipsy, and feeling the beginnings of a hangover, we make it home. Damian follows me into the house, his house, and we beeline to the kitchen. He tosses his jacket over a chair and slumps back against the counter while I put the kettle on. In our brief time together, we seem to have developed the ability to read the room when it's just the two of us. Tea is in order. While I grab the cups, the tea bags, and the milk, he stands there, staring at the kettle, frozen in place, his face scrunched up in a supreme effort to stem more tears.

Holding back grief is like trying to tame a tornado. All you can do is seek shelter. I turn and put a hand on his chest. His tie still hangs loosely around his neck.

"I know it hurts," I say. The statement covers the past, the present, and possibly the future.

He pulls me close, wraps his warm, tattooed arms around me, and I lay my head on his chest where my hand had been. The weight of the day, the rhythm of his beating heart, his ragged breath, and his earthy scent—a heady blend of rain, soil, and a base note of what I've become acquainted with as uniquely Damian—completely undoes me. I look up, cradle his face in my hands, and bring his lips to mine. His response is unexpectedly urgent, and he kisses me back as if providing an answer to a question he's been waiting for me to ask. The first intrusive thought that pops into my head is Sloane's comment from all those years ago: "He's not a good kisser." She couldn't have been more wrong. Every cell in my body throbs with need.

"I just don't want to be sad anymore," I whisper against his lips. I want to jump inside his skin and let him smother my pain.

He kisses me harder. His tongue is soft, probing, letting me know he needs this as much as I do. He easily picks me up and sets me on the counter. His lips never leave mine as he cups my breasts and his breath quickens. He slips my dress from my shoulder. He hesitates then kisses my tattoo. The feel of his lips on my skin, the light pressure of his hands traveling down my body, sliding up my thighs, and the sound of his breath quickening take mine away. I can no longer think, and that's what I want—not to think. My head falls back, and I spread my legs wider. His fingers slowly slip inside me, and we let out a synchronized moan. The only other sound is the desperate in and out of our breath—until the piercing screech of the kettle jerks us apart as if we've been caught in the act. I have the irrational, if fleeting, thought that Cillian is looking down on us and letting us know that what we're doing is wrong. I slap my legs together and pull my dress down.

I lower myself from the counter, stunned that my poor decision-making skills are still firmly in place. The earsplitting whistle of the kettle is still going strong. I turn off the burner and move the kettle to the side.

When I turn back around, Damian is looking at me, seeing through me, and he's standing so close I can feel the effect of our almost tryst pressing against me. Neither of us speaks for a prolonged slice of time. Then he steps back and shoves his hands in his pockets.

"I guess that was a mistake, yeah?"

He sounds so unsure, so tentative, as if he's asking for confirmation that it had actually happened, or maybe he's asking for forgiveness. But I instigated it.

"I think so." I feel just as unsure as he sounds.

"So, maybe I should go…"

I can't tell if he's asking me or telling me.

He's already grabbing his jacket and turning to leave when I surprise us both by shouting, "No!" I grab his hand and take in a breath. In a softened tone, I plead, "I don't want to be alone tonight. Stay. Please?"

He nods and once again pulls me close, but this time he sweetly kisses my forehead. Sex is off the table.

We sip our tea for a while before acknowledging that, despite the early hour, we both desperately need sleep. He reaches for my hand and leads me up the staircase and into the bedroom. We silently slip off our shoes and, still fully clothed, slide under the covers. He scoots close, leaving no space between us, and rests an arm on my hip. The warmth of his body, the rise and fall of his chest, and the very maleness of him are so painfully sweet, I almost cry for reasons that have nothing to do with the day's events. It's the most comfort I've been offered in a very, very long time.

"Thank you, Damian," I whisper, but his slow breath on the back of my neck tells me he's already sleeping soundly.

Before I can count to ten, I join him in a deep, dreamless sleep.

Chapter 37

I wake to the vibration of my cell phone on the nightstand. My eyes pop open, and I glance over at Damian. He's snoring lightly, like a puppy. I slide out from under his arm, take my phone from the nightstand, and glance at the screen. It's Ashlyn.

"Good morning, sweetie," I whisper as I quietly leave the bed. "Wait, what time is it there?" I do a quick calculation—it must be three o'clock in the morning in Austin. "Is everything okay?" I'm still whispering as I slip out of the room, softly close the door behind me, and make my way down the creaking stairs, hoping not to wake Damian.

"Why are you whispering?"

"I was asleep."

"Oh, sorry, but can you talk?"

"Of course. What's wrong?"

"When are you coming home?" she whines.

My initial reaction is exasperation. My twenty-one-year-old married daughter is calling me from across the Atlantic Ocean and waking me up to whine because I'm not there at the exact moment she wants me to be.

"My flight leaves tonight. What's going on?"

"Mama, I need you."

She never calls me "Mama" unless she's sad, and I immediately regret my knee-jerk reaction.

"I'm here, sweetie. What's wrong?"

"It's Jason. He followed me to the dog park and saw me with Dax. We were just holding hands, but I... I thought he was going to kill Dax—and me. If he finds out I called you... I can't do this any-more, Mom. I hate him."

"Oh, Ash, honey."

All my suspicions about Jason are coming true while I'm on an-other continent, helpless to do anything to help her through this.

"Do you feel like you're safe? I mean, he hasn't hurt you, has he?"

"No. I... I think I'm fine. He's just so angry."

Her hesitant tone does nothing to assuage my fears.

"Okay. Listen to me. Call your father and have him come and get you as soon as Jason leaves for work. Act normal. He can't suspect anything. Pack what you can. Grab any money in the house that you can find. Let me think—my flight leaves at five o'clock tonight, my time. I'll have to double-check the arrival time, but it takes about eleven hours with the layover, so I should arrive at eleven in the evening, Austin time. I'll see if I can get an earlier flight. I promise we'll figure it out. I love you so much."

"Me too," she says between fresh sobs.

"Text me as soon as Jason leaves, and let me know what's happen-ing, okay? Now hang up and call your father."

Each time I say "your father," something in my brain hiccups. But I know Elliott will shift into papa bear mode until I get home. I hang up, emotionally wrung out once more.

As I'm in the midst of texting Sloane to let her know what's go-ing on, Damian waltzes into the kitchen barefoot, clothes wrinkled, hair tousled.

"I heard you on the phone. Everything okay?"

"Not really," I say as I hit Send. "Ashlyn called. I told you that she and Jason—that's her husband—are having problems. I think it's reached a crescendo and she wants her mommy."

"Understandable. When does your flight leave?"

"Tonight—if I can't get an earlier flight."

He crosses his arms tightly across his chest and glances at the floor. "Well, it's good you'll be there for her, but I'm sorry you're leaving so soon."

"Me too. I would have loved to see more of Dublin—more of Ireland. But I can't thank you enough for everything you've done. I can't imagine how I would have handled it without you." I take a jagged breath. "And... um... about last night..."

He holds his hand up to stop me. "It's okay. I'm not sorry it happened, well, *almost* happened."

He grins, and I feel my cheeks redden.

He takes my hand, and I hold my breath before he continues. "I don't know—maybe if the situation were different and we didn't live a few thousand miles apart..."

It's my turn to stop him short. "Listen, Damian, you've been lovely, and I think we've been good for each other these last couple of days—but I'm pretty sure any connection we might feel right now has been forged out of mutual sadness."

"But you've taken some of the sadness out of me."

I look away before looking back at him. "You know this isn't real life."

"You don't think this is real life? This is about as real as it gets."

"Maybe, but my reality is that I need to get back to my job—crappy though it may be—and most of all, I need to get back to my daughter and help her figure out the way forward."

He takes a step back and rubs both hands across his stubble. "At least let me drive you to the airport. I'll go home, shower, change, and I'll be back. Just let me know about your flight."

"Yeah, that would be nice. Thank you."

I stand in the doorway and watch him walk to his car. *Am I attracted to him because he reminds me of Cillian? Is it the accent, the memories it triggers? Or is it like I suggested to him—just the intense emotions of the situation we've shared?* I'm in pain, and he's provided me with pain relief. I shake my head, trying to rattle my thoughts loose. In a few hours, I'll be returning to my life, and he'll be returning to his, and we will carry on as if our brief time together never happened.

Getting an earlier flight proves impossible, so Damian shows up promptly at three o'clock, loads my suitcase in the car, and opens the passenger door for me. Aside from my crippling anxiety over Ashlyn's situation, the knots forming in my stomach over leaving Ireland, leaving Damian, take me by surprise. After we've driven a couple of blocks, my phone dings. It's Ashlyn.

Dad picked me up this morning and bought me ice cream at that place on South Congress, like he used to when I was little. :-) I'm at his house. I feel better already. Can't wait to talk in person. I love you, Mama.

The knots in my stomach loosen.

"Everything okay?" Damian asks for the second time that day.

"It's Ashlyn. Elliott picked her up, and she's safe and sound at his place."

"Is she not safe with her husband?"

"It's beginning to feel that way."

"Sounds like a shite situation. I'm really sorry, Zee."

I nod, and in a less-than-subtle change of subject, I say, "I meant to tell you I washed the sheets. They're in the dryer. I didn't have time to put them on the bed."

"You didn't have to do that. I have a cleaning service that does all that when guests leave."

"Oh, yeah, of course." So, I was a guest. That puts things into perspective.

We fall silent for a couple of miles.

I glance at his profile. I can still see the twenty-something guy with the floppy hair and the muscle shirt, just with more well-defined, more appealing angles.

"Please thank Aislinn for letting me know about the funeral, and tell Cillian's family goodbye for me—especially his mother." My voice cracks. My emotions are still too close to the surface. I clear my throat. "Sorry."

He reaches over and gently squeezes my knee, triggering a flashback to the night before when he slid his warm hands up my thighs and—

"These last coupla days have been a lot, and it sounds like you've got quite a lot waiting for you when you get home. I'll tell everyone you said goodbye. I'm sure they'll be sorry they didn't get to say goodbye in person."

I stare out the window until we pull into the parking garage at the airport. It feels like weeks, not days, have passed since I landed and spotted Colin holding a sign with my name on it. It's taken me a couple of decades to make it to Cillian's home, and now, after only two days, I'm leaving.

Damian parks and takes my suitcase from the back seat. I reach for it, and he says, "No, it's okay. I got it. I'll go with you to check in."

It's such a small thing, but it doesn't go unnoticed.

The airport is a hive of activity, but check-in goes smoothly. It's time to go through security. The two of us stand stiffly at the cordoned entrance.

"Damian, I know I've already said it, but you've been great. Really great. I do wish I could stay longer, but—"

"Come with me," he says, and he tugs me aside, away from the crowds lining up for security. He stops abruptly and touches my cheek. "Zee, can I kiss you goodbye?"

I smile. "Of course."

I'm expecting a soft goodbye kiss on the lips, but he leans over and presses his mouth to mine like he's on death row and I'm his last meal. I respond in kind, tugging on his hair, and he pulls me up, forcing me to stand on my tiptoes. I don't care if people are gawking. I don't care if this is the last truly passionate kiss I'll experience in my life. I'm buoyed by the flutter in my center of gravity and the weightless feeling I haven't experienced in over twenty years. He's making it harder than ever for me to leave, harder to go back to my passionless life. But for this brief moment, with his lips pressed to mine, I'm right where I'm meant to be.

Chapter 38

The moment we touch down at the Austin Airport, I turn on my phone. A text from Ashlyn says, *I'm at the luggage carousel.*

I'd told her my arrival time but hadn't expected her to show up at the airport. I thought she'd be concerned that Jason might be tracking her movements. I was planning to take an Uber home.

Just landed. Be there soon.

I need to put my time in Ireland in the past and review my concocted story about a yoga retreat before greeting Ashlyn. I'm going to have to work hard to give off an aura of rest and relaxation, and I need to quickly reorient myself to my current life, my real life, not dwell on a place half a world away that represents all my lost dreams, lost love, and missed opportunities of the past. The mental switch is jarring, like being shoved into a time machine and waking up in another time and place.

The taco stand, the frozen-yogurt franchise, the vending machines with AirPods, and the live music wafting through the terminal leave no doubt that I'm home. When I retrieve my checked bag from the luggage carousel in Austin, I rip off the previous luggage tag that clearly says "Dublin" and toss it in the trash. I see Ashlyn's smiling face as she walks in the terminal—with Elliott beside her. *Shit.* A sad echo of our past reverberates. Ashlyn waves enthusiastically. I hurry down the last few steps and engulf her in an embrace. The comforting scent of her herbal shampoo is a kind of aromatherapy. I kiss her forehead.

I turn to Elliott and mouth, *"Thank you."*

He gives a single, grim nod. "No need."

"I know it's only been a couple of days, but I missed you so much," I say as I step back.

She pulls me into another tight hug. "I'm so glad you're home," she says, her voice strained.

The ride home is not the time for Ashlyn to fill me in on what happened with Jason and Dax or for me to share much about my fictional yoga retreat—not with Elliott in earshot of every whispered word. I don't know how much detail Ashlyn shared with Elliott about her situation, and I don't want to test her boundaries. Instead, our conversation consists of superficial niceties: "How's the weather been?" "How was the flight?" "Are you feeling jet-lagged?"

A text from Sloane dings my phone: *Call me when you catch your breath.*

Tomorrow? I'm with Elliott and Ashlyn now.

She responds with a GIF of Edvard Munch's *The Scream.*

Elliott's presence in the front seat with me feels comfortably familiar, and the good memories tangle up with the bad: when Ashlyn was born; how he would always hold me when I cried, even when I wouldn't share with him why; how he always said, "I love you" with such feeling; how he sang off key in the shower; how he cried when I told him I was leaving him.

When we pull into the apartment parking lot, I thank Elliott again as he hands me my luggage.

Ashlyn takes his hand. "Dad, I want to stay with Mom tonight."

His face contorts into a scowl. "But what about Jason?"

"He knew Mom was gone. He doesn't know she's back. I'll be fine."

Elliott wraps his arms around her and kisses the top of her head. "Okay. But you call or text if you need anything. Promise?"

The concern on his face stabs at my heart.

"I promise."

He gives me a head jerk of acknowledgement and goes back to his car. Before he opens the door, I catch him looking at me. I want to say, "I'm sorry, Elliott," but one more time isn't going to make his hurt go away.

I take a galvanizing breath. Ashlyn insists I hand over my suitcase, and she drags it up the stairs ahead of me, loudly bumping up each concrete step. We stand at the front door of my apartment, the portal to my other reality. She takes the apartment key from her purse and pulls hard on the doorknob as she turns the key just right—a trick she learned long ago as the only way to get the warped door to cooperate.

"You want some coffee or maybe tea?" she asks as she shuts the door and gives it an extra shove with her hip.

"Tea sounds good."

I plop onto the sofa and kick off my shoes. My first ever case of reverse jet lag is doing me in. I lay my head on the back of the sofa and close my eyes. I'm already drifting off when the shriek of the tea kettle bolts me awake. For that fraction of a second, I'm back in Dublin, Damian's lips locked to mine, and—

"You want one sugar or two?" she shouts from the kitchen.

I clear my throat as I clear my thoughts. "Uh, one is good."

She comes in, carrying two mugs, and hands one to me, and I pat the space next to me for her to join me. I take a sip.

"So, do you want to tell me what's going on with Jason?"

Ashlyn is about to share her truth with me, but I wouldn't, I couldn't share mine.

I feel the weight of her sigh. "It's awful," she says with a slow-motion shake of her head.

I pull her beside me, and she rests her head on my shoulder.

"I hate to wreck your calm."

"This isn't about me, Ash. This about you."

She sits up to face me and sets her tea on the coffee table.

"Okay, so Dax and I were in the park, and we were just talking, you know, about our lives, about the future, and we somehow slipped into talking about *our* future..." She stops and clears her throat.

"It's okay."

"Anyway, that's when I heard Jason yelling, 'What the fuck, Ashlyn, and who the fuck is this guy?' He saw us holding hands, and he grabbed my arm and shoved me to the ground. I scraped my arms on the gravel."

She pushes up her sleeves to show me her bruises and scrapes, which have already begun to scab over.

"Oh my God, Ash, let me see."

I gently take her arm to examine the damage Jason has inflicted, and I kiss it like I kissed her boo-boos when she was a toddler. I feel my anger bubbling up, but Ashlyn is dealing with enough without me adding to her emotional load.

"You should have told me! I would have taken the next flight out."

"There's nothing you could you have done."

"You simply have to get away from him once and for all. You once told me that Jason wasn't a monster. But I think that's exactly what he is."

She doesn't disagree. She simply lowers her head, and her tears fall silently.

I hand her a tissue, and she clears her throat before she says, "Poor Dax. He didn't know what to do, what to say. He was trying to help me up when Jason punched him. Dax's nose started bleeding, I was screaming at Jason, Maple and Gretchen were barking, and everyone was staring at us. I was afraid someone would call the police. God, Mom, it was horrible."

"Are you okay?"

"I guess. Dad's been supportive."

"So, he knows?"

"Yeah, and I've never seen him so pissed off. When I told him what happened, I thought he was going to hunt Jason down and kill him."

I can't imagine Elliott being so alpha male, but his muscled paternal instinct must have kicked in.

"And Dax, he's okay?"

"His nose is swollen, but it's not broken. If you can believe it, he came over and talked to Dad, to explain. It was kind of weird, but I think Dad was impressed. He's never said, but I'm pretty sure he never liked Jason. I want you to meet Dax too. He's such a good guy, Mom."

"He sounds like it."

My thoughts are square-dancing across my brain—Jason, Dax, Elliott, Cillian, Damian—partners that have do-si-doed in and out of my and my daughter's lives, but the rhythm has always been off.

I clasp her hand in mine. "So, what is it you want to do?"

"Well, whatever does or doesn't happen with me and Dax, I don't want to be married to Jason any longer than I have to. I'm going to file for divorce." She hesitates. "Dad said he would help with the legal fees."

I wrap my arms around her and squeeze tightly. "It's going to be okay, Ash. I'm here for you, whenever and whatever you need."

She pulls back and tilts her head to her shoulder like she did when she was four and was about to ask for another cookie. "Do you think me and Maple could move in here with you? Just until I can get a job and find a place to live." She rushes the words, "Dad's been great, but I—I want to be here in my old room, with you."

"Of course, of course. But I don't want your father to have hurt feelings."

"I already mentioned it to him, and he's cool with it."

"Wonderful."

I'm already mentally clearing out her bedroom, which I've been using as storage since her wedding day.

She sits back, clearly relieved. "That's enough about me. Tell me about your yoga retreat. The pictures looked awesome."

I set my mug on the coffee table, brace myself, and prepare to fill her in on my fictional trip, providing just enough detail about the place, the classes, and the people to make it seem real.

But before I say a word, she jumps up and says, "Oh, I almost forgot." She goes to the kitchen and comes back with a FedEx envelope.

"It has an overseas address. It looks like it's from a law firm in Ireland, of all places."

She's waiting for my confusion, for my surprise, for an explanation. I don't have enough time to muster an appropriate reaction before she asks, "You don't know anyone in Ireland, do you?"

Hearing Ashlyn utter the word "Ireland" feels surreal, like my long-hidden secret has been exposed to the light and might burst into flames, igniting me along with it. A deep flush creeps up my neck and settles in my cheeks.

"Aren't you going to open it?" Ashlyn asks as she shoves the FedEx envelope in my direction. I want to make like a squirrel and run as fast as I can to avoid being pummeled by an oncoming car.

Instead, I slowly retrieve the envelope and hold it tightly in my hand. The return address reads McAllister, O'Connor, and Murphy, Law Solicitors, Dublin, Ireland.

I swallow hard before I open the flap and inch out a slim document written on the law firm's letterhead. The first line in all caps reads LAST WILL AND TESTAMENT OF CILLIAN JAMES BYRNE.

The room spins around me. I literally see stars.

"What is it?" Ashlyn asks as she shifts toward me to get a look.

I pull the rest of the document from the envelope, turn the pages away from her, and spring off the sofa. The envelope falls to the floor.

"I... I'm not sure," I say as I speed walk my way to the bathroom.

"Mom, what's wrong?" she calls after me. "What is it?"

"Just give me a minute, Ash."

I slam and lock the door and slump to the cold tile floor. My hands shake as I scan the first page. Damian is named as executor in Cillian's will. I feel a flash of anger. He didn't say a thing to me. I flip to the next page.

Cillian named me as a beneficiary.

And, *shit*, Ashlyn is listed as well.

Did he know the truth about Ashlyn? Did Damian know? Was Damian's surprise at my having a daughter all an act? Nevertheless, according to the document I hold tightly in my hands, Cillian has left me—and Ashlyn—a sizeable chunk of his fortune. He's left an inheritance to his family, of course, but he has left us an insane amount of money, as well as a house in Ireland. My heart thrashes in my chest. The will slips from my fingers and lands at my feet. Cillian was thinking of me as he counted down his last days, and now, he's communicating with me from beyond the grave. I begin to sob uncontrollably.

Ashlyn pounds on the door. "Mom, are you okay? Mom?"

I pull a wad of toilet paper from the holder, wipe my eyes, and blow my nose.

"I'm fine. I'll be out in a minute."

I grab the towel rack, pull myself up, and look at myself in the mirror. I don't look fine. *Is this the moment of truth, when everything I've secreted away comes out of hiding?* Another thought bulldozes its way to the front of my brain. *Oh God, what am I going to tell Ashlyn? What* should *I tell her?* I've been privy to Cillian's reflection in my daughter's face every day for the last twenty-one years. Countless times, Ashlyn would frown or smile or laugh, and her resemblance to Cillian rattled my heart. Her face was a constant reminder that he had been a part of my life, that he still is, and always will be.

This will drive the dagger deeper into Elliott's heart. When Ashlyn was in middle school, she had her blood typed as part of a science class project. She came home and showed us her results. "Look. Not sure what it means, but my blood type is O."

"Is that your blood type or your grade?" Elliott teased. "My blood type is the rarest of all. It's type AB."

"Cool. What's Mom's?"

Elliott looked at me for guidance. I cringed. If she was studying inherited blood types, she would learn that it was a genetic impossibility for Elliott to be her biological father.

"Mine is O," I said.

"So, I guess I inherited mine from Mom." She evidently hadn't yet gotten to that part of the lesson.

Elliott was uncharacteristically quiet at dinner.

"You okay?" I asked.

He grunted but wouldn't look at me. I reached out to offer a comforting touch, and he recoiled. It was all very un-Elliott-like behavior.

After we cleared the table and loaded the dishwasher in silence and after Ashlyn retreated to her room, he pulled me into the garage and shut the door to the kitchen.

"Do you think she'll find out?" he whisper shouted at me, his face bloated with fear.

"I don't know, Elliott."

"She believes I'm her father. It'll destroy her if she finds out."

"You are her father in every way that truly matters."

"Shit, you know what I mean, Zee. We've been lying to her all this time." His eyes welled up, and he crumpled back onto the hood of the car, his face in his hands. "If she figures it out, she'll resent both of us, and she'll never look at me the same."

His eyes were rimmed in red. He ran his fingers through his hair as he spewed a string of hurtful words aimed at himself, it seemed, words I never imagined coming out of Elliott's mouth, and for a moment, I thought he might actually hit the wall with his fists, but that wasn't who he was, who he is. He grabbed the car keys from the rack on the wall, got in the car, and slammed the door shut. Then he opened the garage and sped away.

My plan has always been to take the secret of Ashlyn's paternity to my grave. But now, I'm holding Cillian's will in my hands, and I have no idea how I'll explain away the fact that a famous Irish singer has left us more money than either of us could earn or spend in a dozen lifetimes—or that I just returned from his funeral in Ireland.

Chapter 39

I pick up the will from the bathroom floor, still trying to make sense of the words so clearly written on the page, and stand at the door, my hand hovering over the doorknob. *How can I possibly explain this to Ashlyn without shattering her trust in me? If I tell her the truth, will she resent me? Love me any less? Maybe even hate me? Will she look at Elliott differently?* I grasp the handle and unlock the door. When I open it, Ashlyn is right there, her eyes wide, bursting with questions.

"Mom?" She glances at the document in my hand.

I wrap my arms around her. "Ash, you know I love you, right?"

Her eyebrows shoot up. "You're scaring me. What's going on? What is that?" she asks, gesturing to the papers gripped in my hand.

"Let's go sit so we can talk." I lead her to the sofa and hand her the will. "I want you to take a look at this document first."

I never wanted things to get to this point, but I think, deep down, I knew this moment was inevitable. Secrets always have a way of squirming their way to the surface. I watch her expression shift from curiosity to confusion as she scans the first couple of pages. She looks up at me.

"I don't understand. Who is this?"

After a second or two, recognition explodes in her eyes.

"Wait, isn't there an Irish singer named Cillian Byrne? Is that him?"

I simply nod. Ashlyn looks from my bloodshot eyes back to the sheaf of papers in her hand.

"You knew him? But why the hell is he leaving you a fortune? And me?"

She shoots me a well-deserved accusatory look. *This isn't going to end well.*

I clear my throat. "Yes, I know him—knew him—before he got famous, when I was in college."

"Okaaay."

The effort to stem my tears feels like an aneurysm has burst in my brain.

"Ash, this is so hard for me. I don't know if you'll be able to understand why I did what I did."

She nods silently, solemnly and swallows hard, unprepared to hear my full confession. But it's now or never. I reach out and place my hand on hers. She's still gripping the will.

I take a deep breath and huff it out. "He wasn't just someone I happened to know."

"So, what, was he your boyfriend?"

"He was more than that."

She silently waits for me to continue.

"I was a senior in college, and I met him at a bar on Sixth Street. He was a singer, and his band was the entertainment. Anyway, we started seeing each other whenever he was in town. Eventually, an agent spotted them and offered a contract. Things were starting to happen for him and the band, and he asked me to go with him on tour. I applied for a passport and dropped out of college so I could go with him on his European tour that had just been booked. What can I say? We were in love. But then my mother died and—and then he hurt me, and I pulled away."

"So, what does that have to do with me?"

I gather my strength, my defenses, to finally release the truth that with each passing year felt like a bruise spreading under my skin.

"Your father is a good man. He was such a good dad to you, but—" I see the dawning realization on her face before I say the words, "Elliott isn't your biological father."

She jerks her hand back as if she stuck a finger in an electric socket. She quickly stands, her arms folded tightly across her chest.

"Ash, sit back down. Please. Let me explain."

"But you always told me stories about how he was there when you went into labor and when I was born."

"That's all true."

"Wait, you're saying that this guy, Cillian, is my real father?"

"Elliott has been your father since the day you were born, and he loves you more than anything. Nothing can change that. But he's not your biological father. Cillian Byrne is."

"Wow, just wow. Shit! I can't believe you kept this from me my whole life." She holds her breath. "Does Dad know?" she asks, her voice cracking.

"Yes, he knows."

"So, you *both* lied to me?"

"It was to protect you, for us to create a happy family."

"Happy?" She lets out a harsh laugh. "Okay, so, how was lying to me and getting divorced a part of that 'happy family' plan?"

"I tried. I really did. But I couldn't be the wife, the life partner that your father needed, that I wanted to be."

"Did you have an affair?"

"No, I never cheated on your father."

"So?"

"I was pregnant when your father and I first got together. When he asked me to marry him, I told him, but he wanted us to be a family anyway."

"What the fuck, Mom?"

"Ash, you have to see it from my perspective back then. My mom had just died and left me with a mountain of debt that I had no way to pay back. I didn't have a degree or any marketable skills. Cillian broke my heart, and then I found out I was pregnant. And there was your father, telling me how much he loved me and asking me to marry him. I wanted something better for you, for your future. I thought that with time, I would—"

"Got it."

The shock, disappointment, and grief are visibly weighing her down, and she falls back onto the sofa, her head in her hands. But then just as suddenly, she jerks her head up.

"Did *he* know? Is that why he included me in the will?"

"I never told him."

"So, is there anyone else who knows or that you've lied to about me?"

Her comment stings, but I let it go.

"Your Aunt Sloane knows, but I don't think I could have kept it from her. You look a lot like him."

"Geez, Mom, I really didn't need to know that. So, what, every time you look at me you think of him?"

"Ash—"

"Forget it. But what I want to know is, if you never told him about me, why did he mention you *and* me in his will?"

My phone dings with a text. I give it a quick side glance.

Call me!

Sloane's text might as well have shouted, *Liar!* As my dearest friend, she's thrown me a lifeline more times than I can count, but I don't think she can help me now.

Chapter 40

The next morning, I text Sloane back.

Want to meet for coffee?

The deceptively simple message represents a far more complicated conversation. Just as I set my phone on the kitchen table, I hear Ashlyn moving around in her room earlier than usual, at least earlier than when she lived with me. I doubt she slept well. *And whose fault would that be?* I make her coffee the way she likes it—strong with a dash of milk and half a teaspoon of sugar—and set it on the table as soon as I hear the door to her bedroom open.

She shuffles into the kitchen, her green eyes puffy and her long sandy hair askew.

"Morning, Ash. How'd you sleep?"

"Not great."

"Want something to eat? Toast, eggs, bagel, cereal?"

"You know I don't like to eat breakfast as soon as I get up."

I do know that. My offer of breakfast is my lame attempt to distract from the unaccustomed tension between us.

She sits in my chair and mumbles, "Thanks," as she lifts her coffee mug in a gesture of gratitude and takes a sip.

"Ashlyn, honey, I know you're hurting, but nothing's changed."

"Maybe not for you."

"I'm still your mom, and Elliott is still your dad."

She shoots me a look of utter disdain.

"I love you, and I'm so sorry that I kept the truth from you, but I did what I thought was best. If you could just—"

My phone dings with a message.

Ashlyn glances at the phone in front of her on the table then turns to me, her mouth agape. I cast an eye over the words on the screen before they disappear.

Meet you at Get Grounded after work? How was Ireland?

"What is she talking about?"

I know how this looks. On top of my lies of omission about her paternity, she may never trust me again.

"You were in freakin' Ireland? What about the pictures you sent and all that stuff you told me about the yoga retreat? That was bull-shit?"

I finally look at her, and I know she sees the truth in my eyes.

She shakes her head in disbelief. "Man, the hits just keep on coming."

For a second or two, she seems too stunned to speak, but then she says, "If he's dead, then why were you in Ireland?"

I sit in the chair next to her, my eyes burning with guilt and shame. My daughter, the person I love most in this world, is disappointed in me and has labeled me a serial liar.

"I hadn't told you anything about Cillian. How could I tell you that I was going to Ireland to attend his funeral?"

The hard lines that had formed on her forehead softened.

"You went to his funeral? How did you know he died?"

"I read it online, then I reached out to his best friend, Damian. It's been a long time, but he still remembered me. Long story short, on an impulse, I bought a last-minute ticket, and I didn't know what to tell you, so I made up that story about a yoga retreat."

She walks over to the sink and leans against the counter, her back to me.

"It's a lot to take in, you know? You could have just told me the truth." Then she slowly turns to face me. "It's like you had a secret life or something."

She hit the proverbial nail on the proverbial head. I have had a secret life, but it's been happening in my head for the previous two decades. Cillian's death and my desperate need to say one final goodbye brought it out in the open.

"I guess in a way I did have a secret life, one that I never expected to share with you. Ash, I'm your mom, but I'm also a person, a woman, with a complicated history. Ask me anything, and I'll tell you what you want to know, or we can never speak of it again, if that's what you prefer."

I wait for her to decide. Her brows furrow in thought.

"If he was the 'love of your life' and you were pregnant with me, why didn't you just tell him? What did he do that hurt you so much that you couldn't tell him something so important, so life-changing?"

I clear my throat. "It's complicated. You sure you want to know?"

"I think I *need* to know."

I scrutinize her face as I lay out the details of my plans to drop out of school and go with Cillian on tour, my mother's illness, and her words of warning about men like Cillian, like my father. I recount the phone call that made my mother's warning seem like a prediction, then Elliott knocked on my door after the funeral, and later he proposed.

I let out a weary sigh. "The rest, as they say, is history."

"Wow, Mom. It's like you're not who I thought you were and I'm not who I thought I was."

"That's not true, Ash. We're still the same people, just with a more complicated backstory."

She doesn't argue but simply moves on to the next question.

"So, you never spoke to him again after that phone call?"

"He called repeatedly for a while after that, and I never answered, so he finally gave up. But then several years ago, we actually met for coffee."

"Coffee? Is that a euphemism for sex?"

I'm taken aback by her frankness, but that's where we are.

"He asked me to come back to his hotel, but—"

"What a dick."

"No, Ash, he loved me."

"Not just you, it sounds like," she says, her voice dripping sarcasm. "Why did you even agree to meet him in the first place after what he did to you?"

My heart lurches in my chest. "What I *thought* he did to me. When I was in Ireland, Damian swore to me that Cillian never did anything wrong, and he wouldn't have any reason to lie to me now that Cillian is gone. I wasn't willing to listen to what Cillian was trying to tell me back then. My mother's warning was too fresh. The bottom line is I made a mistake—quite a few mistakes, in fact."

I let out a jagged sigh.

"But you didn't know that when you agreed to meet with him."

"A lot of time had passed. My hurt and anger had blunted, and I thought seeing him might allow me some closure."

"And did it?"

"No. I still loved him, but it was too late for us. I never told your father about that meeting. I don't think he would have believed me that nothing happened."

"What about after that? You didn't talk to Cillian again after that?"

It's strange to hear Ashlyn say his name, especially in anger and frustration. She's digging in, wanting to know more.

"Actually, he called me just a couple of months ago. He wanted me to come to Ireland. It was shocking, unexpected. He didn't tell me that he was sick."

He was sick. I've somehow pushed that to the back of my mind and have failed to work that into this already traumatic conversation—a terrible reminder of my making the wrong decision again or at least stewing in my indecision. I missed my last opportunity to be with him.

"What was he sick with?"

"Damian told me that he had a genetic disease that damaged his lungs."

I watch the realization develop on her face, and it hollows me.

"So, I could have inherited it?"

I reach for her hand. "We'll get you tested. It's just a blood test. But it's unlikely. He has seven brothers and sisters, and he was the only one who inherited it."

"Okay." She leans back, and I can almost see her compartmentalizing before she asks, "So, I guess you said no when he asked you to come to Ireland?"

"Not exactly. I thought I had time to decide if there might still be something between us after all these years, if I could change the direction of my life."

"Really? Is that something you wanted to do?"

"It was."

"So, why didn't you?"

"I had decided I would, but—" Here, my voice cracks. "He died before I could tell him."

Chapter 41

The coffee shop is a five-minute drive from Nature's Trail—five more minutes for me to obsess over what I'm going to say to Sloane. My brain is overworked and so, so tired. I pull up in front of Get Grounded and spot her through the glass front. She looks relaxed, sipping her coffee, scrolling on her phone.

"You look tired," she says as I join her at the table after a hug and a kiss on the cheek.

"Gee, thanks."

"I mean are you taking care of yourself? I know that trip had to be incredibly stressful."

"Let me go order some coffee. Be right back." I stand and head to the counter.

When I return, latte in hand, I sit and give her a weak smile. "I don't know where to start. These last few days feel like they've lasted a decade."

"Start wherever you want. It's okay."

Where should *I start? Cillian's funeral, meeting his family, almost having sex with Damian, his passionate goodbye kiss, the will, telling Ashlyn the truth?*

I decide the best place to start is at the very beginning. I take a deep breath and follow up with a couple of gulps of my latte, burning my tongue in the process.

While I'm considering the best place to start my tangled tale, she says, "You never told me. How did Cillian die? He was our age."

I look down into my lap and shake my head with the weight of my answer.

"He had a genetic disease that affected his lungs."

She opens her mouth to ask about Ashlyn, but I answer before she can form the question.

"Ashlyn's getting tested."

"So she knows?"

"Yeah, it was awful. She blamed me and Elliott for lying to her all these years—which leads me to something else I have to tell you."

"Should I buckle up? Get something stronger than coffee?"

"I'm pretty sure there are no seat belts, and they don't serve alcohol here," I say, smiling. I've managed to relax—a little.

"Okay, so continue."

I tell her about the will, and she's overjoyed for me, but I hate that her happiness is the result of Cillian's death. Then I replay everything I told Ashlyn about my time in Ireland, but this time, I add the titillating details of my almost-sex with Damian and his passionate goodbye kiss.

With that reveal, she raises an eyebrow.

"I've read that grief can be a powerful aphrodisiac" is all she says.

"Yeah, my episode with Elliott after my mother's funeral is further proof of that."

"So, Damian, huh?" she says.

"Yeah, I know. But I got to know him better than I ever did when Cillian and I were together. He's not that twentysomething guy out for a good time anymore. He's actually one of the good ones."

"So, what's next—with the will, with Damian?"

"First off, there's nothing that's next between Damian and me. That interlude was simply the result of a combination of grief and close proximity, but I *am* going to call him and ask why the hell didn't he tell me about the will."

Two days later, I'm staring at the WhatsApp video icon on my phone. This call needs to be face-to-face. I want to see Damian's reaction when I confront him. Even I realize how rich that is—me, the gold medalist in the lies-of-omission category, calling him out for his omission. I wake up at five in the morning to leave time for this uncomfortable conversation and my reset before going to work. The prospect of seeing Damian again leaves me as anxious as a teenager about to go on a first date. I remind myself I'm being ridiculous. I'm a grown woman with a grown daughter, and besides, what happened between us was just "one of those things." But then I remember that kiss at the airport, my stomach flips, and I hit the video icon before I have time to talk myself out of it.

I'm not exactly video-call ready. I'm draped in the ratty terry cloth robe that Elliott gave me ten birthdays ago, I haven't brushed my hair or my teeth, and my eyes are puffy from lack of sleep. But then I think, *Why should it matter?* He answers on the first ring, and he looks great. I glance at my own image in the corner of the screen and cringe. I pull my robe tighter before I remember I'm furious at him.

"Did you know about this?" I demand before he even has a chance to say anything besides hello. I have the will gripped in my hand, shaking the papers in front of the camera.

"Well, good to see you too, Zee," he says.

"Why didn't you tell me?"

"Tell you what? What are you goin' on about?"

"This!" I shout as I hold the papers up again.

"I can't read it with you waving it about."

I hold it still in front of the camera. He squints and leans in then jerks back.

"Cillian's will?"

"Like you didn't know."

"I didn't."

Judging by the confusion on his face, he just might be telling the truth.

"He named you as executor. How could you not know?"

"I'm executor? *Shit.*" He leans back in. "What else does it say?"

I huff an exhausted breath. "He left me a shitload of money. And a house in Ireland."

"Wow. And that's a bad thing? What's got you so worked up?"

"He also left money to Ashlyn. Did you know that he knew?"

"Fuck all, Zee. You're talking in riddles. Knew what?"

"Come on, Damian. You were his best friend. How could he not tell you?"

"Tell me *what*?"

"That Ashlyn is his daughter!"

"Wait, what? That doesn't... How?... He didn't... How old is she again?"

Now he wants to do the math?

"Ashlyn is almost twenty-two. I was pregnant when we broke up, when I cut Cillian out of my life."

"And your husband? Ex-husband? Does he know? Does Ashlyn know?" His rapid-fire questions are a reflection of his mental state, his confusion.

"That's a story for another time. Not today, Damian."

"Okay. Well, shit. Give us the name of the law office. If I'm executor, I think I need to know a wee bit more of what the fuck I'm to do."

I text him the name and address of the law firm. He looks down at his phone.

"Ah, the office is close to where you stayed. Maybe my copy went to another address. I've got a few."

"Of course you do."

"Hey, no judgment, Zee. You'll soon have enough money to buy more than one."

He smiles, and the drumming of my heart slows to a steady beat. I finally look at him, and I see what I saw that night in Ireland.

"I'm sorry I jumped down your throat. I was sure you knew about... everything, and I was blindsided by all this as soon as I walked in the door. I have no idea what I'm supposed to do next."

"Email me a copy of the will, and I'll ring the law firm and see what I can find out. I'll ring you back and let you know. We'll get it sorted. Promise."

It didn't escape my attention that he said "we."

Chapter 42

I check my phone. It's eleven thirty at night in Ireland. I don't know if Damian is a night person, and after our last uneasy conversation, I don't want to pull him from sleep only to ask for a favor. I text him first.

You up?

The moment I hit send, I realize that if he weren't five thousand miles away, it would sound like a booty call.

Watching the telly.

Can you talk?

Two seconds later, my phone rings with a video call.

"Hey, Damian."

"Where's the sexy robe?" he asks with a crooked smile. His "sexy" comment triggers another flashback to his feverish kisses. And he's looking at me right now with the same intensity.

"Anyway," I say to get us back on track, "I have another issue that I'm hoping the lawyer can shed some light on."

"Yeah, go on."

"You remember I told you about Ashlyn's husband and their situation? She's going to file for divorce. I need to know if Jason would have any right to her inheritance."

"What a prick," he said. "He wants to nick her money? He needs a good kick in the arse."

"I don't know for a fact he would pursue it, but I want us to be prepared if it comes to that."

"I don't know the answer, but I'll ring the solicitor straight away."

"Thank you, Damian."

He fidgets with his rings, and his Adam's apple slides up and down as he swallows hard.

"You and Ashlyn alright, then?" he asks.

"We will be when all this is settled." I glance at the time again. "So, you're a night owl?"

"This is early for me. All those years of late-night gigs messed with my sleeping. You?"

I raise my hand. "Early bird here. Have to get to work really early most days."

"Think you'll keep working after you get the money?"

"Uh, wow. I... I haven't thought that far ahead. It's crazy to think that I might not have to work. What would I do with my time?"

"Maybe you need a lie-in for a change."

"Sleeping late sounds so decadent, but I don't even know if my body would cooperate."

Decadent. My body. Why does everything that comes out of my mouth sound suggestive? Maybe it's just where my head is at.

He runs his fingers through his hair, clasps his hands behind his head, and cracks his knuckles. He looks uncomfortable, like something unsaid is squirming its way to the surface. He leans in and lowers his voice.

"Zee... I have to know. Have you not thought about us, about what happened—you know, between us?"

"Damian—"

"I haven't stopped thinking about it. About you. There's something here," he says, gesturing between us. "Maybe we owe it to ourselves to find out. What do you think? Come back to Ireland, Zee, and let's see what happens."

Tears sting my eyes.

"Bollocks. I've stepped in it now, haven't I?"

"Damian, I... I..."

Do I tell him how I think I feel and open that door of new possibility? I don't know what would be worse for me now, dwelling on my past with Cillian or a possible future with Damian.

When I don't finish my sentence, he fills in the blank.

"So, that's a no? Fair enough." His disappointment is palpable, even on the screen.

"This is hard for me, Damian."

"It's okay, luv."

"No, it's not what you think." I shift in place and clear my throat. "I've put my emotions on hold for so many years, ignoring them, then Cillian invited me back into his life, and then just like that, he was gone. And there you were. You were so kind, so understanding, so tender, so—"

"Sexy?" he says with a knowing smile.

I feel blood rushing to my cheeks—a dead giveaway—but I give a quick nod. "It was all so unexpected. I wasn't prepared to have feelings like that—not so soon after losing Cillian. Though, I guess it had been a long time since I'd actually had him to lose." I take a shaky breath. "You're asking if I've thought about what happened between us? The answer is yes, I have. Constantly."

He releases a breath and leans closer to the screen. If I were there, I know exactly what would happen next.

"So, just give it a think. I'll wait for your answer," he says in a throaty whisper.

Chapter 43

I walk into my apartment, hyped up on nervous energy, after yet another "session" with Sloane. These days, I fluctuate between feeling sluggish and feeling like I'm about to jump out of my shrinking skin. I have to find a way to release some of my pent-up angst. I've let things go at home. I'm amazed by how much more of a mess two people and one large dog can make, now that Ashlyn is staying with me, compared to living alone. If I can get the apartment back to a lemon-scented state, maybe I'll be able to think more clearly. I determinedly gather my cleaning supplies and set them on the kitchen counter, grab a couple of rags from atop the washing machine, pull the vacuum cleaner from the closet, and get to work. I open my laptop and turn up the volume on my Spotify playlist titled "Hodgepodge." Scrubbing the kitchen sink to the sound of the Backstreet Boys is surprisingly satisfying. I wash and dry the dishes, clean the stove top, and mop the kitchen floor, dancing like no one is watching, because they aren't. Beads of sweat form on my forehead and upper lip, so I decide to take a break before tackling the living room. I pour a glass of ice water, chug it, and refill the glass. I'm about to collapse on the sofa in the living room, glass in hand, when I spot something on the floor, peeking out from underneath the sofa. I sit on the edge of the cushion, bend over, and pull it out. It's the FedEx envelope that held Cillian's will—not the reminder I need right now. I toss it onto the coffee table, and another much smaller envelope slips out. My name is handwritten on the front. I would recognize that handwriting anywhere.

I set my glass on the coffee table and stare at Cillian's loopy handwriting before I grab it and rip the envelope open to find a page filled with more of the same. I cover my gaping mouth with my hand as I scan the first few lines:

Zee, baby, if you're reading this—well, you know what that means. And I can safely assume you've read the will. I hope what I've left you will allow you to live the life you deserve. You and Ashlyn.

The Swifters' song "If I Had You (Wild Love)" cues up on Spotify, and Cillian is singing his heart out about *us*. I drop the pages on the sofa and run to the kitchen, turn off the music, grab a bottle of wine and a glass, and fill it to the brim. I need something to take the edge off before reading any more. I almost call Sloane, but despite our decades-long friendship, some things are just too intimate to share, even with her.

I down half the glass of wine while leaning against the kitchen counter, then bring the glass and the bottle with me to the sofa. I pick up the letter, take a deep breath, and continue reading.

I'm not sure how to say this, and I'm not there for you to deny it, to try to explain it away, but I now know that Ashlyn is my daughter. I've seen recent photos of her on Instagram and Facebook. I can see myself in her face. I mean, just look at her. There's no way you could know this, but she looks exactly like my sister, Margaret, when she was younger—the green eyes, the freckles, the sandy-colored hair.

"I do know, Cillian," I say out loud.

I understand why you chose not to tell me that you were pregnant back then, and I hold no resentment. How could I? She's my daughter. And she's beautiful. But I have to tell you once and for all that I wouldn't have done anything to risk what we had. And I don't want to leave this earth with you believing that about me. I've always wished that we could somehow erase that fateful phone call and that you would be with me now, when I need you the most. I said this to you once before, but I always thought you would come back to me someday. I know that

I was being selfish, asking you to come to Ireland. But I wanted to spend whatever time I had left with you. And I thought there would be much more time. I'm not telling you this to make you feel guilty about not coming. That's the last thing I want. I just want you to know how I feel, how I've always felt.

But I have another, far more selfish request. I want more than anything for my family to know Ashlyn. She is all they'll have left of me. I don't know if you ever told her the truth, but maybe now it's time that you did. What do you say, Zee? Can you make that happen?

More than anything, I hope that I've left you with grand memories of the two of us that make you smile whenever you think of me, of us. Maybe I have no right to have loved you all these years, but know that I never stopped loving you. Ever. And I never will.

All my love,

Cillian

I bring the paper to my lips and kiss his signature, pour myself another glass of wine, and tearfully reread the letter again and again. I can't go back in time, and I may not have been with him in his last days, but he's with me now, and he always will be.

The apartment is cleaner than clean, and Cillian's letter resting on the coffee table is giving off sad sonic vibrations. I want it to stop. I carefully fold it back to its original form, slide it into the envelope, and hide it from myself in the drawer in the end table by the sofa. The sound is muffled, if not completely silenced.

I jump at another sound—three hard knocks at the door. I'm so unfocused that I stupidly open the door without checking to see who it is.

And there stands Jason.

"You two thought you could hide this from me?" he yells as he shoves a FedEx envelope with the Irish law firm's return address in my face.

I'm so confused. "How the hell did you get that?"

"Is she here?" he demands as he easily looks over my shoulder into the apartment.

I'm angry and scared, but I stand my ground, blocking his six-foot-three presence from entering my apartment.

"She's not here. I'm going to ask again—where did you get that?"

"It was in *our* mailbox. I opened it to find out she's inherited a shitload of money from some singer in Ireland. How did she know this guy?"

"You do know that it's a federal offense to open someone else's mail?"

"She's my wife!"

"Not much longer, she's not."

"Fuck! I knew you had something to do with that. She thinks she's going to divorce me? Well, I'll make sure she's left with nothing, not even her inheritance from whoever the fuck this guy is."

"Jason, I think that you—"

"I don't give a fuck what you think. Just tell her that she'll get nothing, nada, zip, not one penny, if she doesn't come home, like right now!"

With his threat still ringing in my ears, he stomps to his Jag, slams the car door, and screeches out of the parking lot and down the street.

I'm shaking so hard I have to sit on the sofa and take a series of deep breaths. I'm in a vicious tug-of-war with myself. *Do I tell Ashlyn of his threat? Should I?* Jason's simply using the will as leverage to get his way, to control her. He didn't threaten her physically, and she insists he's never hit her. But the very idea that I'm considering the possibility frightens me.

The next morning, when I reluctantly slip back into my routine—a bagel in the toaster, jam from the fridge, and my laptop booting up, I hear the ding of a WhatsApp message on my phone. I glance at the screen.

Can you talk?

It's Damian.

"Zezelia!" he says as if my call has taken him by surprise.

I wave to the camera.

"Did I wake you? Did I get the time difference wrong?"

"No, I was just making coffee."

"Well, you're looking grand."

"Damian, you're such a liar."

"I mean it. Remember, I've already seen you first thing in the morning," he says, and it's hard to miss the not-so-subtle suggestive tone in his voice.

"Sorry it's taken me so long to get back to you," he says as he shifts gears. "I had questions, and then I'd think of another and ring the solicitor again."

"It's only been a week," I say. "Listen, before you fill me in, turns out Jason definitely wants to get his greedy hands on Ashlyn's inheritance."

"What happened?"

The memory of the vitriol and hatred lining Jason's face leaves me shaken. "It was shocking, even for Jason. Yesterday, he showed up at my door, threatening to siphon off all of Ashlyn's inheritance and leave her penniless if she doesn't come home."

"Bollocks!"

"Yeah, bollocks." I bite my lower lip. "Damian, can I ask you something first?"

"Go on."

"Do you have any idea how long Cillian might have known about Ashlyn? Do you think he knew when he asked me to join him in Dublin?"

"If he knew, he didn't tell me. But he'd've put her in the will even if he didn't know she was his. He loved you. You love her. I think it's that simple."

"Maybe, but seeing her name in the will was a shock."

"If you don't want to talk about it or if it's none of my business, tell me, but when I asked you if she or your ex-husband knew, you said that was a story for another time. How about now?"

I steel myself and launch into my overly complicated story. I tell Damian everything, beginning with my pregnancy and ending with Cillian's will. He listens patiently, and when I'm done, he exhales loudly and grimaces.

"Zee, I'm sorry. I know that was a shite decision to have to make. How's your daughter taking the news?"

"Elliott doesn't know that Ashlyn knows, and I haven't told him anything about the will. I have all that to look forward to. But it's been hard on Ashlyn. I mean, she grew up believing that Elliott was her father, so it's been incredibly disorienting for her to learn about Cillian. She's still processing it all, I think. But she's coming around. So, what did the lawyer say?"

"You don't have to come to Ireland to finalize things for the money to be transferred to your account in the States. You're to sign the papers digitally."

"Oh, okay." I feel an unexpected twinge of disappointment.

"But the solicitor says it could take up to a year to get the will out of probate. As executor, I'm to submit paperwork for Cillian's assets. I've no idea how long that'll take."

"No worries. Take your time."

I can't decide if I should tell him about Cillian's letter, if I *want* to tell him, but I know I don't want the call to end. We sit there, looking at each other, the silence turning awkward.

"Zee, I..." he says with unmistakable tenderness in his voice. He hesitates, clears his throat, then takes on a decidedly businesslike tone. "I'll be back in touch with more details in a few days." Another pause. "Okay, luv, call or text if you have any questions or need anything else."

"Wait, Damian. There *is* something else."

"About the will?"

"No, Cillian left me a handwritten letter—with a request."

"A request? What kind of request?"

"He wants his family to meet Ashlyn, to know that he has a daughter."

He doesn't say anything right away. I can't tell if he's thinking it's a good idea or a really bad one.

"So, how do you see that going?" he finally asks.

"I don't know. You tell me. I only met his family that once, and it wasn't exactly under the best of circumstances. You know his mom, his brothers and sisters. How do you think they'll take the news?"

"They'll be a wee bit shocked. But I think they'll be chuffed to meet her and know that there's a piece of Cillian left behind."

I nod as if I can actually imagine Ashlyn and me going to Ireland together and me introducing her to everyone—her grandmother, her aunts and uncles, and all her cousins, most of whom I haven't met. The single branch of our family tree would no longer be blowing in the wind all alone.

"So, you're coming back then, are ya? For Ashlyn, I mean."

"Well, I haven't made up my mind when or how, but I'll bring her. I can't really ignore Cillian's dying wish, can I?"

"I want to meet her," he says with absolute certainty. He looks away and rubs his hand over his stubble. "Cillian's daughter," he says softly, his voice full of wonder. He seems to have momentarily forgotten that I'm watching him, then he looks back at me. "Brilliant. I'll show you both around Ireland."

It's the same promise Cillian made to me.

Chapter 44

The next morning, I hear Ashlyn rustling around in her bedroom then the creak of her door opening. I'm determined to protect her from Jason's ire while she figures out her next steps.

It's early. She didn't get in until around two in the morning then tiptoed down the hall so as not to wake me, but I'd been lying awake, my mind in overdrive.

"Morning, Mom."

I'm curious about what she was up to until two, but I don't want to pry. My mother always drove me crazy with her questions and accusations. I won't do the same.

She's wrangling her hair into a hair tie as she glances at the oven clock. "What are you still doing here? I figured you'd be at work."

"I took the day off. Just have a bunch of errands to run."

And things to obsess over, like how and when to tell Ashlyn that her biological father wants her to meet her biological family in Ireland. And whatever the hell might be happening between Damian and me right now, despite what I said to Sloane.

She pours herself a cup of coffee and adds milk and sugar. "Anything I can help you with?"

"Thanks, but it's all stuff that I need to do. What are you up to today?"

"I need to call the divorce lawyer."

"You already have one?"

"Dax gave me a name and phone number. He said someone he works with used the firm, and they said this lawyer was good. A 'pit bull' was how he put it." She manages a weak smile.

A surge of panic overtakes me. I need to know if Jason has any legal claim to Ashlyn's inheritance before she gets too deep into divorce proceedings.

"You feel okay, Mom? You're looking a little pale."

"Fine. I'm fine. I think I just need another cup of coffee."

She sits next to me at the table and cups the mug in her hands as she stares at the taffy-colored liquid.

Her phone dings. She stares at it then looks at me and smiles. "It's the clinic. It says I'm a carrier of the gene, but it won't make me sick."

I'm breathless with relief. I go over and wrap her in a tight hug. "Thank God!"

She takes the good news in stride, pulling back before she says, "Mom, do you think it would be okay if I brought Dax over to meet you?"

I'm surprised at her dizzying change of subject as well as her willingness to bring me into the orbit of her newly developing relationship, but it thrills me that she wants to share her happiness with me.

I sit back down. "I would love to meet him, but..."

"Too soon?"

"No, it's not that. It's just—I didn't want to upset you—but Jason showed up here yesterday, waving the will around. He was livid, threatening to take control of your inheritance, unless—"

"Unless what?"

"Unless you come home."

Her mouth falls open, and her brows arch in surprise. Or is it shock? No, it's fear.

"Well, that's sure as hell not happening. But how did he get hold of the will?"

"A copy was sent to the house, to you, and he opened it."

"Seriously? Shit! Oh, God, Mom. If it's possible, I think I hate him a little more every day. Can he even do that?"

"I'm going to check with the lawyer in Ireland. Your divorce lawyer should speak with her, and together, they can figure it all out."

With trembling hands, she brings the coffee mug to her lips.

"Ash, come here." She sits in my lap like she did when she was little, and I sweep her hair behind her ear. "It'll be okay, sweetie. We'll be okay. Once this is all settled, we'll be more than okay. Jason will just have to deal with it and move on."

She stands suddenly. "He's not going to break me. That's what he wants, you know, what he's always wanted."

I won't let Jason break my daughter. If he were to succeed, the damage might be irreparable. Cillian's death had cracked me open, but I was carefully gluing the pieces back together. While the seams might not be visible to the naked eye, they'll always be there, but I'll be stronger than before.

And so will she.

Chapter 45

The now-familiar ring of a WhatsApp video call has me scrambling to turn off the stove, grab my coffee, and position myself in front of my laptop. Damian's calls have become the bright spot in my days, and I've come to depend on the steady tenor of his voice and his steadfast reassurances. He hasn't pressed me further on when I might be coming to Ireland, and I appreciate that. I don't need another looming decision in my life. I click Answer, and his image comes into view.

"Mornin', luv."

"Morning."

"What's the craic?"

I chuckle. "I don't know if I'll ever get used to that expression. Sounds like you're asking me for drugs."

He looks confused for a second then smiles. "Ah, right."

"Anyway, I'm good. You?"

"Grand."

"So, is there any news from the lawyer about Jason and the will?"

"Good news. Solicitor says he's a gobshite."

"She actually said that?"

"No, that's me. But she says he's talking nonsense. She contacted a lawyer she knows in the States. As long as Ashlyn doesn't deposit the money in a joint account, he can't get his greedy hands on any of it."

I place my hand over my heart and expel a long-held breath. "That's such good news! I can't wait to tell her. I can't believe it—she'll be set for life. She can get her own place, go back to school, buy a car—determine her own future." Tears of relief threaten to spill over. I close my eyes and say a silent thank-you to Cillian.

"And I sorted the mail at my other properties and found the will."

"Ah, okay. Mystery of the missing will solved."

He hesitates. "Cillian left me a note as well."

"Really? What did it say?"

He looks away then back at me. "I can't, Zee. Reading it once was hard enough. Maybe someday, I'll tell you what he said."

He runs his fingers through his hair. It's longer than it was when I was there. But even then, he had enough that I grabbed a thick fistful as we—

"Zee, have you thought any more about when you might be coming to Ireland?"

So much for no pressure.

I take a sip of coffee and fidget with my mug. I'm stalling. I know what I want to say, but his question suddenly feels like a cruel déjà vu.

"I really need to ask Ashlyn if it's something she wants to do. If she does, I'm thinking I should come alone first to talk to Cillian's family and explain. It would be too much of a shock for me to just show up with her: 'Oh, remember me? We met at Cillian's funeral, and here's his daughter that I kept a secret for the past twenty-one years.'"

"Fair enough."

"So, how's his family doing?"

He sits back and crosses his arms tightly against his chest. "His mam is having a rough time of it. Cillian was her baby. But the family is there for her."

"So, do you think it's a bad idea for me to dump this on her? Maybe she needs more time to grieve and get back to a new normal before learning about Ashlyn."

"Ah, luv, grief never goes away. It just becomes a part of you, and you carry on, yeah?"

The thought of carrying the grief of Cillian's death until the day of my own is a weight that feels too much to bear, but I know that's how this works. More than twenty years after my mother's death, a full-body sadness overtakes me if I dwell on it for any length of time.

He leans into the screen again. "Zee, why don't you come and see what happens—stay longer than just a few days."

"I know it's probably hard for you to understand, but even if I can get the time off, another trip like that would be expensive, and I've already maxed out my credit cards. I don't have the inheritance yet, and like you said, it could be several months before I do." Even I can hear how ridiculous I sound.

"You said you hadn't decided if you want to keep working, and I can help you until the inheritance comes through."

I shake my head before I say anything. "Absolutely not."

"Alright, so what if I come there?"

"What? Why?"

"Zee, maybe I haven't made myself clear. I want to be with you, and it has nothing to do with the will or with Cillian's family."

I blink repeatedly. This time, I want to make the right choice, a choice that I won't regret for the rest of my life.

"Damian, I—"

"If you're thinking you're somehow being unfaithful to Cillian's memory, don't. I know Cillian would have wanted for you and me to be happy, and if us being together is what makes us happy, I think he would be happy *for* us."

"What... what about my telling Cillian's family about Ashlyn?"

"We can fly back together and tell them."

"Oh, Damian, I don't know. I—"

"Mom?"

I jerk my head up so suddenly that my neck cracks.

"Zee, what is it? You okay?" Damian's voice fills the kitchen as Ashlyn walks in with a young man I've never seen before.

"Who are you talking to?" Ashlyn asks.

She comes around and stands next to me, peering at the screen.

"Um, Ashlyn, this is Damian, a friend of Cillian's. Damian, this is my daughter, Ashlyn."

Damian's eyes widen, and he gives Ashlyn a nod and a single wave.

I turn toward the young man standing next to Ashlyn. "And this is...?"

"Oh, Mom, this is Dax. Dax, my mom." She looks at Damian then at me. "I guess I should have called first."

"Zee, maybe I should ring you later," Damian says.

Dax inches closer, and his mouth flies open. "Is that who I think it is?"

Clueless, Ashlyn turns to Dax. "Who do you think it is?"

"Ash, this is Damian O'Leary of The Swifters." He looks at Damian. "Am I right?"

There's a pause as we each take in the situation and decide what to say next, then I hear the front door slam shut.

"Ashlyn? I know you're in there!"

Ashlyn squeezes Dax's hand, and her lips turn white as she frantically scans the room for an escape route. There is none.

Her eyes widen, and she looks at me in panic then up at Dax. "Oh my God, it's Jason."

Jason appears in the doorway, and he's pissed. Maple had been sniffing around the kitchen, but now she positions herself next to Ashlyn and emits a low, rumbling growl in Jason's direction.

"No fucking way," he bellows, pointing an accusatory finger at Dax. "What is this asshole doing here?"

"More to the point, what are *you* doing here?" I demand. "How did you get in?"

"The fucking door was open. Not smart."

"Is that Jason?" Damian asks, with equal parts confusion and concern.

"Who the hell is that, and how does he know who I am?"

He's inching closer to Ashlyn, but Dax positions himself between them.

Jason's frown deepens, amplifying his dark demeanor. "She's still *my* wife. Maybe you fucked her a couple of times. Doesn't mean shit."

"Jason, I want you to leave. Now!" I say in the most authoritative voice I can muster.

"Zee, what the fuck is happening?" Poor Damian is a bodiless voice, helpless to do anything, and now is not the time for me to stop and explain.

"I'll leave when, and only when, Ashlyn comes with me." Jason reaches out and takes another purposeful step toward Dax, who's puffing out his chest and standing taller. He's not Jason's six-foot-three, but he looks like he could take him on, based on the grim determination on his face.

Just not in my kitchen. Please.

The tension is palpable as they size each other up, and Jason inches ever closer. I jump out of my chair and pull Ashlyn out of harm's way. At that exact moment, Jason lunges for Dax. Maple joins the fray, barking and jumping on Jason, pulling at his leg. Dax ducks, narrowly escaping Jason's fist.

And the full force of it lands squarely on my face.

The words "knocked senseless" come to mind, a fitting description for the disorienting assault. The sound I make as I hit the floor is the anguish of a wounded animal.

I open my eyes. The back of my head and my face are screaming with pain. I hear Jason bellowing, Ashlyn shouting, and Maple whining before I drift off again. The next thing I'm cognizant of, the police are dragging Jason from my kitchen in handcuffs, the paramedics are taking my blood pressure, peppering me with questions, and Ashlyn and Dax—and *Sloane?*—are hovering. As the paramedics help me up and onto a stretcher, I glance at the darkened computer screen.

Damian had checked out of this dumpster fire of a family disaster, and I can't say I blame him.

Chapter 46

I can't wrap my head around the fact that Jason decked me. His punch was as forceful as I would have expected, given his size and his fury. I wasn't his intended target, but I'm more certain than ever that if Ashlyn had stayed with Jason, she would have eventually become his target.

The ER doc says I have a mild concussion but no broken bones and I don't need stitches, but that assessment belies the excruciating physical and emotional pain I'm experiencing. My split lip, which already feels like I've overdosed on lip plumper, is being treated with a cold compress, and I have instructions to apply petroleum jelly and rinse with salt water when I get home.

As I wait for my discharge papers, I'm able to convince Ashlyn that I'm fine, or at least I will be, and that she and Dax don't need to stay. She reluctantly agrees to leave and gives me a soft kiss on my good cheek.

Before they pull back the curtain to walk out of the cubicle, Dax turns to me and says, for no less than the third time, "I'm really, really sorry, Ms. Owens. I'm the reason things got out of hand and you ended up here."

"Dax, you did absolutely nothing wrong. It's all on Jason. I plan to press charges, and if there is any justice, he'll spend some quality time in jail."

Dax gives me a wan smile and nods in agreement, but when I smile back, I immediately regret it. My lip is bleeding again.

"Sloane, can you hand me that gauze?"

"Mom?"

"I'm fine, Ash. Go, go. Y'all get some coffee or maybe a stiff drink."

She's not happy with her banishment, but the last thing she needs right now is to sit around, watching me cringe in pain.

"Okay. Love you, Mom. Promise to call me when you get home."

I carefully blow her a kiss. "I will. Oh, is Maple okay?"

"She broke the skin on Jason's leg when she came to my defense, but she's fine."

I hold the gauze to my lip, fall back onto the pillow, and close my eyes. The throbbing in my cheekbone feels like the thrum of a bass drum keeping time with my heartbeat.

Sloane sits on the edge of the bed and takes my hand.

"You sure you're okay?"

"Define 'okay.'" I open one eye. "So, are you going to tell me how you knew to call the police? Ash said it was you. Do you have telepathic powers that you've somehow forgotten to mention?"

Sloane purses her lips. "Hardly. Damian called me, and he—"

"Wait. What? How the hell…?"

"You gave me his number when you were in Ireland for the funeral. Remember? You said it was in case anything happened to you since no one else knew you were there, and I texted him, so he has my number."

I don't remember. My brain was overcooked with the wake, the funeral, and meeting Cillian's family. I close my eyes again. Keeping them open is such an effort.

"God, Damian saw the whole thing. I can't imagine what he thinks of me right now."

"Are you kidding me? You were Wonder Woman, the way you pulled Ashlyn away just in time and took the hit. But he was totally freaking out when he called. He was only thinking about keeping you and Ashlyn safe. At first, I couldn't understand what he was say-ing. Evidently, his accent gets thicker when he's excited."

I reach up to touch my swollen, tender face and gasp. "Do you have a mirror?"

"I wouldn't do that if I were you. It's going to take a while for the swelling to go down, and I doubt it's even peaked yet. You're going to have a lovely kaleidoscope of colors on the left side of your face in another couple of days. The doc said she called in a prescription for painkillers. Peter or I will pick it up."

"Thank you, Sloane. I can't imagine what would have happened if you hadn't called the police."

But I actually *can* imagine, and it makes me sick to my stomach.

The nurse swings the curtain aside, comes in, and hands me my discharge papers. "Okay, you're free to go. Just keep this ice pack on it—fifteen minutes on, fifteen minutes off—keep your head elevat-ed and take the pain medication the doctor prescribed. Don't skip a dose, and rest as much as you can. You're going to have an impressive shiner in a day or two."

Rest? I need to call Clyde. I can't go to work looking like this.

"Listen, why don't you come and stay with me and Peter for a couple of days—at least until you're feeling better."

I'm easily persuaded, and I jump at Sloane's offer. "I think I will. Thanks."

"Wow, that was easy," she says. "I was expecting an argument."

"I honestly don't have the energy to argue right now."

I gingerly walk out of the building and into the parking lot with Sloane, who's slowed to keep time with my sluggish pace. Lowering myself into the passenger seat of her BMW raises my pain level a cou-ple of notches, and I moan like I'm in the early stages of labor. Sloane reaches over to help me with my seat belt, and I lean my head back onto the headrest.

She hands me the gel ice pack the nurse gave me, and we sit in silence in the hospital parking lot for a few minutes while I wait for the ice and the pain meds to do their thing. When my moaning stops, she asks, "Better?"

"Yeah, a little. Thanks."

She starts the car and says, "I'll be sure to hit all the potholes."

"Shut up. Don't make me laugh."

In the drive to her place, we're stopped at a red light, and she turns down the volume on the radio. "So, I didn't know you were still in touch with Damian. What's going on with you two?"

The pounding in my face picks up. "Yeah, I was going to tell you about that."

"So, there *is* something to tell?"

I dive into the details of Damian's help with the will, his daily calls, his invitation to join him, and his offer to come here. A car behind us honks, and she presses on the gas.

"You're getting really good at keeping things from me."

"I wasn't keeping it from you as much as I was keeping it from myself. It's been hard to accept that I have feelings for Damian."

With that, her eyes widen, and she whips her head in my direction.

"Eyes on the road, Sloane!"

She quickly pulls onto the shoulder and puts on the flashers. "Oh yeah? What kind of feelings?"

"You're going to make me say it?" I sigh dramatically. "Okay, I want to be with him to see if we should be together."

She lets out a little grunt. "I'm going to say something you may not like, but I'm your best friend, and it's my job to keep you from making bad decisions—though I haven't exactly been good at my job so far."

"Sloane—"

"Shhh. Just listen. Are you absolutely certain that what you're feeling is for Damian, or is he a Cillian clone? I mean he's Irish. He was in the same band as Cillian. He was Cillian's best friend, for Chrissake."

"Believe me, I've asked myself the same question a million times over. But Damian is his own person, and I haven't felt this way about anyone else in over twenty years. I haven't given him my answer yet."

"But you haven't even slept with him yet unless that's something else you haven't told me."

"You know almost everything."

"Almost?"

I'm so tired of explaining myself to everyone. I squirm under the seat belt.

"The other reason I want to go is... Cillian left me a note asking me to bring Ashlyn to Ireland to meet his family."

"Wait, wait—what do you mean Cillian left you a note?"

"It was in the same envelope as the will. It was his last wish, Sloane. I have to honor that, so I'm thinking I'll go to Ireland alone first to be with Damian for a while and then pave the way with Cillian's family to meet Ashlyn."

"Wow. Anything else?"

I shake my head—slowly.

"Does Ashlyn know about this family reunion?"

"No, but I'll tell her. I've been waffling, but I think Jason's fist may have jarred loose my indecision."

When we pull into Sloane's driveway, I spot Peter's lanky silhouette on their porch. Sloane comes around to the passenger side, helps me out, and motions to Peter to assist.

His shocked expression lets me know that Sloane made the right call by refusing my request for a mirror. When I stand, I'm dizzy and a little nauseated from the pain pills. Sloane and Peter sandwich me between them to help me up the front steps, and they guide me to the downstairs bedroom. I settle on the bed, my head propped up on a collection of pillows. It feels like heaven, and my ears ring in the absence of hospital noises. Sloane removes my shoes and tucks me in.

"Thank you."

"I'll get you some tea. Do you want something to eat?"

"Maybe something soft—yogurt or soup?"

"Coming right up. Peter's gone to pick up your pain pills from the pharmacy, and Ashlyn went to get you a change of clothes, your toothbrush, everything you'll need for a few days."

I'm not used to people taking care of me. Despite my aching face, this feels positively luxurious.

"I need to call Damian. And Clyde." I sound drunk.

"Right now, you only need to rest. I'll call Damian. You can call Clyde in the morning."

Through a mental fog, I hear her set a cup on the nightstand and turn off the light. I'm out within seconds.

I wake to Sloane's soft voice nudging me.

"Zee? Zee, honey, Damian's on the phone. He's insisting that he speak with you."

"What time is it?" I'm completely disoriented. I realize it's dark out. I must have been asleep for hours.

"Uh, okay." I reach out for the phone.

"It's a video call."

"No way." I push the phone away. "Tell him I'll call him later."

"Zee? Take the phone." It's Damian's voice. "I want to see if you're okay, see what that prick did to you."

Sloane shrugs and pushes the phone in my direction.

I sit up straighter. I can't even imagine how awful I look.

I take the phone, and before I can say hello, he gasps.

"Fuckin' hell! Are you in a lot of pain?"

"Not too much. They gave me a couple of pain pills at the hospital, and I think I'll have more soon."

"You went to hospital. Good." He pushes his hair back from his face, and leans closer to the screen, scrutinizing my face and frowning.

"Was he arrested?"

"The police took him away in handcuffs, but I think I have to press charges or something. I'm not exactly sure how all that works." I shift my position, and the phone slips from my hand.

"Zee? Are you okay? Zee?"

I grab the phone from my lap. "Yeah, sorry. I dropped the phone. Damian, I wanted to tell you how grateful I am that you were there and that you let Sloane know what was happening. It could have been so much worse."

"Why don't you tell me that in person? I can catch the next plane out and be there by tomorrow morning, your time."

The idea of his comforting presence almost has me saying yes.

"Damian, that's so incredibly sweet of you to offer, but Sloane and Peter are taking good care of me. There's no need for you to come here."

"But I want to."

"It's really not necessary."

He pauses, looking hurt, but I can't really tell because my left eye is swollen shut.

"Please don't come," I say.

"Right, yeah. I'll check on you tomorrow."

He hangs up, and I realize I've made another mistake. Sloane is standing in the doorway for a second before she sits next to me on the bed.

"Hon, I couldn't help but overhear. Look, I've been thinking. Maybe I was wrong. If this is what you want, just go for it. You deserve this. Don't push him away because you think it's too risky. Just go to Ireland. If you're worried about Ashlyn, I'm here, and I'll help her with whatever she needs going forward. Maybe Damian's offering the life you've always wanted, always deserved."

"It's hard, Sloane. I feel like this is some kind of twisted déjà vu."

"Okay, I'll give you that." She chuckles. "Just promise me you'll seriously think it over before you close the door on Damian and the life you've always dreamed about in Ireland."

The next morning, I call Damian, and he answers the video call on the first ring. We say awkward hellos before we start talking over one another.

"Go on," he says.

"Damian, I'm really sorry about yesterday. Things have been so crazy. It's not that I don't want you here... It's that I've decided... I want to come to Ireland. It'll have to wait until I'm better, of course, but I'm ready to see what happens with us and to talk to Cillian's family, tell them about Ashlyn."

Now, I know what Damian looks like when he's genuinely happy. His happiness is infectious, and I forget about the pain and about Jason for a moment, but if I smile back at him, my lip will split again.

"That is, if you still want me," I say, pointing to my bruised and battered face.

"Of course. I want to be with you, bruises and all. Zee, that's grand. Let me know when, and I'll get you a ticket."

I still have to tell Ashlyn—and Elliott—which makes me want to back out, to call the whole thing off before it's even begun.

Chapter 47

Three weeks later, my lip is healed, and the lingering yellowish bruising is easily covered with makeup. It's close to midnight when I stand in the parking lot of my soon-to-be ex-apartment with Sloane and Ashlyn. Sloane's hug lingers as she whispers in my ear, "Don't you dare second-guess yourself. Just do it."

I sometimes wonder if she really does have telepathic powers. I back away, look down, and nod. I grab my suitcase.

"Mom, got your passport, your phone, your chargers?"

"Check, check, and check."

Sloane leans in. "Sexy lingerie?"

I cock my head and click my tongue at her. "Just don't." But then we snicker like a couple of middle school girls passing notes about the cute guy in history class.

Ashlyn rolls her eyes dramatically and sighs. "Okay, 'girls,' I really didn't need to hear that."

I ignore her response. "Ash, got the keys?"

She rattles them in my face.

"Don't forget to water the plants, and see if you can get the rest of the packing done. There are more boxes in the storage closet."

Ashlyn salutes me. "There won't be much left to do when the movers come. Promise."

"I texted you the lawyer's name and number in Ireland," I say. "You still have to sign some papers."

"And please try to spend more time with your father. This has been so hard on him. He's still trying to accept it all."

I don't know what shocked Elliott more, the fact that Ashlyn knew the truth about Cillian or that I was leaving for Ireland to be with Damian. Maybe my being five thousand miles away will allow him to finally move on and find someone who loves him in the way he deserves.

Ashlyn rushes me, almost knocking me over, and my suitcase falls onto the concrete. Her farewell hug guts me when she refuses to let go.

"I love you, Mom. Be happy. And let me know when you want me to come. I'm ready when Cillian's family is ready."

She steps back, swiping away a tear, and Sloane steps forward, pulls Ashlyn to her side, and kisses the top of her head like I used to do when she was little.

"Don't worry, *Mom*," Sloane says. "Peter and I will help her and Dax get settled in their new place."

"Okay, I guess I'm heading out. Don't want to miss my flight. I'll let you know when I land."

The driver throws my bags in the trunk, and I climb into the Uber and stick my head out the window. I wave frantically as we drive away, then I twist around to watch them through the rear window. As the streetlights fade and bleed into darkness, we turn the corner, and I lose sight of Ashlyn and Sloane. I face forward and stare at the back of the driver's head in silence all the way to the airport, my thoughts too scrambled to form actual words.

"We're beginning our descent into Dublin" are the words that wake me, and I straighten myself and wipe drool from the corner of my mouth. I can't believe I slept almost the whole flight. Emotional exhaustion apparently works better than a sleeping pill. But now, my skin is buzzing with anticipation of what lies ahead in the coming days, in the coming weeks—in the coming years. I don't possess an imagination wild enough to conjure up the reality of my life right now. But the explosion of hope that hits me is stronger than my imagination could ever be.

Up until Cillian invited me back into his life, my heart had been in atrophy. While fate had other plans for us, I'll always be grateful to him for bringing it back to life and allowing me to open my heart to Damian. But before Damian and I can have the slightest chance at a future, I need to tenderly pack up my love for Cillian and put it in the past, where it belongs. But I'll never forget him. I couldn't even if I wanted to.

The wheels hit the tarmac and bounce once, twice, three times, and I look out the window at a breathtaking sunrise and the Dublin airport for the second time in my life. I take a deep breath and turn on my phone to find texts from Ashlyn and Sloane.

Ashlyn: *Landed yet?*

Sloane: *Is he there?*

I don't have a chance to answer either text before it's my turn to stand and shuffle down the aisle to the exit.

As I enter the terminal, I hear the ding of another text and a selfie of Damian next to the luggage carousel. His image both soothes and excites me.

Damian: *Where are you now*?

The irony of him asking that question doesn't escape me, and it brings to mind an old Irish proverb that Cillian once told me: "Your feet will take you where your heart belongs."

I speed walk to the escalator, and as I step on, I spot Damian below, staring at his phone, waiting for my reply. My fingers fly across the keypad.

I'm here.

He looks up and rakes his fingers through his hair, and his lips form a smile that unties the knots in my stomach and warms my heart. This time, there will be no second-guessing, no paralyzing self-doubt. I know what I want. When I reach the bottom, he sprints to me, and before we've even said a word, he pulls me close, throwing me off balance, but he simply pulls me tighter and kisses me as deeply, as passionately as he did the day I left.

"Welcome back, Zee," he says, his lips a hair's breadth from mine, his voice a lusty rumble. And I know more than I've ever known anything in my life that I'm right where I belong.

I'm home.

Acknowledgements

It takes a village to create a novel, and I'm thankful to my writing village for helping me create this story that I adore. A special thanks to my critique partners, Janet Rundquist and Lynn Haraldson, who read endless revisions and tirelessly provided valuable feedback. Thank you to my beta readers—you know who you are. And a special thanks to fellow author Barbara Conrey, who read an early version and always had a kind word to push me forward. While two of my characters are Irish, I've never had the opportunity to visit Ireland, so I have to thank Sharon Ritchey, who put me in touch with Gavin O'Reilly, a native of Ireland, who so kindly offered invaluable insight on how my Irish characters would speak. I couldn't have pulled it off without him. Though I've never spoken with Kevin Toolis, author of *My Father's Wake: How the Irish Teach Us to Live, Love, and Die*, I have to thank him for his book, which told me everything I needed to know about old Irish customs around death. Gratitude goes to Jessica Hopper, who filled me in on the music world of agents, tours, and the like. Lastly, I have to express my gratitude to Red Adept Publishing for taking on another of my stories, for doing a bang-up job of editing that helped steer the story in the right direction, and for creating a breathtaking cover. If I've left anyone out who helped me along the way, just know that you are greatly appreciated!

About the Author

Densie (not Denise) Webb has spent a long career as a freelance non-fiction writer and editor, specializing in health and nutrition, and has published several books on the topic. She grew up in Louisiana, spent 13 years in New York City, and settled in Austin, TX, where it's summer nine months out of the year.

Densie is an avid walker (not of the dead variety, though she adores zombies, vampires, and apocalyptic stories). She drinks too much coffee and has a small "devil dog" that keeps her on her toes. She has arrested development in musical tastes, and her two grown children provide her with musical recommendations on a regular basis.

Read more at https://wordpress.com/view/densiewebb.com.

About the Publisher

Dear Reader,

We hope you enjoyed this book. Please consider leaving a review on your favorite book site.

Visit our site to find more quality books!

Read more at https://RedAdeptPublishing.com.